GOOD GUYS DON'T LIE

MICALEA SMELTZER

GOOD GUYS DON'T LIE

PROLOGUE

One Year Ago

CREE

THE BONFIRE BLAZES HIGH, the smell of smoke, alcohol, and sweaty bodies filling the air. I've been hanging with my friends for the last hour or so, currently nursing my second beer. But I'm feeling antsy. Big gatherings like this aren't usually my scene, I only come because I know my friends would roast the hell out of me if I didn't. I can't help it that I'm not a social butterfly.

"I'm going to go for a walk," I yell to be heard above the music.

My friend Daire gives me a bleary-eyed look. When the weed came out, I passed but several of the guys indulged. "A what, man?"

"I'm going for a walk."

"It's a party." He throws his arms out wide. "Who goes for a walk at a party?"

"Me." I stand from the tree stump I was using as a seat. "I'll see you later. Don't do anything stupid."

"Me?" He points to himself, giving a dopey grin. "Never."

Slapping him on the shoulder, I head off away from my friends with no plan in mind. I toss my empty beer in one of the many trash bags along the way—the school turns a blind eye to us using the old football field for parties if we clean up after ourselves.

Shoving my hands in my pockets, my eyes follow my feet and the ratty orange Vans I'm wearing. If I keep my head down, there's less chance of someone trying to talk to me. Being in the popular crowd has its perks, but I'm not much for socializing with people I don't know well. It can be a bit much at times, but it comes with the territory. That doesn't make having social anxiety any easier though.

I'm sure it would be shocking to most of the school

population to learn how much social situations stress me out—especially considering I play hockey and have no problem being on the ice or interviewed after games. But for some reason my brain catalogs that as something different than this.

Looking up, my gaze is drawn to a tall slender girl swaying beside a tree. A solo cup is clasped in her hand and long red hair cascades halfway down her back. She's beautiful in a unique way. It's ethereal, the way she moves to the song—Electric Love by BORNS—but there's something in her eyes that tells me she's as uncomfortable here as I am.

I can't help it as I take the necessary steps closer to her.

She startles at my approach, eyes dropping to her drink. "Hey."

She bites her lip, tucking her hair behind her ear. "Hi."

"Sorry to bother you," I start, rocking back on my heels. "It's just ... you looked as out of place as I feel."

She laughs in an endearingly awkward way. "Is it that obvious?"

"A little." I grin and she smiles back, her eyes dropping to her shoes. "What's your name?"

Hazel eyes twinkle with the reflection of the bonfire. "I don't give strangers my name."

I nod my head, trying not to laugh. "Fair enough. What about a fake name then?"

She thinks for a moment, her nose scrunching and making the freckles sprinkled there move. "Daisy," she settles with. "You can call me Daisy Buchanan."

My heart skips a beat. As an English major and a fan of novels in general, I've had a special place in my heart for *The Great Gatsby* ever since I read it in high school. I always reread it every Christmas. Sometimes twice a year if I feel moved to. The fact that she's mentioned one of the main characters does something to me.

"Gatsby fan?"

Her cheeks flush. "Maybe."

I hold a hand out to her, bowing with a flourish. I don't know what makes me do it, I'm not normally like this. "I'm Jay, then. Jay Gatsby."

"Bad choice," she stage whispers. "He dies in the end."

She slowly fits her hand in mine, and I bring it to my lips. "It's worth it if I get to have a pretty girl like you."

She throws her head back and laughs.

I've never experienced lust at first sight, but this girl … I'm fucking enraptured.

"Did you eat a whole bucket of cheese before coming over to me? Because that was extra cheesy."

"I'm bad with the ladies."

She snorts, looking me over. "I doubt that."

"Why?"

"Because you're hot."

I try not to grin, but it's pretty difficult not to. "You think I'm hot?"

She thinks it over, seeming at war with herself. Her shoulders straighten with a resolve. "Sure, why not?"

She dumps the contents of her cup in the grass and gets rid of her cup when we pass a trash bag.

Extending my hand for hers, she hesitates a second before taking it. Her hand is tiny in mine, her skin several shades lighter and cool to the touch from the night air. "This isn't like me," she feels the need to admit.

"Me either."

Not that I haven't had hookups, that would be a lie, but it's rare for me and usually after at least one or two dates. I'm not like some of my friends who can sleep with anyone. I blame it on growing up with parents who are madly in love with each other. I can't help searching for the real deal.

I reach my old Ford Bronco, painted a sage green color. It's entirely redone, inside and out, and cost a pretty penny, but was a gift from my grandpa. 'Daisy' arches her brow in surprise.

"I've always wanted one of these. But my parents would never approve of something that's considered an antique and not a Mercedes."

"Mercedes is overrated." I give a small shrug.

"Tell them that."

"Mercedes or your parents?"

She smiles at my teasing. "Both."

The door creaks slightly when I open it. Still gripping tightly to her hand, I help her inside the lifted Bronco. She looks around longingly and I know it wasn't a line about wanting one herself.

"What got you into cars?" I ask before I close the door.

"My brother. It's kind of his thing. Do you have any siblings?"

"One—a sister."

"Younger or older?"

"Younger. She's planning to attend here next year."

"Is having your little sister around going to cramp your style?"

"Nah. I love her. She's cool."

Closing the door, I jog around to the driver's side and hop in. Putting the key in the ignition 'Daisy' seems to hold her breath, listening with her eyes closed as the engine turns over.

"So, Jay," she begins, as I maneuver out of my parked spot, "since you don't do this often, what exactly are you assuming *this* is?"

I chuckle, grinning at her. "Whatever you want it to be."

We drive around for a while, windows down. Her hair blows in the wind, and there's a peace in her eyes that was missing before. There's a calmness between us in the quiet, like we've known each other for a long time, but that's far from the truth.

"Pull in there." Her voice permeates the silence, a purple painted nail pointing to the turn off for a local pond. I've been here before. It's nothing huge, but it's plenty deep and nice to look at.

The tires crunch over the gravel as I park. No one else is here—nobody else crazy enough to be at a pond at two in the morning.

Daisy hops out, and I follow her to the edge of the water. "What are you doing?"

She smiles coyly, unbuttoning her tiny pair of shorts. The zipper slides down and she says, "I'm living, Gatsby. Do you want to live with me?"

I don't answer her, not with words. Hooking my thumbs into the back of my shirt, I yank it off and drop it onto the ground at my feet. Daisy is already down to her bra and panties and heading for the water. She lets out a shriek when the cold water hits her toes, but she keeps going, looking back at me over her shoulder.

I remember my dad telling me the first time he met my mom, he just knew instinctively, like every cell in his body recognized her as his other half and that I'd know too.

I've always wanted that perfect love I saw growing up, but I never really believed him.

Not until now.

I follow her into the water in only my boxer-briefs. I'm pretty sure my dick shrivels as soon as the water touches my skin, but I keep going. She swims over to me, wrapping her arms around my shoulders and legs around my waist.

Her hair is soaking, looking less red and more brunette now that it's wet.

"Hi." Water clings to her lashes.

"Hi," I say back, both of us grinning dopily at the other.

She makes the first move. The second our lips connect, I lose myself in her.

Kissing someone new for the first time can be weird, but not with her. It's like we were born to kiss each other, each of us anticipating what the other's going to do and following. Her nails scratch against my skin, while I hold on tighter to her hips. When she gasps into my mouth, I feel like I might lose my mind.

"Tell me your real name," I beg, chasing her lips.

"No," she giggles. "This is more fun. I can be anyone I want to be."

"Are you trying to torture me?"

Her eyes sparkle with humor. "Maybe."

I shake my head, but she stills me, her hands moving to hold onto my cheeks. She kisses me again, biting my bottom lip.

I have no clue how long we make-out in the water since I lose track of time, but I know when we climb out and back into my car, that I want more than one night with this girl.

She kisses me deeply, passionately. Almost like she's trying to prove something to herself. Cupping her cheeks, I pull her back slightly. Her eyes are hooded with lust, but she's coherent. Definitely not drunk.

"Are you sure you want this?" I know where this is headed, and I don't want to do something she'll regret in the morning. I'd hate myself if that were the case.

"As crazy as it sounds," the end of her small pink tongue sweeps over her lips, "I've never been surer of anything."

Climbing into the back of my Bronco, she unclips

her bra and shimmies out of her panties. I follow behind her, saying a silent prayer that I have condoms in here since I don't carry any on me.

"Please, I want you," she begs, lying back. Her fingers trace down her body to her clit. Her nipples are hard and pink—begging for my mouth.

"Hold on." I lean over the front seat and rifle through the glovebox, triumphant when I find a condom.

Sliding it onto myself, I cover her body with mine. Kissing her neck, she wiggles and pleads with me for more, but I want to take my time. Swirling my tongue around her nipple, I capture it in my mouth. She gasps, her body arching up to meet mine.

"Don't be greedy," I chide playfully, and her cheeks flush, making her freckles stand out even more.

I kiss my way down her body, lifting her hips when I reach her pussy. There's not a whole lot of room in the back of my Bronco, but we make it work. Her fingers delve into my hair, pulling and tugging as I work her over with my mouth. I can tell she's getting close, the way she wiggles and the little noises she makes.

When her orgasm hits her, she cries out. "Oh my God, yes! Oh my God, oh my God, oh my God." She slaps her hand over her mouth, and I yank it away, our eyes connecting.

"I want to hear what I do to you."

Her lashes lower over her hazel eyes—more green than gold now.

Double checking the condom, I guide myself to her entrance and sink inside, both of us letting out long, drawn-out moans.

"Fuck, you feel so good," I groan into the skin of her neck.

She wraps her legs around my waist, pulling me impossibly closer. "Fuck me like you mean it." I don't have to be told twice. Lifting her hips, I rock into her. Her head falls back, and she moans. "Holy shit."

"Baby, your pussy is squeezing me so tight." Her fingers rake down my chest, leaving marks behind. Yanking her body into my arms, I hold her in my lap. "Ride me."

She smiles at my command. Leaning back as far as she can in the space of my car, she rests her hands on my knees, lifting and lowering herself. I surge forward, capturing one of her nipples in my mouth. With one hand she clasps the back of my head, holding me there.

Wrapping my arms around her back, I lose all control and pump into her hard and fast. Her pussy squeezes my cock and I know she's close. I say a prayer that she comes before I do, and thankfully it's answered.

She cries out and I kiss her as she does, absorbing the sound into my own body as I come.

Her body collapses into mine, both of us damp from the pond and sweat.

My arms are still around her, and I hold her against my body. She's so small compared to me. I could nestle her here forever.

Pulling back slightly, she gives me a lazy post-sex smile. "Gatsby, you sure do know how to make a girl feel special."

I chuckle, the movement rattling her body along with mine. "I try."

After a few more minutes, we extract ourselves from each other and redress. "Can you take me back to the bonfire?"

"I'm sure it's over by now. I don't mind taking you to your dorm."

"I know, but I left my car there. I'd rather get it tonight."

"All right."

We're quiet on the way back to campus, but it's not awkward. The radio plays softly in the background, and, 'Daisy' since I still don't know her name, looks out the passenger window with a soft smile. Her hair whips around her pale shoulders, but she doesn't seem to mind that it's getting tangled.

There are a few cars left outside the old field. "Which one?"

"The Mercedes SUV." She points to a white one.

"Ah, right—your parents are Mercedes enthusiasts."

I park beside the big white SUV.

"So, our night ends," she muses with a tiny smirk.

I grin, not missing the way she stares at the dimple in my cheek. "This isn't the ending, Daisy, not by a long shot."

She laughs softly, reaching for the door. "You're very sure of yourself."

"I trust my gut. There's a difference."

"Sure." She gets out of the car, heading toward hers.

"Do I get your real name or not?"

She pauses, looking back at me over her shoulder. Her hair has dried in natural soft waves. She reminds me of the Little Mermaid. "If you trust your gut so much, then why don't you trust it to find me again? *Then* I'll tell you my name."

I wet my lips with my tongue. "I like a challenge."

She wiggles her fingers over her shoulder. "Good luck, Gatsby."

ONE

"DO YOU SMELL THAT?" My sister stands beside me on the sidewalk, inhaling deep breaths of air.

My brows furrow as I look down at her. "The promise of too much alcohol and debauchery?"

She rubs her hands together, looking a little too eager for a freshman. "That too—but mostly freedom."

"Millie! How much did you pack?" Our dad's voice interrupts us, and she turns to where he's standing behind the small moving truck, packed to the brim with her stuff.

15

The off-campus house my parents bought when I started college, stands in front of us looking a little too picturesque to be in a neighborhood filled with other college kids. It's white, with stately columns, and a wraparound porch that extends to the second floor as well.

"Dad," Millie heads away from me and to his side, "this is my first year, I needed a lot of stuff. Remember when Cree first moved in? He had even more stuff because the whole house was empty. What I have in comparison to that is really nothing. You should be proud."

My mom pulls up then, parking on the street and hops out with a fresh coffee in one hand and a paper bag in the other. She passes the bag to me, and I peek inside, finding it filled with muffins. I devour one in practically two bites. I'm *starving*. Then again, I'm always hungry, so it's not new.

"Let's help your father, shall we?" She smiles at me, eyes the same color as mine crinkle at the corners. She takes the bag back to pass it to Dad and Millie.

It takes hours to get everything brought in and set up for Millie.

I can't even gripe because she really didn't over-pack, but building furniture for her room while my dad mumbles about lost screws and holes not fitting right—had to snicker at that one—made things drag on.

Millie's room is down the hall from mine on the opposite side beside what was my friend Murray's room, but since he graduated, it'll now be my friend Jude's room, with a shared bathroom between them. I have the master and the room beside me is Daire's.

It's late by the time we get Millie's room done and order pizza since none of us feel like cooking—not to mention that would require a run to the grocery store.

We hang out in the family room, the pizza on the coffee table as we all sit around it. Dad has his arm around mom, rubbing her shoulder. He looks at her adoringly, like he's still in the honeymoon phase despite the fact they've been together for thirty years. Sometimes my sister and I pretend to be grossed out by them, but I know we're both thankful to have parents who love each other like that.

"How are you feeling, Mills?" My mom eyes my sister across from her. I can tell she's worried about her youngest kid going off to college. I'm not a parent yet, not even close to being ready to be one either, but I can imagine it's a strange feeling watching your youngest kid leave the nest.

"I'm excited." Millie bounces where she sits. She's

always had a hard time sitting still. "I've been looking forward to college for forever."

My mom gives a laugh, shaking her head. "It's not all fun and games, sweetie. You have to do schoolwork too."

"And no getting pregnant," my dad adds.

"Dad!" Millie cries, her cheeks turning red. "Shut up!" She pretends to gag.

"All I'm saying is, I'm too young to be a grandpa."

"Leave her alone," mom admonishes, smacking him lightly in the stomach, "you don't say this stuff to Cree."

"You're right, you're right." Then he turns to me with a serious look, "Don't get a girl pregnant."

Now we're all groaning at him. "Dad, trust me I don't think that's going to happen."

I've had sex one time in the past year. Mind-blowing, out of this world, never going to forget it sex—but damn if I haven't been disappointed, I never found 'Daisy' again.

"Enough of this talk." My mom stands with her plate. "I'm exhausted and heading to bed. We need to hit the road early in the morning." She taps my dad's shoulder.

He rubs a hand over his tired face. "Right."

"Don't worry about cleaning up. Mills and I can handle it."

"Are you sure?" Mom hesitates, eyes bouncing between the stairs and the mess.

"Of course, Mom."

"All right." She passes me her plate and my dad does the same.

They head up to bed—they'll be staying in my room tonight, and I'll be taking Daire's since he's not here yet.

Grabbing another slice of pizza, I eye my little sister. "How do you really feel about school?"

"Excited," she repeats, "*and* a little nervous."

I chuckle. "You're going to do fine."

"I know." She nibbles on the end of her pizza crust. "It's a different world than high school, though."

"I'll look out for you."

"That's what I'm afraid of." She sticks her tongue out.

I poke her cheek, making her giggle. Most guys would probably be pissed they're forced to live with their little sister for their senior year, but Millie and I have always been close. Leaving for university was an adjustment at first for me. Our family has always been close, and suddenly, I was on my own.

Millie stands, gathering up some of the trash. "Don't worry, big bro. I'm going to be just fine."

I shake my head, trying to hide my amusement. "You think so?"

"Pssh, I know so."

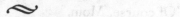

OUR PARENTS LEFT at the crack of dawn to head back to Massachusetts which left the two of us to wash the sheets and get things back in order. The house was cleaned once a week by a maid over the summer, so things aren't in too bad of shape which is nice, but Daire should be getting in sometime today and Jude has to move in too.

"I can't believe I'm going to be living with a houseful of dudes," Millie grumbles good-naturedly, helping me put clean sheets on Daire's bed since I crashed in here last night. "What was I thinking?"

"That you wouldn't have to live in a dorm room?"

"That," she agrees, snapping a corner into place, "and the closet space."

I chuckle, grabbing the comforter. "Mills, you don't even have that many clothes."

"Doesn't mean I don't want space for them."

I shake my head.

Sisters.

We finish with Daire's bed and then I move onto mine, sending her to answer the door when the doorbell rings.

She comes back a minute later, snickering at my Spiderman bed sheets. I ignore her amusement. "Who's your hot friend that's moving in?"

"Excuse me?" I arch a brow.

She rolls her eyes. "I'm eighteen with a pulse, Cree. Give me a break."

"He didn't introduce himself?"

"No, he just said he was a friend of yours and is moving his stuff in."

Sometimes I forget that my college life has been so separate from my home life. But that's what happens when you move too far away for your family to visit you regularly at university.

"What did he look like?"

"Tall. Big shoulders. Dark hair. Brown eyes."

"That'd be Jude," I answer. "Daire's blond. But stay away from him—both of them, but especially Jude. He's … not been the same since a bad break up, and he fucks around."

Millie laughs, helping me finish my bed. "I like them broken. Means I can try to fix him."

"Mills," I growl.

"Kidding." She bats her eyes. "But I can still look. I'm only human."

I drop my head. Something tells me this is going to be a long ass year.

"I trust you. It's *him* I don't trust."

She pauses, giving me a funny look. "You don't trust your own friend?"

"Not with you."

She snorts, putting one of the pillowcases on. "I'm a big girl. You worry too much." She tosses the pillow down and dances toward the door. She pauses, looking back at me. "I'm going to see if your hot friend needs any help."

"Mills!" I yell after her, but she's already bounding down the stairs.

I let my head fall back with a sigh. Finishing my bed, I figure I might as well help Jude too—and make sure he doesn't hit on my sister while I'm at it.

Between the three of us—and four when Daire arrives—it doesn't take long to get all of Jude's stuff brought to his room. Afterwards, Millie heads out wanting to check out campus. I offered to go with her, but she didn't want her big brother tagging along.

Plopping on the couch, I turn the TV on. It's still on the Home and Garden Network my mom had it on this morning while she sipped her coffee. That already feels like a lifetime ago.

Jude comes downstairs and saunters over to where I am, taking the chair in the corner.

"Thanks again for offering me a room. I'm sick of the dorms."

"They're crowded," I agree, watching him carefully.

"Why are you looking at me like that?"

"No reason."

He makes a noise in the back of his throat. "Is this about your sister?"

"Why would it be about her?"

It totally is.

"I'm not going to go after your sister, dude." He sounds sincere enough, but I see the look in his eyes — the one that says he's attracted to her.

"She's a good girl."

He ignores that comment. "When are we throwing the first party?"

I rub a hand over my face, annoyed with myself, not him. I've never been much of a partier, but last year after my hookup with 'Daisy' I started throwing parties in the hopes that she'd show up. Every single time it ended with disappointment from me. Daisy never came, and I had to wonder if I'd imagined the whole thing. I know that's not true, though. She's out there. I don't want to consider the possibility that she graduated or transferred.

A part of me doesn't want to continue the parties this year, that way I don't have to deal with strangers in my space and things getting out of control. But I can't say no. Not on the off chance that I finally find her.

"Let's get through the first week of classes, and then Friday night it's happening."

Jude grins in triumph, rubbing his hands together. "Excellent."

TWO

Ophelia

"I COULD GET you your own apartment, sweetheart. Or even a house," my father reminds me, looking around my shared dorm apartment with contempt. "Why you want to share a space with two other girls when you don't have to is beyond me? Why couldn't you have gone to Harvard? Or Yale? Aldridge is decent, but—"

I hold up a hand to shut him up. "Because I wanted a true college experience," I explain about the dorm, "and this is the school I always wanted to attend. You know that."

"John, leave her alone," my mom speaks up from my room where she's putting my clothes away. I told her a million times that I would do it, but she doesn't trust me not to live out of boxes for the entirety of the school year, so she's doing it herself.

"Don't worry, sir," my roommate Kenna wraps an arm around me, "we'll take good care of her." She's referring to our other roomie, Li.

Originally it was Kenna, Li, and a girl named Rory until she moved in with her boyfriend last year, and I got paired up with them. Luckily, they've been great roommates and do their best to include me. It's me who struggles when it comes to friendships. Ever since I was a little girl, I've always had trouble on that front. Getting close to people isn't the easiest for me.

My dad smooths his hand down the front of his suit —why he wore a full suit in August when it's one-hundred degrees outside is beyond me. "I'm sure." He sounds doubtful, eyeing Kenna with contempt, but she brushes it off easily. Not much ruffles her feathers.

I don't know why my dad acts like Kenna and Li are beneath him. Both are from families almost as wealthy as ours, but if my dad hasn't handpicked every single person in my life, then he doesn't approve. Sometimes I think he's that way because he's protecting me; other times I'm convinced it's because he's embarrassed of me and wants to make sure that someone is on his payroll if I do or say something stupid.

Growing up, I was always different. Not in the ways one might want to think they're unique. I struggled to learn certain things while others came incredibly easy. Making eye contact was near impossible and is still a struggle at times, and communicating can feel like pulling teeth.

It wasn't until I was in my early teen years that I got my autism diagnosis.

Things started to make sense then, why I had my little quirks, but it also became a label I didn't want to bear because I wanted to be seen as *me*. Sure, autism is a part of me, but so are so many other things. It's just a piece, a tiny one among the puzzle that shapes me, but suddenly it felt like my entire being.

I felt like maybe my parents were ashamed that I wasn't 'normal' like my brother or their friends' kids, but what *is* normal? Does such a thing even exist?

Stepping out of my room with a yellow sweater, my mom holds it up. "Do you actually wear this? I've told you yellow isn't your color."

"Mom," I groan. "I like it." I swipe it from her and march past, hanging it in my closet.

Again, I know my mom doesn't mean to be hurtful, but she is. I know much of the way she is, is because of how she was raised, but that doesn't excuse her lack of tact.

"I'm sorry," she sighs, picking up the next item in the box.

"Seriously, Mom. I can handle this." I take the jacket from her. "You and Dad don't need to stay."

My freshman year I attended completely online from home because neither of them wanted to let me be on campus. I had to fight tooth and nail to be allowed to transfer to campus last year. I struggle with learning, and passing tests can be damn near impossible even when I understand the material, but I wanted a normal experience … and a break from my parents. God love them, but the hovering can be way too much. Plus, I hate feeling like a disappointment, especially when my older brother is a whiz.

She frowns, picking up another sweater. "But we were going to take you to dinner."

I bite my lip. I hate disappointing my parents. I feel like I always have. I'm not a brainiac like my brother. I don't excel in school and at everything I touch. The only things I've ever been good at are horseback riding and reading. Neither of which is going to help me when it comes to my own path in life. Granted, my family owns luxury hotels all over the world, so money is never an issue, but I don't want to be dependent on my parents for the rest of my life.

That was the whole point of *this* — college, living away from home. But even now my parents don't want to cut the umbilical cord.

Rubbing a hand over my face, I sigh. "We can do dinner, Mom."

I know I should be grateful for parents that care, and I am, but sometimes I want them to look at me and see the adult I've become and understand I don't need their constant hovering.

Deciding not to fight this battle today, I help my mom unpack while Dad takes phone calls and chats with my roommates. Bless them for entertaining him.

"Are you sure you want all these lights? It might be a bit much." My mom asks, helping me hang up the curtain fairy lights that will be across the entire wall.

"I'm sure."

"I do quite like all the plants. Don't forget to water them." She looks around at the various plants I've placed around my room — on the desk, bookcase, my dresser.

"I won't forget."

With the lights up, one of the last things we needed to do, we step back and assess the space.

There's a fluffy white rug covering the floor, plush

enough to sink your toes into. My bed is elevated, allowing for storage underneath. I've used it for my surplus of paperback books. The bedspread is the same as last year—white with tiny flower detailing—and blanket draped on the end because I like to wrap myself in one like a burrito.

On my desk is my laptop, a lamp, and more books. My closet houses the obvious—clothes—and other miscellaneous things. In the corner of the room is a basket filled with more blankets and a fluffy chair I can sink into when I want to get lost in a novel.

It's a small room, but it's *mine*.

"It's … cozy." My mom has to search for her choice of word. I know this isn't her taste at all. She opts for a more glam style—lots of white, marble, and gold.

"Thank you," I say, even though I'm not sure it's a compliment. Over the years I've learned the proper things to say in situations, and now it's automatic to respond the way others expect.

She gives a smile, then squeezes me into a hug. "We're so proud of you, Ophelia."

I'm slow to hug her back, sometimes not entirely comfortable with these nuances that seem natural to others.

Releasing me, she pats my cheek and heads from the room, leaving me alone for a blissful moment.

I inhale a breath, letting it fill my lungs before I let it out slowly.

"Do you ladies want to join us for dinner?" Dad asks my roommates.

They both look to me, not wanting to step on any toes. I give a tiny shrug. I don't care, so I leave it up to them.

"That would be great, Mr. Hastings," Li replies. "We appreciate the offer."

"Yes, thank you."

"Aw, ladies, I told you to call me John."

"And Alice for me. Don't make us feel older than we already are," my mom giggles.

"What do you want to eat?" Dad lobbies the question at me.

I loathe being put on the spot, so I blurt out the first thing I think of. "Pizza."

WE END up at a pizza parlor near campus—the kind with the red and white checkered tablecloths and traditional choices, none of the weird fancy pizzas you might find at a place my parents would choose.

Li and Kenna sit on one side of the booth, with me stuffed on the other side between my parents.

I pick at my Hawaiian, my appetite lacking.

"Ophelia," my mom nudges me with her elbow, "are you feeling well?"

"I'm fine." I fake a smile.

More like bothered by the ridiculously loud music and cacophony of a million conversations going on.

I force myself to eat so my mom won't worry so much. I can't afford to give her any excuse to decide that I'm better off doing my studies at home. I need to be out on my own, to grow and thrive. It's hard to do that when you're constantly suffocated with someone else's worry.

After we finish with dinner, my dad insists we grab ice cream from a place across the street.

"I'm so sorry about this," I mumble to Kenna as she looks over the choices.

She gives me a funny look. "Don't be sorry. Your parents are sweet."

"Oh." I wrap my arms around myself. "Okay, that's … great. Cool."

Kenna laughs, nudging me with her elbow. "Loosen up, Ophelia."

We place our orders and I wait patiently, but excitedly, for my chocolate with rainbow sprinkles in a waffle cone. I don't think I'll ever outgrow my love of rainbow sprinkles. They make everything better.

Sitting outside at a table, we enjoy our ice cream while my dad regales my roommates with stories of our family. He wasn't this enthusiastic last year, but I think both of them were sick with worry about leaving me. This time they're still not thrilled, but they do feel better about it.

I lick happily at my ice cream, deciding it wasn't such a bad idea to get dessert.

"How are you girls feeling about your junior year?" My dad asks, mixing chocolate chips around in his strawberry ice cream.

"I'm happy to get to focus on my major," Li responds. "It feels like I'm finally going to do what I came here for."

"It's a step closer to graduating." Kenna shrugs, more focused on her ice cream than my dad's questioning.

"Hmm," he hums, nodding. "I remember when I was your age —"

"John," my mom laughs, tipping her head in my direction. "Don't embarrass Ophelia with any more of your stories."

Dad chuckles, setting his cup on the table. "All right, all right. But what about the time —
"

"John."

AFTER HUGGING MY PARENTS GOODBYE, I say good-night to my roommates and shut myself in my room. I close my eyes, savoring the blissful quiet that washes over me. This evening has been over stimulating to say the least.

Changing out of my clothes into a pair of sleep shorts with sheep jumping over clouds and an oversized t-shirt I stole from my best friend Logan during high school, I pick out a book to read.

Climbing into bed, I burrow beneath the covers and read with only the glow of my fairy lights. Calmness settles over me and my body relaxes, finally at peace after the chaotic day of moving back into the dorms. Flipping to the first page, I start to read, fully planning to stop after a few chapters.

But the next thing I know, I've finished the book, and it's three in the morning.

Setting the finished book aside, I pull my covers beneath my chin and hope for a few hours of sleep. At least class doesn't start for a few more days.

THREE

CREE

DAIRE BURSTS OUT of the hall bathroom just as I'm coming up the stairs.

His eyes connect with mine, his hands on the towel at his waist. He's soaking wet. It's obvious he grabbed the towel and ran.

"Dude," he glares at me, holding up a purple razor, "why the fuck does your sister need so many razors? There are like twelve in there, and half of them are on the floor of the shower. I cut myself." He turns, showing me his heel. It's barely bleeding, he's just being dramatic. "And why does she even need them in *my* shower? She's supposed to be sharing a bathroom with Jude!"

"Calm down." I shake my head, pausing outside my room. "I've seen you bleed worse on the ice."

"Yeah, but that's fun. Stepping on a razor isn't."

"I'll tell her to get rid of them and clean her stuff up. I don't know why she's using yours." I pinch the bridge of my nose.

Daire runs his fingers through his wet blond hair. "You do that. Millie is cool and all, but living with a chick is weird." He shudders. "There's so much hair around the drain I thought there was a rat for a second when I got in."

Daire only has brothers and was raised by a single dad. His experience with women extends to the physical kind and that's it. This final year spent living with Millie will be eye-opening for him.

I chuckle, amused at his disgust. "You better get used to it. One day you'll be living with a chick permanently."

"Nah." He smirks, shaking his wet hair at me like a dog. "I'm an eternal bachelor."

"We'll see."

He laughs like the idea is ludicrous, closing his door behind him.

Bypassing my room, I knock on Millie's door. "Come in."

Opening it, I lean against the doorway. "I hear you have a ton of razors in the bathroom. A bathroom that isn't even yours."

"Not a ton—there's like three. One for my legs, the backup for my legs, and the one for my lady bits."

"Ugh, Mills." I gag like I sucked on something sour. "I don't need to hear about your lady bits."

"Why are you asking me about my razors?" She arches a brow, her face highlighted from the glow of her laptop on her bed.

"Because Daire cut his foot on one."

"Aw." She mock pouts. "Should I kiss it and make it better for the poor wittle baby?"

"Don't even joke about kissing my friends in any way." My friends are great—until it comes to the idea of one of them with my sister, then they're public enemy number one. "Just keep your razors picked up and hair from going down the drain. Oh and all in *your* bathroom." I point a finger at the closed door that connects her bedroom to the Jack and Jill bathroom between her room and Jude's.

Rolling her eyes, she waves her hand in a shooing gesture. "Ugh, but I hate sharing a bathroom with *him*." I glare at her because it's a fucking bathroom.

"All right, whatever, now go. You're getting on my nerves."

I pale with realization. "Jude didn't do anything funny did he?"

"Oh, God. No! Nothing like that! He just annoys me. Tell Daire I'll move my crap back later."

Shaking my head, I close her door behind me.

In my room, I grab my computer to go over my schedule again in preparation for the first day of classes tomorrow. Something my friends and team-mates roast me for is how much of a nerd I am. I love school and learning in general. I read all the time and would rather watch documentaries than most other things. Despite that, hockey is still my great love. Much to the disbelief of almost everyone, I haven't made up my mind if I want to pursue the pros—they showed interest last year but I didn't bite—or do my own thing. Life's short, with endless possibilities. How can I know if I'm making the right decision?

"Knock, knock." Daire pokes his head in my open doorway.

"Don't worry I talked to Mills, and she said she'd take care of the razors."

"That's not why I'm here." He grabs the top of the doorframe.

"Then what do you want?" I close my laptop and swivel my desk chair in his direction.

"Let's go to Harvey's. I want a drink and a chick in my lap."

I chuckle, leaning back in my chair. It lets out a long squeak of protest. "That so?"

"Yep. Grab your wallet. I'm not taking no for an answer."

"All right. See if Jude wants to go."

Daire gives a nod and heads downstairs, feet thumping on the stairs as he goes.

Grabbing my stuff, I knock on Millie's door again.

"What?" she snaps, swinging the door open before I can.

"Whoa." I hold my hands up innocently. "I wanted to let you know the guys and I are headed to the bar."

"Of course, you are." Her tone is sassy, and I narrow my eyes.

"What's that for Millicent?"

She makes a sour face at my use of her full name. "Nothing, I'm just in a bad mood." She rubs a hand over her face.

"About what?" My sister is usually easy-going, always ready with a smile. It's rare for her to be sassy or admit to not being in the best mood.

"Nerves."

"Aw, Mills." I pull her into a hug. "Don't be nervous."

"College is scary, Cree."

"You've got this. Besides, you have three awesome roommates to help you through it."

"Ha," she says snarkily. "You guys are seniors. You'll forget all about my poor pathetic freshman self." She looks away, staring off into the distance. She's really in her head about all of this.

"Not a chance." I ruffle her hair. "I gotta go but text me if you want me to bring you back something."

"I have a car." She rolls her eyes. "And I'm capable of using the kitchen."

"Hey, it's just an offer. Take it or leave it." I throw my hands up in an innocent gesture.

She laughs, stepping back into her room. "Have fun with the boys."

Downstairs, I meet the guys in the kitchen where Jude's making a sandwich.

"Dude, why are you eating?" I chuckle, eyeing his monstrosity of a sandwich. It's turkey, ham, lettuce, pickles, and what looks like ketchup, mayo, *and* mustard. Barf. "Can't you eat at Harvey's?"

"I'm starving, that's why." He takes a massive bite. "Besides, the Uber is still twenty minutes away."

"You called an Uber?"

"Duh." Crumbs of food fall out of his mouth. "I don't think any of us wants to be the designated driver."

I shrug indifferently. I'm not a huge drinker, so it doesn't matter much to me, but if an Uber is already on its way, I'm not going to complain.

Millie comes down before we leave, eyeing us suspiciously on the way to the fridge. "You guys haven't left yet?"

"Uber's late," I explain.

"Ah." She bends over, grabbing a La Croix. I have no idea how she drinks the nasty stuff. "Enjoy your night boys."

I catch Jude checking out my sister as she leaves the kitchen and slap the back of his head. "Dude, you can put your dick anywhere you want but not in my sister. Don't look at her like that."

Daire laughs, nearly falling out of his chair. "Don't ask for trouble by fucking your friend's sister. It's in the bro code, dumb ass."

Jude rubs the back of his head, mumbling something under his breath about how he was just looking. Asshole. I'm really regretting the decision to let him move in. When I asked him if he'd want to room here, I didn't think about him being around Millie. I'm not typically the overprotective type, but when it comes to Jude, I'll do whatever the hell it takes to keep him away from her. He's not the sort of guy she needs to get tangled up in. Too much baggage he needs to deal with.

Jude's phone vibrates. "Car's here."

~

HARVEY'S IS PACKED with students, but as soon as we enter, the crowd parts like we're a bunch of Gods. Daire and Jude eat it up, but I keep my head down as we head back to our usual horseshoe-shaped booth in the back. Some guys are already there and quickly make room for us.

"Hey." I clap hands with Caesar when I settle beside him. He's a cool guy, on the football team with Jude, and we hangout some.

"How was your summer, Creature?" He chortles at the nickname the guys on the hockey team gave me.

"Not bad. Spent a lot of time on the water."

"Lucky bastard." He picks up his glass of beer, downing a long gulp. "My parents shipped me off to my grandparents farm to help out. Manual labor is a bitch, but those country girls sure are nice."

"Whatever you say."

"Oh, it's true." He waggles his brows. "What do you want to drink?" He lifts his hand, signaling the waitress.

"Just a Sprite."

He blinks at me and down at the other end of table Jude slams his hands onto the wood surface. "This is why I got an Uber. Eat, drink, be merry!"

I sigh, scrubbing a hand over my face. "I'll have a Guinness." Yeah, I'm giving in to peer pressure, but one drink would be kind of nice. I'm feeling stressed about this year and the decisions I need to make. Not to mention, it's been a year since my run in with the mysterious Daisy. I still find myself thinking about her. Even though I haven't meant to, I've already been searching for red hair in the bar on the off chance she's here.

It's pathetic and I need to get over it.

I know what my friends would say if I told them about this. After they recovered from laughing their asses off, they'd tell me to get laid and get over it.

"You look like you have a lot on your mind." Daire sits on my other side, looking over the menu even though we have it memorized after three years. "Wanna talk about it?"

"Nah. The beer should help." And like a beacon in the dark, the waitress appears with drinks for us and refills for some of the others.

"Things already seem quieter this year," he says only to me. "It's weird having Mascen, Cole, Teddy, and Murray gone."

"Yeah, it does feel weird. Teddy and Murray always made things interesting."

I sip slowly at my beer, and the next time the waitress comes by I order tacos.

"Tacos? At a bar? Sacrilegious." Caesar chortles, emptying his drink.

"I like tacos."

There's a commotion at the end of the table and then Rory, Mascen's girlfriend, and her two friends join us.

"Where's Mascen? He's not on guard duty tonight?" Jude calls out, already on his second beer. There's a girl beside him getting cozy, her lips suctioned to his neck.

Rory rolls her eyes behind her glasses. "I can go places without him. He's in Malibu right now staying with his cousin and his wife. They had a baby not long ago, and he wanted to meet her."

"Ooh, do you have pictures?" The girl who was sucking on Jude's neck extracts herself to ask. "I *love* babies."

She eyes Jude eagerly like he'll whip his dick out and say, "All right, let me give you one."

Instead, he gets a haunted look and scoots away from her.

"Sure," Rory chimes, oblivious to Jude's discomfort and gets her phone out, showing off photos of the baby.

"Aw, wow. She is precious. Look at all that dark

hair. Don't you think she's cute?" The chick tries to show Jude, but he stares blatantly at the table ignoring her. Rolling her eyes, she gives the phone back to Rory. "Thanks for showing me. She's adorable. What's her name?"

"Her first name is Annie, and her middle name is Hope."

The girl clutches her chest. "I love that."

"So, when are you and Mascen popping out some kiddos?" Daire jokes, trying not to laugh.

Rory pretends to gag. "Not for a good long time. Let me get through this and law school. And he better put a ring on it before he knocks me up too."

Jude pushes against his chick of the night. "Move. I gotta piss."

She quickly gets out of his way to let him out of the booth. He bolts like he can't get away from us fast enough, and I really don't think it's entirely about having to pee.

"Let me out, too." Something tells me to go check on him. Feelings and shit aren't really my thing, but if there's anything I learned last year when Teddy told us about all the crap he'd been dealing with, it's that even if it makes you uncomfortable, you need to be there for your friends. "Don't eat my tacos," I warn, Daire as he and the girls sit back down.

"No promises." He smirks, stretching his arm along the back of the booth.

I check the restroom and find it empty of Jude.

Shaking my head, I know it could take me a while to find him if he's disappeared into the crowd in the middle of the room, but something urges me to go outside.

Using the side exit, I step out and look around. I spot his form pacing up and down in the gravel lot, hands clasped behind his head.

"Hey," I call out. His body visibly tenses at the sound of my voice.

He ceases his pacing, letting his hands drop. "What?" His jaw is granite. For a second, I think he might punch me for no reason.

Shoving my hands in my pockets, I toe the front of my sneaker into the dirt and rocks. "Are you okay?"

"I'm fine." He puts his hands on his hips, angling his head back. "Just got shit I need to sort through. That's all."

"You know you can always talk to me if you want. I'm not going to tell anyone."

He snorts. "Let's not try to act like a bunch of Girl Scouts that are going to sit around in a circle and spill our feelings or whatever it is that they do."

"I'm pretty sure that's *not* what Girl Scouts do. I'm not saying you have to. Just that I'm here."

46

"Go back in, Cree. Be merry. Have some fun for once in your life."

"And what are you going to do?"

Jaw pulsing, he looks to the side. "I called an Uber. I'm going home."

"Are you sure you're all right?"

He makes an okay gesture with his hand. "Fucking dandy. Oh." He rifles through his pocket and pulls out some cash, smacking it into my hand. "For my drinks."

"I would've paid for them."

"It's fine." He waves me off when I try to give the cash back to him. Lights streak across the lot and a minivan pulls up front. "That's my ride."

He doesn't give me a chance to say anything else before he strides for the car and gets in.

I watch it pull away, puzzled over what the fuck just happened.

FOUR

Ophelia

"ARE you sure you don't want to come with us? Rory's meeting us there." Kenna adjusts her tank top, making sure her boobs look even better than they do already. "Harvey's is great. You'll love it."

"I don't think so. But thank you for the invite."

The last place I want to be is a loud, crowded college bar, but I hope neither of them stops inviting me. It feels good that despite me turning them down all of last year, they keep trying. I couldn't have asked for better roommates when it comes to Kenna and Li. I lucked out in so many ways.

"One of these days," Kenna wags a finger, "you're going to say yes."

Not likely.

"Maybe," I say instead.

Her smile is small, like she knows it probably won't happen either. But Kenna is a bright ray of sunshine that can't help but try. "If you need us for anything just text."

I brighten. "Can you bring me back an order of potato skins?"

She laughs, shaking her head. "What is it with you and potato skins?"

I shrug. "They're yummy."

I get up to grab my wallet, but she waves me off.

"Don't worry about it. I'll text you when we leave the bar."

"Thanks." I really do appreciate her effort. Over the years I've found that most people don't put in the time or energy it takes to get to know me. I find it difficult to open up, afraid that if people know the real me, they won't like what they find.

The door closes behind them as they head out. That leaves me with the entire dorm to myself. As much as I know I've been blessed with good roommates, being here by myself is my favorite thing. Back home, my parents rarely left me without either their company or the housekeeper, even when I was in high school.

I felt like I'd committed a crime just by breathing if I always needed supervision.

I know my parents didn't mean for it to feel that way, but that doesn't change the fact that it did.

Grabbing a blanket from my bedroom, I burrow onto the couch in a cozy cocoon and put on the first Hunger Games movie. I don't know why the books and movies have always been a comfort of mine. Maybe it's because I relate to Katniss—her quiet pondering and desperate need to fade into the background—but then I envy her poise in handling the spotlight and her strength, wishing I could channel that.

The first movie starts, and I lay with my head pillowed on my hand. I only make it halfway through before I'm interrupted with a Facetime from my best friend Logan.

I'm already smiling before I swipe to accept his call.

"There's my girl," he says right away when my face appears on screen. My heart warms at his greeting.

Logan and I have been friends for a long time. So long, in fact, that at one point we tried to be together. We realized after a handful of hours that we're friends and nothing more, that's just the way it's meant to be.

"How are you doing?"

Logan is off at Aldridge's top rival school when it comes to sports. We had originally planned to attend the same college, but there was no way my parents were ever going to agree to let me go all the way to Harding University in Alabama. So, I ended up at Aldridge and Logan stuck with the original plan.

"Good, good," he chants. He's in his room in his tiny studio apartment above the pottery place he works at. Logan doesn't *have* to work. His family is paying his school tuition and gives him money, but Logan always does his own thing. "Just had dinner with a couple of friends."

My chest pangs at the mention of friends—friends I haven't even met. I barely saw Logan this summer. He was only back home for a couple of days a handful of times. When he wasn't home, he was jetting off to different places exploring. That's how he is. He's not appeased by any one place.

"What are you up to?" His question brings me back to the land of the living.

"Oh, I'm watching *The Hunger Games*."

His chuckle is warm and amused. "Of course, you are. You've only watched it five-thousand times."

"And I'll watch it five-thousand more."

He shakes his head, dark floppy hair bouncing. "You should be out. Go do something, Filly."

I hate the stupid nickname he gave me because of my name and love of horses. But at the same time, I think I'd be sad if I asked him to stop and he listened.

"I would if I wanted to." And it's true, even if it makes me uncomfortable there are times I push my boundaries. "Tonight, I want to watch Katniss be a bad ass."

He chuckles. "You're a bad ass, too."

I roll my eyes playfully. "I know that."

Logan's shoulders sag. "I miss you."

"I miss you, too."

Besides my brother, Logan is the only person in the world who knows me inside and out, every rotten detail and loves me anyway.

"I'm sorry I didn't get to see you more this summer."

"You have a life, Logan. I get that."

"But you're part of that life." He rubs a hand over his stubbled face. He looks tired despite the fact his classes haven't begun yet either. "I'm going to make a trip up to see you one weekend."

"Don't be silly."

"It's not silly. I miss my best friend."

"I'm not going to stop you if you really want to."

He grins triumphantly. "Cool. It might be a few weeks but I'm going to make it happen."

I don't tell him, but I'll believe it when I see it.

I hang up from him and get back to the movie, but it isn't long until my mom begins texting me. Frustrated, I turn my movie off, unwrap myself from my blanket burrito and throw on some workout clothes and tennis shoes.

As I walk outside, my steps long and quick, I reply to each and every one of my mother's texts as they come in. I do my best to pacify her worries, despite wanting to chuck my cellphone into the nearest trash bin.

Once my mom is sufficiently appeased, I keep walking, not in the mood to go back and attempt to finish watching my movies.

Eventually I end up at one of the coffee shops on campus. It's empty at this hour so I'm able to walk right up to register.

"Hi." The cheery barista greets. "What can I get you?"

"Um." I study the menu. "How about a java chip frozen coffee, please?"

"What size?"

"A medium."

She reaches for a clear plastic cup, writing my order on the side. "Anything else?"

"Nope, that's it."

Normally I would get a brownie with sprinkles, but I think the chocolate in the coffee will satisfy my sweet tooth.

She rings me up and I pass my card over. Returning it with a smile, she says, "We'll get this ready shortly."

"Thanks." I put my card away and sit down at a table.

It's dark outside, the carriage top streetlights glowing warmly. I've always liked the golden glow they emit versus the stark bright white of the ones in other places.

Tapping my fingers against the top of the table, I wait for my order. A few more texts come through from my mom, and I respond as kindly as I can despite her wearing on my last nerve.

Not for the first time I wish I was normal like my brother. That way neither of our parents would worry so much about me.

As if my thoughts have conjured him, a phone call interrupts my mental spiral.

"Hello?" I answer just as the barista sets my drink down on the counter. I take it, mouthing a thank you and head outside to make the trek back to my dorm.

"Hey, sis. I just wanted to check in."

I close my eyes, letting my brother's soothing voice

wash over me. Gus—short for Augustus—is the best big brother on the planet, of that I'm certain.

"Settling back in, nothing too exciting. Classes start tomorrow."

"Ophelia," he says, his tone playful but still warning. "You don't have to sugar coat things with me. I'm not mom and dad."

"I'm doing okay." I take a deep breath, sitting down on a bench while I talk to him. "I just picked up a coffee."

"What about your friends?"

"Well, you know Logan—"

"You know I'm not talking about Logan. What about your friends there?"

"My roommates went to the bar tonight, but you know that's not my thing."

Gus's weary sigh echoes over the phone. "I want you to try to put yourself out there more. Get to know new people, make actual friends."

I wish it was easier said than done.

"I'll try," I vow. And for Gus, I mean it.

"I love you. Remember you're more than you think you are. You're not different. You're *you*."

"Thank you." My voice cracks annoying with emotion. "I love you, too."

"I've gotta go, but I'll talk to you soon."

"Bye."

Hanging up the phone, I close my eyes and tilt my head back, letting the cool night breeze wash over me.

You're more, I say to myself, echoing his words. *Stop letting other people's insecurities turn you into a shell of who you really are. You are light. You are magic.*

FIVE

CREE

LEAVING my first class of the day, British Literature, I head for the dining hall. I want a snack and some coffee. Glancing at my phone, I find a string of texts from Millie that I missed while I was in class.

Millie: This campus is HUGE

Millie: <GIF Attachment>

Millie: I think I'm lost.

Millie: How hard can it possibly be to find the science department?

Millie: Dude, help me.

Millie: I bet you have your phone off in class. You goody two shoes.

Millie: Never mind, I was in the right place all along. Tata.

Shaking my head in amusement, I get in line and text her back.

Me: Glad you got it all worked out.

She replies back almost instantly.

Millie: No thanks to you.

Me: I was in class.

Millie: And I needed help.

Me: You better pay attention to your class.

Millie: Meanie.

Returning my phone to my pocket I grab a sandwich and bottle of water. Scarfing the sandwich down, I head to the nearest coffee shop. After ordering a black coffee with one creamer, I find a quiet seat and pull out the latest book I'm reading. Technically it's a reread, but I never get tired of the Percy Jackson series despite being twenty-one. Flipping the book open, I tuck my head low and start reading. I have time to kill before my only other class of the day, and don't feel like going back home for such a short amount of time. After my next class I need to hit the gym too. There's a home gym in the basement of the house, but I still prefer the campus one for athletes.

A flash of reddish hued hair catches my eye, causing my gaze to jump from the pages of my book to the café around me. The girl breezes behind the counter, and I realize her hair isn't the right shade.

Scrubbing a hand over my face I curse my pathetic ass for still pining over a girl I haven't run into in a year. I don't know her real name, or if she even still attends this school.

It's beginning to feel more and more like Daisy was a figment of my imagination.

Taking a long swallow of my coffee, I force my eyes back to the pages of my book, but I can't fucking focus anymore for the life of me. Slamming the book closed, I shove it back in my bag.

It's the first day back on campus, and I'm already losing myself to thoughts of her again.

I can't let this be my ruination.

Throwing my bag over my shoulder, I shove my way out of the shop, earning more than a few glances of concern at my weird behavior.

I haven't gone very far when I'm stopped by my name being called. "Cree! Hey, Cree!"

I groan internally when I see Rosie Thomas waving as she walks toward me.

Raven-haired, curves for days, and downright gorgeous, she's most guys dreams ... and she knows it too. She's been with most of the guys on my team, and that's cool, she can do whatever she wants, but where I draw the line is putting up with her endless pursuit to get with me.

"Hi, Rosie." I keep it short, my tone implying I'm not in the mood for small talk.

She laughs like I've said something so funny as she comes to a stop in front of me. The black v-neck tee she wears shows an abundance of tits and yeah, I can't help but take a look. I'm a guy. Sue me.

She smirks, having caught my glance despite my quick diversion.

"How was your summer?" She puts a hand on her hip. "I missed seeing you around." She smooths her hand over my shirt, pressing against my chest. It annoys me that she thinks she can touch me without my permission. My parents raised me to always respect a woman's personal space, to never assume something without asking or her telling me she wants it, but Rosie doesn't understand personal space.

Grabbing her hand from my chest, I let it drop. Immediately she pouts her bottom lip. I'm sure she means it to look somehow seductive, but she looks like a toddler about to throw a tantrum.

"It was fine. How was yours?" I hope I don't sound as pissed off as I feel. Or maybe I do because she might be more likely to leave me alone.

"It could've been better." There's a seductive glint in her eyes.

A part of me says I should go for it and take what she's been offering for the better part of two years now —that it might help me erase Daisy from my mind. But I know it's a lie. If anything, it would make me feel worse.

"Sorry to hear that."

"We should catch up sometime. Maybe over coffee or dinner?"

I commend the girl for putting herself out there, but I don't want what she's offering. "Thanks, but my schedule is pretty packed. You should hit up Daire."

She wrinkles her nose, and her full lips turn down like the thought of seeing Daire is sour on her tongue. "Some other time then. I'll see you around."

She doesn't wait for me to respond before she's trotting off, eating up the attention when a guy literally turns around to check out her ass in her tight denim skirt.

I walk around campus for a while before I can't stall any longer and have to go to class.

My creative writing class drags by. I've never been

that great at writing unless it's an essay. It's like there's a block in my brain that doesn't allow me to be imaginative. Despite reading the books I do, when I sit down to write something of my own creation I freeze. I love reading about fictional worlds, but creating them? It doesn't seem like I can.

When class ends, I feel exhausted over the prospect of what I might be enduring over this semester. But no matter, this is my last year to get through.

Daire beats me to the gym, already changing in the locker room.

"I see you survived." He yanks his shirt off over his head.

"Barely." I set my bag down and yank out the shorts I'm going to change into. No point bothering with a shirt. I'll soak it with sweat quick enough.

"Hey, hey, hey," Caleb Richardson and the goalie on our team cajoles as he strolls into the room. "If it isn't the dynamic duo." He gives both Daire and me a shove. "What trouble have you been up to already?"

"Not much yet," Daire laughs, slamming the locker closed. "But there's gonna be a party Friday night at our place. Spread it around."

Caleb fists bumps Daire. "I've fucking missed your parties, man." He turns to me, giving his fist as well. I bump it back.

"Glad to be of service."

At least some people like the parties even if, ironically, I'm not one of them.

Changed, I head into the gym and start my warmup. Some teammates are already there, and I give a head nod in greeting since they're busy.

Daire isn't far behind me and joins me in my corner of solitude. I'll give the guy credit. He's always known without me saying that I prefer the quiet, and for the most part respectful of that.

After warming up, we start on sprints, an integral part of our training for endurance on the ice. So much of hockey is having to go all out one moment and coming to a dead stop the next. They help a lot, even if I fucking hate doing them.

Both of us are dripping with sweat by the time we finish, and we haven't even gotten to the weight part of our workout yet.

I keep up with a decent regime over the summer, but one day back and it already feels like what I've been doing is inadequate. Coach Hawkins is going to whip my ass our first day back on the ice.

The workouts, bruises, and blood are all worth it for the love of the sport.

I still remember the first time I put on skates and got on the ice. No one in my family had ever been an ice hockey player before, but from a young age I begged to try until my parents finally relented when I was six. They saw immediately what I'd already known—that's where I belonged. I started ice skating lessons and from there I joined my first team.

An hour later Daire and I get back home, stepping inside to the smell of garlic.

"Who's cooking?" Daire calls out, passing by me and heading straight for the kitchen.

"I thought I'd make dinner!" Millie calls as we round the corner into the open layout kitchen. We find her standing at the stove, stirring alfredo sauce while noodles are going in a pot. Jude is with her cutting up already cooked chicken for the sauce.

"How'd you get this one to help?" Daire tosses a thumb at Jude.

I grab a bottle of water from the fridge and chug it down. I already had a decent amount of fluid before leaving the gym, but I know more won't hurt anything. I turn, waiting eagerly for my sister or Jude's response.

"I told him to get off his lazy ass and help me, that this isn't the 1950s and he's just as capable being in the kitchen as I am."

"That true?" Daire holds back laughter, gripping the back of a chair at the table.

"Unfortunately." Jude tosses the cut-up pieces of

chicken into the simmering sauce. "She wouldn't even let me use frozen garlic bread — no, I had to make actual garlic butter, slather it on some kind of fancy bread, and now it's in the oven, so you better fucking love it and if it tastes like shit, I don't want to hear it."

Millie swats him with her spoon — one covered in sauce and it goes all over him, including his hair.

We're all silent, staring at the mess on Jude. He stares my sister down, her lips thinning and her expression melting into one that very blatantly says *oops*.

Daire is the first to crack, his snort piercing the silence. Then my own laughter breaks free.

"I am so, so sorry," Millie tells him. Jude's massive beside my tiny sister, but she doesn't cower.

He shakes his head slowly. "Who's gonna clean this mess up, Little Madison?"

"Um…" She bites her lip. "You?" He dips the tip of his finger into the sauce where she can't see and then flicks it into her hair. Her jaw drops. "I know you did *not* just get sauce in my hair?" She shrieks and lunges at him.

The next thing I know, Daire and I are ducking out of the way. Millie chases Jude out of the kitchen, swatting at him with a dishrag.

"I just washed this hair! Do you know what that

means? I shouldn't have to wash it for three more days, but thanks to you, I have to wash it again!"

Their feet pound up the stairs, voices growing distant.

Daire glances at me, shrugging. "Guess we're finishing dinner then, huh?"

SIX

Ophelia

MUD SQUELCHES BENEATH MY BOOTS, squishing with every step as I make my way to the barn.

No matter how many years I've spent around horses, I've personally never gotten over the smell. Some people love it, but I'm not one of them.

What I do love is being in the presence of a horse. Even when I was small, their big forms were never imposing or scary. I've always found them magical in a way. They're extremely intelligent and warm, smart too. The first day my parents ever brought me to a barn to see if I'd be interested in lessons, I knew this was where I belonged. I want to own land and have horses for myself one day. They're hard work, but that's another reason I love them. When I'm tending to a horse, my mind quiets. It's one of the few times it's not buzzing with chaos and worry.

"Ophelia!" Mary cries out, the older lady who owns this farm with her elderly husband Tom. They don't have much help around here, can't afford to, but luckily the farm is small enough that they've been able to manage with help from their grandson Callahan. "Oh, how I've missed you!" She sets down a bucket filled with water and closes the distance between us, hugging me. Holding my face between her wrinkled hands, she smiles. "It's not the same without you."

"I missed you, too."

I really did. Mary and Tom have treated me like family, and being around Callahan makes me feel like I have another brother.

"Are you able to stay for dinner?" She bestows upon me a smile that reminds me of the sunshine, extraordinary and warm.

"I don't have plans."

"Great!" She steps back. "The horses have missed you too." She winks, picking up her bucket. "I'm certain you share some sort of secret language with them. It's amazing to see."

"Maybe I do."

Mary laughs, waving over her shoulder as she walks away. "You know what to do and where everything is. Nothing's changed. I'll see you later, dear."

A year ago, I saw a flyer looking for help on their farm. When I came to inquire about it, Mary told me she was sorry, but circumstances had changed, and they didn't have the funds to pay for an employee. I explained, practically begging, that I didn't want nor need, to be paid. She still tried to turn me away, but when I continued, I think she sensed my desperation to be near the animals and relented. She's tried to slip me cash, which I always refuse or find a way to give back if she sneaks it into my bag. She doesn't understand what being around the horses does for me. Besides, getting to have her home-cooked meals is payment enough.

Walking up to one of the stalls, I smile when I see my favorite horse. "Hello, Calliope."

She grunts in response, almost like she's trying to say, "It's about time you showed up."

"I know," I reply, holding out my hand and watching her cues before I touch her. "I had to go home for the summer, but I thought about you every day. All of you." I give the horse, Indigo, in the next stall a smile. His coat is a blue-black which is how he got his name. Calliope is an Appaloosa. Her muzzle and most of the front of her body is a silvery gray, where the rest of her is white with gray spots. I think she's beautiful and her spots make me feel more confident about the freckles that cover my body.

She finally lowers her head, letting me pet her muzzle, and I nearly cry the moment my hands make contact with her. The feeling that washes over me is indescribable. It's calming and grounding, stilling everything inside me. I close my eyes, soaking up the feeling.

A loud noise startles me and my eyes pop open to find Mary has returned, the empty bucket hitting the dirty floor.

Her hands go to her hips. "The bond you have with them is incredible." She pauses, watching me. "But get to work."

I throw my head back and laugh as she walks away. "You got it, Mary."

I'M HOT AND SWEATY, my shoes and jeans caked in mud by the time I finish up with my duties and take Calliope for a ride. I kick as much gunk off my shoes as

I can before giving up and removing them on the porch stairs.

I knock on the door, and I'm not surprised when Mary hollers, "Ophelia, I've told you time and time again that you don't have to knock. Just come inside."

Opening it, I inhale the scent of a home-cooked meal. Heading back to the kitchen, like always, I pause for a moment to take in the family photos that litter almost every surface of wall. Mary and Tom have lived a long and exciting life. With five kids and tons of grandchildren, they've always been busy. It makes me feel sad that despite this huge family, Callahan is the only one who helps them out.

Reaching the kitchen, I smile at the image in front of me of Tom cutting up the pot roast Mary has had cooking in the Crock Pot all day, the oldies station playing softly in the background from the radio plugged into the wall. Callahan sits at the table, watching them with amusement. He hears my steps and smiles my way.

With wavy brown hair bleached blond on top from time in the sun, green eyes crinkled at the corners from all his laughter, and a smile that can make any girl go weak in the knees—he's exactly my type. But I refuse to cross that line, despite his flirting, because I love and value my time here too much to risk it.

Except that one time we made out by the stream in the back, but that's beside the point.

"Hey, Ophelia," he says in his exceptionally deep voice. He waved earlier from the tractor when he spotted me, but our paths haven't crossed other than that today.

"Cal," I say, dipping my head. "How was your summer?"

He's deeply tanned from all his time outdoors, his large hands weathered from hard work. It's been so long since I've been with another person that the idea of his roughened hands on my bare skin sends a shiver down my spine.

But no matter, it won't be happening.

"It was good." He rubs his fingers over his mouth, looking me up and down.

Tom reaches over and swats Cal on the back of the head. "Boy, we taught you better than to check out a lady so blatantly."

"Granddad." He rubs the back of his head. "Was that necessary?"

"Yes," Mary answers for him without turning around. "Grab a plate, Ophelia. You first."

I know better than to argue with her. Mary always gets her way.

Plates are already sitting out on the tiled counters

along with utensils. I grab what I need and pile my plate with enough pot roast and veggies to feed three people. That's another thing about Mary, she's going to make sure no one leaves her house hungry.

With my plate full I sit down beside Callahan. He bumps my shoulder playfully with his, giving me his signature dopey smile. "Missed you."

I warm at his words, sensing the sincerity in them. Oftentimes I doubt my importance to people, but there are moments when I see the genuineness and all my doubts melt away. Emotions can be one of those things that's tricky for me to decipher.

Cal gets up for his plate, joking with his grandparents about his late nights out.

I'm sure he's quite the ladies' man—another reason for me to stay far away and keep things platonic.

Once everyone's seated, we eat. I missed Mary's cooking more than I originally thought.

"I might have to come over for dinner every night."

Mary smiles at the compliment. "You're welcome any time. You know that. We love having you around."

"Yeah, Ophelia, you're fun to have around." Callahan winks and my cheeks heat, reminded of our kiss last year.

After dinner is finished, I have to fight Mary to help wash the dishes. They don't have a dishwasher, Mary claiming that she has two goods hands to wash things with and that's more reliable than a machine.

"How's school going?" she asks softly, passing me a plate to rinse and dry.

I confessed to Mary last year that sometimes I struggle to learn the material. It's not that I don't understand but applying it can be difficult.

"We're not even done with the first week, so not much to report." I stand on my tiptoes to put the dried plate away before taking the next from her.

"What are you going to do when you graduate and get your fancy degree?"

"I always thought maybe I'd be a teacher," I admit quietly. I hate that my shoulders automatically curl up in protection, like I expect her to tell me there's no way I could be a teacher. But this is Mary and she'd never say that.

"I think that's a wonderful idea." She scrubs the sink while I put the final plate away. "I can see you making a great teacher."

"Really?" I tuck a piece of hair behind my ear, shy beneath her praise.

Mary, who's even shorter than my five-foot-four stature—grabs me gently by my shoulders, forcing me to look down at her. "I would never lie to you. You're a beautiful, smart, capable young lady. Nothing, and I mean nothing, is stopping you from realizing any dream you have."

"You're going to make me cry."

She scoffs, pulling me into a hug. "We can't have that now, because then *I'll* cry and I don't cry, I blubber. It's ugly." She pats my cheek before letting me go and stepping back. "I wish you saw yourself as you truly are and not what you've deluded yourself into believing."

"I'm getting there."

She grips my hand, eyes crinkling with a smile. "That you are, my girl."

SEVEN

CREE

THE PARTY RAGES in the house, all the downstairs rooms packed with bodies. I keep the upstairs strictly off limits and that rule has always been followed—not without some reinforcing, but it's rare for anyone to try to go up there now.

Still, I urge everyone to lock their doors because you never know.

Sitting on the couch, I nurse a beer. It's warm and doesn't taste that great, but I don't feel like getting up for a new one. My eyes scan the room, ghosting over every girl. I don't only search for red hair, because I know Daisy could've dyed her hair since that night, but none of the girls I see are her.

It's like she's a myth. Some figment of my imagination.

In the front window, the green lava lamp mocks me for my stupidity of thinking it was so fucking perfect when I saw it to put it there like a beacon for my mystery girl.

Stupid.

Stupid.

Stupid.

I swallow another mouthful of beer as the song changes over and some of the girls start scream-singing it. My eyes close and I pinch the bridge of my nose. I'm not in the mood for this tonight, but I know I need to get over myself and stop wallowing.

"Dude." Daire's voice has me cracking one eye open.

"Yes?"

"Stop acting like a miserable prick. Get up and ask one of these lovely ladies to dance."

My lips thin. I want to argue, but I know he has a point.

Standing, I thrust my half full beer at him. "Take this."

He grins triumphantly, clapping a hand on my shoulder. "That's my boy."

Scanning the room, I move through the throng of bodies until I find a girl that catches my eye. Blonde hair cascades over her shoulders, long and thick enough to grab onto in the right mood. She turns, feeling the music and oblivious to me. In that way she reminds me of Daisy—unbothered by those around her.

Her eyes open, a dark blue shade. "Hey." I smile at her.

She looks me up and down with a flirtatious gaze. She drapes an arm over my shoulder, moving her body to the beat of the song. Her hips sway sexily. Reaching out, I place my hands on them, moving with her. I try my best to let myself get lost in the song, in the moment, in this nameless girl. I have to give things a real shot if I have any hope of giving up on my ridiculous quest.

The girl moves even closer to me until I'm not sure where my body ends and hers begins. Her breasts press into my chest, and her eyes suggest if I wanted to move things up to my room then she'd be more than willing. But while she feels nice in my arms, and I'm enjoying dancing with her, there's no desire stirring inside me. I don't want to kiss her, and I definitely don't want to fuck her.

She turns in my arms, shimmying down my body

and shaking her ass. The girl knows how to dance and move her body, but I still feel absolutely nothing. I close my eyes, focusing on the way she feels against me. The song changes, and with it she moves her body differently. I groan and that excites her, but it's not for the reason she believes.

I think my dick is broken.

Opening my eyes, my surroundings come into focus once more.

"I'm Ariel," she says, swinging around to face me. Her arms twine around my neck.

And now I'm thinking of Daisy again and her Little Mermaid hair.

"Cree."

"Cool name."

"So is yours."

Fuck, I have no game whatsoever.

If Daire is somewhere watching me right now, then he's fucking cringing at my inability to flirt.

Ariel must sense my awkwardness because she's determined to dig us out of this hole. "I haven't seen you around before, and trust me, I would've remembered you."

"Uh ... too bad."

I'm not helping her get me out of this whatsoever.

She giggles, running a finger down my chest. Nothing inside me stirs.

"You need to loosen up," she croons, batting her eyes. "You're tense. Relax." Her hips grind into mine. "I'm just a girl. You don't need to be afraid." Standing on her tiptoes, she whispers huskily into my ear, "I don't bite but you can."

"I'm sorry." I take her hands and gently push her away from my body.

She looks at me quizzically. "Recent breakup?"

"No. Nothing like that." I run my fingers through my hair.

"Gay?"

I laugh. "Definitely not." Wetting my lips with my tongue, I force myself to say, "It's cliché, but seriously it's not you, it's me."

She throws her head back and laughs. "Definitely cliché, but I'll forgive you. Have a good night, Cree." She wiggles her fingers in a wave as she walks away from me.

I sigh, the kind that's heavy with frustration.

"What the fuck?" Daire comes up, tossing his arm around my shoulders. "She was hot. I can't believe you're letting her leave."

I shrug his arm off. "There was no attraction."

"But she was fucking gorgeous. How can you say

she's not attractive?"

I glower at my best friend, wishing he'd lay off my case. "I didn't say she wasn't attractive. She's fucking gorgeous. But I'm not *attracted*. There's no ... feeling of want or desire."

He frowns. "You sound like a chick."

"I don't care." I flee from the room, but he follows me anyway. In the kitchen, I grab a fresh beer from the fridge—also off limits to guests. They can drink the shitty keg beer.

"I don't get what's up with you? You were suspish last year, but we've barely been back and you're even weirder this year."

"Suspish? What kind of word is that?"

He crosses his arms over his chest. "Don't try to deflect."

I scrub a hand over my face, knowing I've avoided this conversation with my friend for too long. "Fine, but I'm not having this conversation here." I look around the kitchen where people idle, drinking and laughing, not giving a fuck about anything.

Daire follows me out onto the back deck and down to the edge of the yard where there aren't any people.

"Tell me what's up because I'm tired of your weird behavior." He leans against the fence.

"It's stupid." I take a swig of beer, bracing myself for his inevitable hysterics.

"Well, you're stupid, so I'd expect no less." I shove him, not hard but he still stumbles and nearly falls in a dip in the yard. "Asshole," he grumbles.

"There was a girl last year at the bonfire party. We hit it off and hooked up. We didn't exchange real names and said if it was meant to be we'd meet again, but we never have. I started these parties in the hope that she'd come to one, but she never has. You're going to think I'm crazy, dude, but no other girl makes me feel this weird thing that I do. It's not love that would be crazy, it's something different. Like my soul recognized hers. That maybe we've met in another life."

He stares at me, mouth parted. He blinks, blinks again. His brain must be having a reboot.

"I think you've been reading too many books."

"Don't mock me."

"Listen to yourself, Cree. You've been what? Abstinent since you hooked up with this chick? One, might I add, you don't even know the real name of. You've just been sitting around waiting for her to appear. It's…"

"Pathetic?"

"I was going to say odd, but yeah pathetic works too." He chuckles, shaking his head. "Pining for a girl you don't even know? It's kind of weird."

"It does sound weird." I cross my arms over my chest, annoyed with how much of a fool I've been. "But that night, it was … I can't describe it, but it was like my dad always said about my mom. He just knew."

He scratches his head, eyeing me skeptically. "Maybe it's because my parents are divorced but I can't relate. I've never felt insta anything for someone. Well," he frowns, looking down at his boots, "insta-hate with Rosie, but that's not what we're talking about here."

Running my fingers through my hair, I mumble, "I know I'm never going to see her again but give me a break. I've never slept around like you and some of the other guys."

Daire mocks offense. "And I don't sleep around like Jude does. That guy's a pig. He grabbed some random girl, stuck his tongue halfway down her throat and then drug her up to his room. Listen, I've had my fair share of one-night stands, but that dude is off the deep end."

We all know Jude sort of lost his shit when it comes to women after his longtime girlfriend cheated and left him. He's not awful to the girls he's with and up front about what it is, but that doesn't mean it's not fucking annoying to witness.

"Anyway, good chat." Daire claps me on the shoulder. "I'm going back in to have fun. You … you do whatever it is you do." He waggles his fingers at me, loping off toward the deck.

Sighing, I bring the fresh beer to my lips.

I have to forget about Daisy. Focus on school, hockey, anything but searching for a girl who's more like a ghost than reality.

EIGHT

Ophelia

I BLINKED and we're already in the middle of week three of our first semester.

And I'm already struggling.

It's no surprise to me that I'm teetering into the failure category when it comes to my Critical Approaches to Literature course. Professor Lindon is nice enough, but a stickler, and a tad overly critical. When I failed last year, I was devasted. It was more than not passing the class, it felt like proof to my parents and everyone else that I'm really not cut out for this thing.

Class comes to a close, and before I have a chance to tuck my books and laptop back into my bag, Professor Lindon is calling my name.

"Ophelia?"

My head jerks to attention like one of those cute bug-eyed meerkats on Animal Planet. "Yes?"

"Please come see me before you leave."

A few of my classmates glance my way questioningly but mostly I'm ignored. With a sigh, I heft my backpack on and trek down the stairs to him.

He looks up from his papers, pulling his reading glasses off. "Ms. Hastings." His voice is gravelly. Shaking his head, he tsks softly. "I was hoping this year you'd be better prepared for my class, but I fear not and your failure is imminent. If you have no plans to change your degree, then I'm afraid you're dependent on passing this class."

"I know." My voice comes out annoyingly small. I try to keep my shoulders back, my head held high, but on the inside, I feel like crumbling.

His face softens. "Look, I know this material can be difficult for some to grasp." I wince and he frowns, probably realizing that his attempt to be kind is anything but. "I'm not making any promises here," he presses on, "but I'm going to reach out to a former student, he's a senior now, and I think if he's able to tutor you, it'd be a great help to you in understanding the material."

I bite my tongue, tears stinging my eyes. I don't want to cry in front of my professor, for him to realize how badly this is getting to me.

Clearing my throat, I say, "That would be great. I appreciate you reaching out to him on my behalf."

"Of course." He dips his head. "I know I can be a bit of a stickler, but Ophelia, I never want to see any of my students fail."

I nod, knowing if I open my mouth I'll start crying.

He seems to sense this and returns his attention to his cluttered desk once more. "I'll email you tonight if I hear back from him."

Taking a couple of steps back, I give out a timid, "Thank you."

Rushing up the stairs, I burst through the doors and dash to the nearest exit where I inhale gulps of fresh air.

You are enough, I remind myself, trying not to break down. *You are enough*.

I chant it over and over, hoping to drill those three words through my skull.

〜

PROFESSOR LINDON EMAILED me last night with the good news that the student agreed to meet with me today to see if he'd be able to help me. He didn't want to say yes right away, which worries me, but I guess it makes sense to see if we even get along. If he's some stuck up know it all prick, I know there's no way I'll be willing to let him tutor me.

Trekking across campus, I keep my eyes trained on the cobblestone pathway. We're supposed to meet at the main coffee shop on campus at three. It's two-fifty-five and I *loathe* being late. It doesn't set a good first impression. I tap my finger impatiently against my book clasped in my arms—today's choice is a retelling of Beauty and the Beast.

I reach the coffee shop at two-fifty-eight which leaves me with two minutes to order a drink. The only kind of coffee I'll drink is the frozen, practically dessert kind, so I can't exactly call myself a coffee drinker. Regardless, I need something to help with my jitters.

While I wait in line, my eyes dart around the room trying to figure out if my tutor is already here. He said he'd be at a table in the back, but what if all those tables are full and he had to pick another one.

I hate this.

I do notice a guy that is indeed at a back table, his

head lowered as he pours over a book, and I have a feeling this is who I'm looking for.

Once I have my coffee I trek carefully to his table, nervously biting my lower lip. If this isn't who I'm looking for, I'm going to be embarrassed and feel terribly sorry for disturbing his reading time.

Stopping beside the table, I clear my throat readying to introduce myself. Ice blue eyes move from the text on the yellowed book pages to me, his face emptying of color, lips parting. His eyes get bigger, and his expression is the definition of shock.

Those blue eyes light up, getting even brighter while a grin breaks over his face revealing dimples in his cheeks. "I've been looking for you."

His words make sense, considering we're supposed to be meeting up—but his expression and connotation to his words leads me to believe he's saying more than that.

"Um … yes … I'm sure you have. I'm a few minutes late, but not much, so hopefully you haven't been waiting too long."

"Daisy," he murmurs, his eyes gliding over my body in a way that sends a shiver down my spine.

"No … I'm Ophelia. Did Professor Lindon give you the wrong name?"

"Professor Lindon?" He repeats slowly, forming the name carefully in his sensual lips.

"Y-Yeah?" I stutter and it comes out sounding like a question. "He emailed you about tutoring me." I pause again. "For Critical Approaches to Literature."

The guy's brows furrow and he appears thoroughly confused. He seems to be thinking something over before coming to some sort of resolve. "Yes," he smiles, nodding slowly, "he did contact me. Sit, please." He waves his hand at the empty chair in front of me. I pull it out and plop down, laying my book on top of the table and my frozen coffee beside it. He glances at the cover, a slow smile spreading. My shoulders hunch, bracing for some sort of judgmental comment on the fantasy romance I'm reading, but he shocks me by saying, "I love that series."

I sit shocked for a moment, absorbing his words. "You've read it?" I shove my finger against the cover. "This?"

He nods. "All of them."

"And you ... liked it?" He chuckles, his long fingers wrapping around his hot cup of coffee. I take a moment to study him.

Chiseled cheekbones, long nose with a slight bump like it has been broken in the past, veiny hands that connect to arms that are even more veiny and muscular, lips that aren't full but aren't thin either but somewhere in the middle. Dark brown, almost black hair that has a natural wave and falls over his forehead in an annoyingly effortless way.

He's without a doubt, the most gorgeous guy I've ever seen. So much so that I feel my breath catching and my heart rate speeding up. It's been a while since I've felt attraction this acutely. Longer than a year, easily.

"I loved it."

I frown, wracking my brain to remember what I'd asked him.

Oh! The book!

"Even the romance bits?"

"Especially the romance bits." He smirks, my stomach dipping with excitement.

Tucking a piece of hair behind my ear, nerves easing slightly I take a sip of my chocolate chip frozen coffee. "As much as I love talking books," I place my hand over the red and yellow cover, "and truly I could go on about them all day long, but I really need to know if you're willing to tutor me? I failed this class last year, and I can't afford to not pass again."

Vulnerability sinks into my chest as I wait for him to answer. I know plenty of people fail classes for various reasons and need extra help, but it doesn't stop me from hating that I'm put in this position.

He waves his fingers lazily through the air. "Not a problem, Daisy."

"I told you," I say slowly, like maybe he didn't understand the first time, "my name is Ophelia."

He grins. "And what a beautiful name it is." He cocks his head to the side, looking at me funny. I hate being scrutinized in such a way. Like a bug beneath a microscope. "Jay and Daisy, remember?"

I stare blankly at the guy in front of me.

Is he sane? What is he talking about?

"*The Great Gatsby,*" he supplies, pausing for a breath. Almost desperately, he adds, "Remember?"

But I don't remember. I haven't met this guy before, but he seems to think he knows me.

I open my mouth to tell him he's mistaken, but then I shut it.

I'm not a liar, never have been, but if him thinking he knows me helps this tutoring thing then maybe I should.

"Right, yeah, of course. *The Great Gatsby*. A classic. It's a favorite of mine." He looks at me quizzically, so I find myself continuing to ramble. "So, Jay, then? Is that really your name or is it something else? Truly, a tragedy that happened to Mr. Gatsby. Completely avoidable too. All those lavish parties, filled with people, and in the end … well, there was no one who really cared."

Jay—though I'm assuming that's not really his name—watches me with a look of awe, one I've never seen directed my way before. He looks at me like I'm more than beautiful—I am the universe, a complex and mesmerizing entity. But it doesn't make any sense to me why a guy I haven't met before is gazing at me like someone in lust.

But he seems to know you or at least he thinks he does.

"Nah, Jay isn't my name." He leans back, draping a tanned muscular arm along the back of the chair beside him. "It's Cree."

"Nice to meet you, Cree."

He grins, those dimples popping out again. "Nice to meet you, Ophelia." He rolls my name around his tongue like he's dancing with it.

"So," I drag out the single word, drumming my fingers on my book. "We should set up a plan for tutoring. How busy is your schedule?"

He winces, and mutters, "Busy." Clearing his throat, adds, "But I'll make time."

Relief floods me. I need his help more than anything. "My schedule is flexible, so I'm sure I can work around yours."

Besides classes, all I do is visit the farm to help Mary and Tom.

"I really can't believe it's you." He runs his fingers through his ink-dark hair. "Just when I gave up hope of running into you, here you are."

"Here I am." I waggle my fingers stupidly in the air.

I'm not this girl he thinks I am. I'm not Daisy. But am I willing to lie to him if it means passing this class?

Yeah. I am.

I never thought I could be such a thing—a liar—but desperation makes monsters out of all of us.

He chuckles, rubbing those long fingers against his chin. "Here you are."

I take a sip of my drink for lack of anything else to do, wracking my brain for what the right thing is to do or say in this situation and coming up entirely empty.

His icy blue eyes follow the movement of my lips around the straw. My stomach dips in that delicious way I haven't felt in so long—*too long*.

Sexual tension radiates between us. For a moment I worry I'm the only one feeling it, but the way his gaze trails over me and his tongue slides out ever so slightly to moisten his lips, I know I'm not alone in this.

Heat flooding my cheeks, I rifle through my bag and procure a piece of paper and pen. Scribbling my phone number down as well as the name of my dorm, I slide it across to him.

He takes it in those long fingers of his, studying my penmanship. "You could've just told me your number and I would've put it in my phone." I flush with embarrassment. He's right. That would've been the normal thing to do. "But I like this better. Old fashioned." He tucks the piece of paper into his jean pocket. "I want a brownie." He points to the case by the register. "You want anything?"

The polite thing would be to say no but fuck polite. A brownie sounds like the best thing ever right now. "A brownie would be great."

He grins like my answer pleases him. "You got it." Bracing his large hands on the table, he pushes to a stand and goes to order, leaving me alone at the table and to my own devices.

Rarely a good thing. Especially when I'm uncomfortable.

Reaching across the table, I slide his book over to me. He has it flipped over so I turn it to the front. It's the final book in the Percy Jackson series. I read them when I was in middle school. I look over my shoulder at the wavy-haired, blue-eyed heartthrob. He talks to someone in line, smiling and laughing. Someone else comes up to him and says something to which he replies with a grin and nod. I narrow my eyes. It seems Mr. Tutor is also Mr. Popularity.

Turning around, I slide his book back to where it was previously placed.

Thudded steps sound behind me and I *feel* his approach—the space he takes up in the world with his large body and enigmatic personality. He sets a brownie covered in chocolate frosting and rainbow sprinkles in front of me on a little white plate, placing a matching one down in his spot as he folds into his chair.

"Percy Jackson, huh?" I blurt giving myself away with my snooping.

He grins, those dimples making my stomach flip upside down. "Curiosity got the best of you, did it?"

I shrug, feigning indifference. "I read those in middle school."

"I did too." He takes a bite of brownie, getting chocolate frosting in the corner of his lip while sprinkles rain down onto the table. He chews and swallows. "But I thought it was time for a reread. What else did you read in middle school?"

"A lot of Sarah Dessen books. I still read her new ones."

"I can't say I've read those, but I do know of them. My sister has read a couple."

"They're good." I pull off a bite of brownie and pop

it into my mouth. My eyes fall closed at the delicious goodness.

Why does chocolate, especially brownies, have to taste so freaking good? It's not fair. Why can't broccoli taste like this? Oh, right. Because it's healthy.

Cree's eyes sparkle with amusement at my display with the brownie.

"I like chocolate." I keep my tone reasonable, not letting loose the chocolate fiend inside that will cut a bitch for a sweet.

"I can see that." His lips quirk. "I do too." He takes another massive bite while I break off another piece.

"These are my favorite," I admit, saving an errant sprinkle with my finger before licking it off. "And everything is better with rainbow sprinkles."

He presses his lips together, suppressing a laugh as he nods at the tiny smattering of sprinkles on the whipped cream in my drink. "I can see that, too."

I give a tiny shrug, sipping my drink. "I don't mean to keep you here. I can go." I reach for my bag to gather my things.

His hand flies across the table, landing on mine and halting my movements. His hand is warm, rough and well-used. I don't think he's aware of it, but he rubs his thumb slowly, softly against the tender skin where my thumb and index finger meet.

"All right." I slip my hand from beneath his. "I'll stay then."

And I do. We spend hours talking about books, school, classes—*everything*.

I've never felt so seen in all my life.

But as we say our goodbyes, I remind myself it's all a lie. I'm not who he thinks I am. I'm not Daisy.

I envy the girl who really is.

For now, I'll fake it.

NINE

CREE

GRABBING A BEER, I head out back where Daire sits on the deck.

"Hey." He looks up from his laptop and closes the lid. "You're in late for you."

Plopping into the chair across from him, I kick my feet up on the railing and take a long swig of my drink. "I found her."

"Who?" His brows knit together.

"Daisy. *The* girl."

His eyes widen, mouth dropping open. "Well, fuck. Talk about an eventful day." He takes a drink.

"What are the odds that I give up on looking for her and today she walks into the coffee shop and sits down across from me?" I shake my head, still flabbergasted and reeling. To be honest I've had to pinch myself a few times to make sure I didn't dream the whole thing. "She thought I was the tutor she was looking for, and dude, I know it was wrong, but I said I was. So, looks like I'll be tutoring this semester."

He eyes me skeptically. "You got time for that? And isn't kind of fucked up to pretend to be her tutor?"

"I'll make time. Besides she needs an English tutor and since that's my major it shouldn't be too difficult. I look at it as the universe giving me a helping hand."

He shakes his head, looking at me pityingly but also annoyed. "Dude."

"I can handle it. It's really not a big deal."

"We'll see."

"Why are you being an asshole about this?" I snap, my bottle slamming against the table.

"Because you're so fucking worked up about a girl you've met once—*twice*—," he corrects when he sees it on the tip of my tongue, "and it baffles me to be honest." He runs his hand through his hair. "Look I'm not trying to be a hard ass, or whatever, I just … don't get it."

"And you don't have to," I gripe, wrapping my fingers around the bottle. "You don't have to approve either."

"Fuck." He shakes his head. "Seriously, I don't want to piss you off, but it doesn't make sense. What is it about this girl?"

I gulp down half the beer, staring at my friend across the table. "You don't get it now, but you will."

He snorts. "Not likely."

"Believe me. Someone will knock you over one day. It might not be in the same way, but at some point, you're going to look at a girl and you're going to know."

"Know what exactly?"

"Trust me, I don't need to tell you. You'll feel it."

He rolls his eyes, doubting me. He can think what he wants. I know he won't be a bachelor forever. Daire doesn't date, not seriously anyway, but I have heard him talk about marriage and wanting kids, so I don't know why he acts like it's such a far-fetched idea.

The sliding door creeks open behind me.

"What are you two bitches gossiping about?" Jude joins us with his own drink. Instead of pulling out a chair and sitting down like a normal person, he hops up on the deck railing.

"Cree's got it bad for some chick."

"She's not some chick," I snap bitingly.

"He's only met her twice," Daire talks over me. *"Twice,"* he emphasizes, holding up two fingers.

"So?" Jude surprises both of us with his reply.

"So?" Daire repeats disgustedly. "It's fucking weird, that's what."

"Nah." Jude shakes his head. "I've had the same thing happen before." His eyes grow distant and neither of us says a word, knowing he's thinking about his ex. "Just because you haven't experienced it doesn't mean it doesn't happen." He points his bottle at Daire, tipping his head. "Don't be such a judgmental asshole."

Daire snorts. "Yeah, but look how that shit turned out for you."

Jude's eyes narrow dangerously. "It went to fucking hell. I know. I was there. I lived it. It fucking hurt losing her, but that doesn't mean just because things ended badly that I would trade all the good times we had."

Daire looks appalled. Poor guy. He can't believe he's on the losing side in this situation.

"What the fuck is in your drinks?" He eyes our bottles. Shaking his head roughly, he stands and grabs his laptop. "Both of y'all are fucking crazy. Insane. Off your mother-fucking rockers."

Still muttering under his breath, he shoves open the door and disappears inside.

Jude and I sit in silence for a while before he speaks. "Don't let him drag you down. He's in a shit mood today."

"Why?"

He snorts. "Apparently Rosie chewed him out real good in the dining hall. Wish I could've seen it." His head lowers, and he seems to be thinking, so I don't make a comment. "I have my own shit to work through when it comes to women after what happened with Macy. But I know not all women are like that. Bro, if a girl makes you happy then see where it goes."

"Daire's right," I admit. "I've only met her twice. It's crazy to feel this way. I'm not in love or anything, that's stupid, but there's just this feeling like I'm supposed to get to know her."

Jude's feet land on the deck. Cracking his neck, he looks down at me where I'm seated. "Then do that and see where it goes. Not everything needs a label and not everyone has to understand."

"You don't think I'm crazy?"

He snorts, looking down at the bottle clasped in his fist like he's forgotten how it got there. "No, I don't." His lips thin and he pats me on the shoulder as he walks by me for the door. "But girls can make you get that way."

I throw my head back and laugh. He's gone before I

sober. Nursing my beer, I look up at the stars in the night sky.

Fuck, I really am Gatsby. I just hope this doesn't turn out like his story did.

TEN

Ophelia

TAKING the steps up to the library, I try to dispel my nerves over my first tutoring session and my tutor. I haven't been able to get my mind off Cree in the three days since I met him.

Firstly, because the guy is too gorgeous for his own good and those *dimples*.

Secondly, because of his familiarity with me despite the fact I'm certain we've never met. He's not the kind of person I would forget.

Wrapping my hand around the door, I pull it open

and head in search of a table. The first floor is mostly full, too loud for my liking. Taking one of the old spiral staircases to the second floor, I inhale the scent of old pages and thousands of stories I'll never have enough time to read.

Wandering down aisles, I skim my fingers over the spines imagining the words inside them.

Eventually I come across a small table in a darkened corner that's quiet and claim it. Sending Cree a text with my location, I wait for him to respond. Thankfully I don't have to wait long to hear from him.

Cree: Running late. Be there in less than ten minutes. Sorry.

Me: It's okay. I'll get set up.

He sends back a thumbs up.

Pulling out my laptop, I start it up and put in my password bringing up a blank Word page and then digging out the first book we're doing an analysis on this semester. The abridged—thank God—version of *Les Misérables* by Victor Hugo stares mockingly up at me from the table. The sketch-like drawing of young Cosette seems to look at me and say, *"Is all of this really as difficult as you make it out to be?"*

I've read the book multiple times, practically have entire passages memorized, but asking me to decipher why a book was written the way it was and what it's trying to convey about society and culture itself is where my brain shuts down. Last year, Professor Lindon told me to think about the different layers to a story, the various meanings woven inside, and I blinked at him before blurting, "How do you expect me to know what an author was implying without asking them? Anything I come up with is circumstantial, a guess at best, and that's not fair. It's all hearsay without the author coming out and saying it themselves."

He simply hung his head, sighed, and walked away. He gave up on trying to get me to understand. He's not the first one to do it either, and I doubt he's the last.

As promised, not that I'm timing him or anything, Cree shows up ten minutes later with coffee and brownies.

I narrow my eyes on the goodies. "You're late because of a coffee run?"

He sets everything down, sliding the same frozen drink I ordered the other day my way and then a box with a single brownie in it.

"Yes, but can you really say that this isn't necessary for studying?"

I open the brownie box and inhale the heavenly scent of chocolate. "You're right. This is one-hundred percent necessary."

He grins triumphantly. "Told you." Pulling out the

chair, he somehow manages to fold his large body into it. He doesn't look comfortable, but it'll have to do. "Look at you all prepared." He nods at my set up, taking a drink of his hot coffee.

"Are you mocking me?" I narrow my eyes on him, trying not to be swayed by those dimples.

"No." His smile falls the tiniest bit. "I wouldn't do that." Undeterred, his smile returns, and he says, "What are you reading today?"

"Isn't it obvious?" I slap a hand on the thick book that resides on the table like an unwelcome beacon reminding me why we're here.

"That's for class. If you're anything like me, you're reading something for pleasure."

I can't help the way my eyes watch his lips when he practically purrs the word pleasure.

Sighing, I reach back into my bag and set the book on the table between us. He places his massive hand on the glossy cover, it nearly engulfs the entire thing, and slides it in front of him.

He takes in the bright orange cover with pops of green. He reads the title aloud, flicking through the pages. "Can't say I've heard of this one."

"It's good. Alex is top tier book boyfriend level."

Cree closes the book, passing it back to me. "Have

you ever met a real guy that reaches book boyfriend potential?"

I start to say no but decide to be a little coy. "I haven't decided yet." I give him a significant look.

He chuckles. "You gonna ask me what I'm reading?"

Placing an elbow on the table, I rest my head in my hand. "What are you reading?"

Like me, he doesn't answer with words. He rifles through his backpack and produces a thick hardback. "I started this morning."

I pick it up, looking where a bookmark is placed. My eyes widen in surprise. "Just started, huh?" The book is more than a quarter read.

He shrugs, leaning back in the chair. I'm surprised he doesn't topple right on out of it. "I was bored in class this morning."

"I think I've heard of this one." I trace my finger over a red leaf on the cover.

He takes the book back, his fingers grazing mine in the process where a shiver skates down my spine. "It's popular so I'm not surprised. You should check it out. What happened to the other series you were reading?"

"I finished them."

"You were on book one." He blanches. "You read them all in three days? They're huge books. Plus, there's the novella that's still technically novel length and the spin-off book too."

I stare at him, a peculiar feeling settling inside me. I've never met anyone I can talk books with like him.

Drumming my fingers on the table, I answer, "I read fast."

Years and years of feeling like an outcast has helped me master the craft of speed reading.

"What did you think of them?"

"I loved them." I fan myself in response and he chuckles. "Anything with a dark-haired brooding hero who you think is the bad guy, but turns out to be good, gets me every time."

"I can't believe you've read them all already. And I thought I was a fast reader." He hangs his head in mock shame.

"Not everyone can be as talented as I am," I joke, feeling like I've accomplished something monumental when he laughs in response. Sobering, I exhale a sigh. "As much as I could sit here and talk books all day, I really do need the tutoring help."

"Oh, right." He shoves a massive bite of brownie— practically the whole thing—into his mouth. "I suck at this. I've never actually tutored before."

My brow arches. "And Professor Lindon still thought you'd be a good fit?"

His chest puffs out. "Yeah," he squeaks, voice higher than normal. "I'm good at this."

"This what?" I prompt, hopefully playfully.

"English and stuff," he says awkwardly, bowing his head. "That's probably why your professor thought of me."

"Well," I pat the top of *Les Misérables,* "let's get started then, shall we?"

ELEVEN

CREE

DAIRE'S ANNOYED WITH ME. That much is obvious. He skates furiously down the ice, barreling toward me. I'm fast, but not fast enough, and he rams me into the board. The reverberation zips through my entire body and know I'm gonna feel that for the rest of the week, no doubt I'll be icing my ribs tonight.

"Motherfucker!" I yell after him, the curse muffled by my mouth guard. Some players think you're being a pussy if you wear one, but I'd like to keep my teeth in as decent shape as possible. Hockey players are notorious for losing teeth, the on-ice fights are legendary.

I catch my breath easily enough and get my head back in the game. Today's our first day on the ice to prepare for our upcoming season start, and everyone's eager to be back together. Adjusting to the loss of players from the previous year and getting used to the feel of the new arrivals is always interesting, and practices like this are exhausting but necessary.

"Madison!" Coach Rogers yells at me. "You gonna let him get away with that?"

I play the right-wing position, meaning I'm on the offense and typically stay on the right side of the center forward player—on our team that's Jake Boworth or Bowie as we call him. My position means I'm also a forward, and it's my job to focus on the puck and scoring.

Whereas Daire is a defenseman, and his job is to keep the other team from scoring. He's a fucking beast at what he does, the best defenseman I've ever played with, but that doesn't mean I'm cool with him taking his anger out on me in practice.

I don't understand his mood since nothing I'm doing affects him, but he acts like I've screwed him over. He doesn't even know Ophelia.

By the time practice has finished up, I'm pretty

pissed off at my so-called best friend, and since each breath I take burns my ribs from where he slammed me into the boards, it's impossible for me to get over it any time soon with that constant reminder.

Ridding myself of my gear takes longer than normal, but I don't let a single grimace slip through. The last thing I'm willing to have happen is Daire to feel satisfied that he fucked me up.

Bowie opens his locker beside mine, his gear dropping to the floor. "You down for a beer tonight, Creature?"

I roll my eyes good-naturedly at the nickname. "Nah."

"Oh, come on," he cajoles, slapping my shoulder. I have to bite my lip not to make a sound. Apparently that part of my body took a hit too. "We're celebrating being back on the ice."

I'm tired, but I can't think of a good enough excuse to deny him a second time. "All right, sure, but first round is on you."

He chuckles. "Whatever you say."

"You two better not be plotting anything dangerous," Justin Stevenson—also known as Stevy and The Biebs—is our team captain and left winger.

"Ah, just some drinks at Harvey's. Join us, Cap."

Stevy shakes his head, fighting a smile. "Fuck, I

can't turn down a drink—but no overdoing it. That goes for all of you," he bellows. "If I hear about any of you fucking around this year and not taking shit seriously then you'll have hell to pay."

I know he's not kidding either. Stevy will kick the ass of anyone who steps out of line. He's a scholarship student, dependent on the team performing above and beyond this year so he can get drafted.

Grabbing my towel, I shed the last of my gear and head to the showers.

Maybe a drink won't be such a bad idea.

HARVEY'S IS PACKED, not shocked about that, but what does surprise me is Jude's absence since he's usually hanging here most nights and Daire's sullen expression. He's been nursing the same beer since we got here, so I know he isn't drunk.

Shit's going on with him that has nothing to do with me, but if he wants to keep being an asshole before he fesses up then that's on him.

Beneath the table, I pull my phone from my pocket and shoot a text to Ophelia.

Me: How's your night going?

I grin when she replies quickly.

Ophelia: Did some studying. Now I'm in bed reading.

Me: And what's your choice of reading material tonight?

Ophelia: My namesake—Hamlet by the one and only William Shakespeare. It's for my playwright class.

Me: Good ole Willie.

Ophelia: What are you up to?

Me: At the bar with my team. I'd rather be home.

Ophelia: Then why don't you leave?

I frown at her text, taking a second before I reply.

Me: I guess I didn't think I could.

Ophelia: You're a big boy, you can leave when you want.

Me: Good point. Maybe I'll order some food to-go.

My stomach growls with approval at this thought, but I shouldn't be eating the crap Harvey's sells.

I decide to head out and not overthink things or I might end up here all night. Slapping some cash down on the table I say my goodbyes and head out to my car. Daire's eyes follow me, but he doesn't make a move to do the same.

Blasting music on the way home, I'm in a marginally better mood by the time I arrive.

I've only been inside the house for zero-point-three seconds when Millie storms toward me, fury written all over her face. Her hair is in a wild bun on top of her head, her glasses she wears in the evenings perched on her nose.

"He has to go!" she shrieks, stomping her foot like she's five years old.

"Who?" I ask dumbly.

I didn't expect to be ambushed like this before I can even close the garage door, so my brain isn't firing on all cylinders.

"The football playing, womanizing, annoying, dick-headed, mother fucker upstairs!" Her fists sway at her sides.

"Language, Mills!" I chide, shutting the door and edging toward the kitchen so I can search for some dinner.

She storms after me.

"Don't fucking reprimand me when Casanova over here is running a brothel! I share a bathroom with him," she reminds me of the Jack and Jill bathroom between their rooms. "I got out of the shower to some chick *peeing!* I was naked, Cree! Sure, we share all the same bits, but I don't need some stranger seeing all of them!"

I slam the fridge closed. "What?" I blink at her, fury building inside me—not at her, but my friend.

"I know, I should've remembered to lock his side of the door, but in my defense who expects a strange girl to be there peeing when they know someone is in the shower? Besides, there's a hall bath too!"

I hold up a hand, silencing her. "I'm not mad at you, Millie."

"Oh." I see some of the fight go out of her.

"Is the girl still here?"

Her eyes roll so hard I'm surprised they don't end up on the floor. "Yes. They've been going at it for hours now. Honestly, I would be impressed with his stamina if it wasn't so fucking annoying."

Ignoring that last comment, I pinch the bridge of my nose, thinking about what I need to do. I've never banned hookups in the house. I might not fool around as much as some of my friends, but I've had my fair share of one-night stands. But I also didn't have my little sis living here, nor was I dealing with any of my friends fucking around as much as Jude does.

"Wait here," I command.

"Don't tell me what to do," she storms after me as I head for the stairs.

The moans and banging of the headboard get louder with each step I take.

"Millicent," I flip back around, leveling her with a look that I know rivals the one our dad gives when he's about to blow up, "again, I'm not mad at you, but I am asking you to stay down here and respect that. Okay?"

She crosses her arms over her chest. "Fine, I'm just upset. This isn't cool. If you can't get him to stop, then I'm going back to Daire's bathroom."

I'm sure with the current state Daire is in he'd be thrilled with this news.

"That won't be necessary."

Bounding up the stairs, I brace myself for whatever fall out I'm going to have to deal with.

And to think I just wanted to come home to eat some food and relax. So much for that.

With the side of my fist, I bang it against Jude's door. "Dude, put your dick away and get the fuck out here."

They keep going at it, undeterred.

I bang again. "Dude, I'm fucking serious. I'll kick this door down right the fuck now and don't think I can't."

I knock again, but they just keep going at it.

"All right, you asked for it."

Kicking down a door isn't easy, and it's going to be especially difficult since I'm sore after practice, but I'm pissed, so at least I have anger on my side. Bracing myself, I slam my right foot into the door, and it rattles on the hinges, groaning. I can't fucking wait to explain this shit to my dad.

I kick again, and this time the sounds inside the room quiet. Regardless, I get ready to kick again, figuring another strike or two will get the door off. My foot is about to slam into the wood when the door swings open and I hit air instead.

"What the fuck, dude?" Jude snaps, looking at me like I've lost my mind, which maybe I have, but I'm not down with this amount of drama.

"Tell your girl she needs to leave."

His fingers tighten around the blanket he tossed around his waist. "She's not my girl."

"She's *a* girl and she needs to leave. She walked in on my sister in the bathroom. This isn't cool, and I won't tolerate your toddler bullshit of fucking everything that moves. So, your ex screwed you over? It's been a year and a half, Jude. Get the fuck over it already." His jaw flexes at my rant. "See a therapist, because pussy isn't helping you."

I don't see his fist coming until it slams into my face, rocking me back a few steps.

And then the whole world goes dark.

TWELVE

Ophelia

FEELING CALLIOPE BENEATH ME, the power in her body as she runs through the pasture sends a feeling of calm through me that I can't find anywhere else. Horses have the ability to put me at ease. Sometimes I wonder what would've become of me if I hadn't discovered my love for them. And it's not just riding that I love, it's the horses themselves, all the varying personalities among them and even the hard work that goes with it.

Mary watches me, her arms draped over the fence. Her head shakes, a small smile on her lips.

"I tried for years with that one, then you showed up and look at her."

I ride up the fence with Calliope, bringing her to a halt. "She's a good girl." I pat her neck in her favorite spot. "She just needed the right person." Not that it was an overnight success story getting her to trust me, she threw me off more than a handful of times, but we've gotten here and that's all that matters.

"We all need the right person. I'm glad she found you."

Mary's words send warmth through me. "I am too."

"Are you staying for dinner tonight?" she asks, shielding her eyes with her hand from the sun. Mary refuses to wear sunglasses despite desperately needing them on the farm.

"I can't." Sadness fills me at the loss of one of Mary's delicious home-cooked meals. "As soon as I finish up with Calliope I have to meet up with my tutor."

"Why don't I make up some Tupperware to-go for you and your tutor. Do you think she'd like fried chicken?"

"What kind of monster doesn't love fried chicken?" I dismount from Calliope, keeping a hold on her reins so I can guide her back to the stable. "And I'm pretty sure he'd love some."

"He?" Mary's brows rise with interest, walking alongside the fence with me.

I roll my eyes. "He's only my tutor. Don't go getting any ideas."

"I would never." She laughs in a way that I know means trouble.

Our paths dissect when she heads for the house while I guide Calliope into the barn.

I've finished up with her, and I'm exiting the barn when I run into Callahan.

"Hey." He grins but it's a little more subdued than normal, his hands shoved into the pockets of his worn and dirtied jeans, a ratty baseball cap pulled low over his eyes. His shoulders are drawn up, head tilted to the side. "I heard you can't stay for dinner."

"No, not tonight." I rub at a spot of dirt on my shirt. I'm not sure if I'll have enough time to run by the dorm and change before meeting Cree, but I hate the idea of showing up sweaty and gross.

"Plans?"

I give him a funny look. "I'm studying."

"My grandma said you have a date."

I can't help the awful sounding snort that comes out of me. "A date? No. I'm meeting my tutor to study. But if she said I was on a date, why are you asking?"

In other words, I can't understand why he wouldn't have believed her?

He shrugs, his jaw pulsing. "Don't know."

My eyes narrow on him, trying to decipher the emotions warring across his face. Sometimes they're not easy for me to read or understand.

"I think you do know. Why don't you be honest with me, Cal?"

He removes his cap and ruffles his hair before replacing it, backwards this time. "I was jealous."

"Jealous?" I blurt incredulously. "What were you jealous of?" Baffled doesn't even begin to describe how I feel.

Sure, we've kissed and flirted some, but it's all seemed so harmless and never led to anything more.

His chest inflates with a hefty sigh. "Of the idea of you on a date." The *obviously* is implied while I continue to stand there blinking at him like some frozen wide-eyed cartoon.

"I don't understand."

He chuckles, but it's lacking the normal humor. "I like you. I was jealous of the idea of you on a date because I want to be the one to take you on a date."

Oh.

"Oh." I gasp. "I … you … me … a date? Whoa. I … wow…"

When he laughs this time, it's light and carefree. Amused. "I see I've rendered you speechless, and I haven't even asked yet." He reaches out, grasping a strand of hair that escaped my braid and wrapping it around his tanned finger. "Ophelia, I'd love if you'd go on a date with me."

"I..." I'm shocked. Flabbergasted. Lost for words.

Callahan is a good-looking guy, kind, a hard worker. There's no reason to say no, except I feel ... *nothing*. No spark. No crackle. Not even a small flicker. I've only been around Cree, not even kissed him like I have Cal, and he sets my whole body on fire. But ... maybe flames are a bad thing. Flames burn, obliterating everything in their path. It could be better to feel next to nothing. Is that a better foundation to build upon?

But if I go out with Cal and it ends badly, I don't want it to affect my time here on the farm. It's one of the few things I look forward to.

"I'm sorry," he says, shaking his head. "I've sprung this on you."

"No, no. It's okay. I ... I'm just surprised is all."

Yeah, he's flirted with me over the past year, but I figured he just has a flirty personality and that it has nothing to do with me when it never went anywhere else after our kiss.

Rubbing a hand over my face, I look up at his

familiar face and start nodding. "Sure, yeah. Let's go out."

"Yeah?" He seems shocked that I agreed.

Frankly, so am I. But I think it's the fear of that fire I'm feeling around Cree that makes me do it.

"Yep." I nod with more surety.

"Cool. I'll text you with the details when I have them."

"Great. That's ... great."

Can you get any more awkward Ophelia?

Callahan sends a disarming grin my way before he goes into the barn. I can't move for a full minute, still trying to figure out what just happened. When I finally get my feet to move, they carry me to the house where Mary is already coming out the door with those Tupperware containers, she promised me.

"Cal ran out of here so fast when I mentioned you were going on a date." Mary smiles triumphantly like this is amazing news. "I think my grandson might have a crush on you."

"Why'd you tell him I was going on a date? I told you it's my tutor."

Her smile grows impossibly larger. "Sometimes men need a fire lit under their ass, and my grandson definitely did. I've seen the way he looks at you."

But what about the way I look at him? Does that matter at

all? I don't think I've looked at him in any particular way that would lead anyone to think this is a good idea?

I close my eyes for the briefest of moments, recentering and refocusing myself.

"Thank you for the food, Mary." I take the paper bag from her that she has everything in. "I need to go."

"Good luck with the studying, dear."

I give her a tiny smile, walking down the driveway to my waiting car.

I set the bag on the floor in the backseat, using a sweatshirt left there to keep them from sliding around too much.

Starting up my car, I turn my music on and let it distract me on my drive back to campus. I don't really have the time to spare, but I run into my dorm and take the world's quickest shower and put on fresh clothes.

I tell myself it's because I was sweaty and dirty, not because I want to look put together for Cree.

Dashing back out to my car, I drive over to the student commons building he asked me to meet him at today since it's close to the ice rink and he had practice.

The irony that I'm being tutored by a sports player isn't lost on me since they're notorious for needing the help, not the other way around.

Grabbing the bag of food and my backpack, I carry everything inside. After my conversation with Cal, I'm feeling particularly exhausted. Encounters like that suck the energy out of me.

Inside, I find Cree already waiting at a corner table by the windows overlooking one of the many pathways lined with trees that snakes through campus. His hair is damp from a shower, curling against the collar of his blue polo shirt that matches the color of his eyes.

My stomach dips, that fire crawling up my spine. He turns from the guy he was chatting with and looks over his shoulder at me. Is it possible he can sense my presence? That charming grin of his surfaces, along with his dimples.

Butterflies take off inside me.

Attraction slams into me, pulsating through my body. It's entirely unfair that my hormones have to choose the guy I desperately need in order to pass this class to want to bang.

"Hi," I say breathlessly, setting the bag on the table. "I hope you're hungry. I work for this older lady and her husband on their farm sometimes, and she's always cooking, so when she found out I was headed for tutoring, she boxed up some food for us."

I'm rambling, embarrassingly so. I flatten my lips together as I plop into a chair. The guy Cree had been chatting with is walking toward the exit.

"Friend of yours?"

"Just someone who wanted to chat hockey."

I gasp when he turns the other way a bit. "What happened to your face?" I finally get a good look at the left side of his face and nasty bruise he's sporting. "Is that from hockey too?"

"Ah. This." He tenderly brushes his fingers over his face. "Um … altercation with one of my roommates."

"Oh, wow. That's awful. I take it you two don't get along?" I pull the containers of food from the bag to busy my hands. I'm not surprised to find that Mary has included utensils. She thinks of everything.

"He's actually a good friend of mine. We just had a disagreement." He adjusts his position in the uncomfortable plastic chair. They're all white. As are the tables. The commons building is new, and I think the old school was aiming for a more modern look opposed to the original buildings which are usually rich with warm woods and classical detailing. But I hate this clinical look. It looks like we're in a hospital, not a learning facility.

"A disagreement about what?"

Now that the food is set out, I grab my books and laptop. My stomach rumbles, reminding me I need to eat first before I think about studying.

"I was pissed at him about something and said some not nice things, so he clocked me. I think I deserved it."

"Did you hit him back?" I crack open my container of fried chicken and then the mashed potatoes she put in another. Not a veggie in sight. I'm not mad about it either.

He chuckles like he finds my question amusing. "No. Despite the sport I play, I'm not keen on violence. I keep it on the ice and that's it."

"So now you're stuck with that?" I wave my fork at his bruised face. "While he has nothing?"

"Well, he's banned from having chicks over to the house, so I think he's suffering enough."

"Tragic." I take a bite of the homemade mashed potatoes, the monster in my belly settling the tiniest bit. "Aren't you hungry?" I wave my fork at the containers he hasn't even opened yet.

His smile spreads, lips tilting upwards. "Right now, I'm enjoying watching you too much."

I lower my head in mortification. "I skipped lunch," I mutter defensively.

"A good appetite is nice. I didn't mean to make you feel ashamed."

"Sorry … it's just … as you've probably noticed I'm very thin. I've been called all kinds of names growing up, girls accused me of having an eating disorder all through middle and high school, spreading rumors of me throwing up in the bathrooms after lunch." Shaking my head at the awful memories, I forge on. "I got called to the guidance counselors office so many times because of it. Even my parents would have to come to the school. I've just always been super skinny where I can't put weight on no matter what I do. And I think people assume if you're thin then life's great and dandy, just because the media seems to value skinny people over average-sized human beings, but I would give anything to put on even ten pounds."

Cree stares at me with a tender-hearted expression. I lower my eyes to the table, unable to believe that I not only spoke so much to someone who's a relative stranger to me still at this point, but that I did so about one of my biggest insecurities.

"I'm sorry." He opens his Tupperware filled with chicken. "I didn't mean to make you feel like you had to defend yourself. That wasn't my intention."

"I know it wasn't. It's just a sore topic for me, and I get too defensive about it."

"Ophelia," he says my name softly, carefully, like a lover's caress. "There's nothing wrong with sticking up for yourself."

"But I know you didn't mean—"

"Shush." He hushes me, an electric current sliding down my spine at the touch of his finger to my lips. "No, I didn't mean anything by it, but it triggered some-

thing for you, and you have every right to express that."
He pulls his finger away and doesn't seem nearly as
affected by the touch as I was. "Now," he picks up a
drumstick, "let's eat this delicious fucking food and
study."

"I CAN WALK you back to your dorm," Cree offers,
holding the door open for me as we leave.

"That's okay. I drove over since I didn't want to
walk with the food and my stuff."

"Oh, of course." He ducks his head almost shyly,
which surprises me. He seems like such a confident guy.

"Do you need me to walk you to your dorm?" I
volley back.

He grins in amusement. "If I lived in one, I'd take
you up on it, beautiful." He winks, sending my stomach
spiraling and twisting through my body. "My parents
bought a house off-campus, so I've lived there since I
started here."

"That was nice of them." My parents would've done
the same in a heartbeat. I had to beg to live in the dorms
—to have any sort of normal college experience. "Are
you free to study tomorrow? I want to make sure I pin
down this first paper so Professor Lindon will stop

breathing down my neck. He knows I'm trying, but..."
I end with a shrug.

Cree worries his bottom lip between his teeth. "I
have a late practice, but I can help you after. Just have
mercy on me, I'll be tired."

"Thank you. I can't afford to fail this class again."

He looks me over carefully, something in his eyes I
don't understand. "I won't let you fail, Ophelia. Not on
my watch." Sighing, he looks at his phone. "I have to
get going."

"That's fine." I hold out my hand for the bag of
containers and leftovers, but he steadfastly shakes his
head.

"I can still walk you to your car."

"I'm just over there." I point to the SUV.

Cree's long legs carry him in that direction, and I
hurry to follow—well, maybe hurry is an exaggeration
because I can't help but take in his delectable ass and
thick thighs in his jeans. Clearly, hockey is good for the
body.

"I've never been on the ice before," I blurt out
thanks to the trajectory of my thoughts. He pauses,
glancing at me over my shoulder with an arched brow.
"You know, ice skating. With the blades. And stuff."

His lips quirk, one dimple winking at me from his
cheek. "I'll take you some time."

"Y-You would do that?" I stutter in shock, not expecting him to offer. "It was just a random thought I had about never having been and—"

"You're cute when you ramble."

Did Cree just say I'm cute? I'm not sure I can handle him flirting with me and Callahan asking me out all in the same day.

"I've rendered you speechless," he muses, walking backwards to his car. "Interesting."

I don't tell him, but the interesting part is the fact that I speak so freely around him. Normally I'm quiet, shy. I keep to myself and it's hard for me to get to know people because I *don't* talk. But there's something about him that pulls words from me.

Unlocking my car, he sets the bag on the floor of the passenger side. The door closes and he turns, studying me. There's a look in his eyes, like he's trying to puzzle me out.

"What?" I prompt, feeling like a bug pinned beneath a microscope.

"It's nothing." He runs his fingers through his thick hair, now dry from his shower. "Have a good night, Daisy."

This time when he says Daisy it triggers something, a crackle in my memory, a flash of fire—literal fire—but before I can grasp onto it, it's gone again.

I open my car door and look at where he stands in wait on the sidewalk. "Night, Jay."

I back out, the headlights of my car fanning over him.

Baffled.

That's the only way to describe how I feel.

THIRTEEN

CREE

I STRAIGHTEN everything up downstairs as best I can. I already cleaned my room in case I end up having to study with Ophelia in there, but I figure right now staying downstairs is the safest option. As much as I'd love to recreate the night we met, I know she actually needs the help with her class and besides, since I like her, it's probably best to dial things back and get to know her better. Take things slow and see if she actually wants the same things I do.

The weirdest part is it's like she doesn't remember

that night at all. I guess she could be embarrassed about it. Like me she might not do casual hookups often and since I'm tutoring her, she doesn't want to toe that line. I respect that, but I wish she'd give me some sort of acknowledgment that she feels this too. Whatever *this* is.

As much as I don't talk to my dad about girls anymore, I'm realizing I might need his advice in this situation.

"What are you doing?"

I scream at the sound of Millie's voice, tossing the pillow that was in my hand. "Jesus Fucking Christ, Mills. Don't sneak up on people."

She rolls her eyes. "I wasn't sneaking. I'm going to grab a drink. You're the one who's being weird."

She's right, I am. I think between Daire being a dick to me because of Ophelia as well as feeling confused about these feelings for someone, I hardly know I'm a fucking wreck.

I set the pillow down and follow my sister into the kitchen. She opens the fridge, grabbing a Sprite. The can hisses when she pops the tab.

"The girl I'm tutoring is coming over tonight," I say by way of explanation of my erratic behavior.

She tries not to laugh. "Is that what the cool kids are calling it these days, bro? Tutoring?"

"Mills," I groan.

She clucks her tongue. "I'm going back up to study. Have fun tutoring." She makes air quotes with her fingers that aren't wrapped around the can.

I don't have a chance to argue back with her because the doorbell chooses that moment to ring.

At least Daire and Jude are out for the night at Harvey's.

Glancing up the stairs where my sister disappeared, I go open the door before Ophelia has to knock again. Swinging the door open, I find her standing there toeing her shoes against the welcome mat my mom left there. Her backpack is on her shoulders and whatever book she's reading for pleasure today is clasped to her chest. The freckles sprinkled across her nose are high-lighted from the glow of the porch light.

"Hey," I greet, stepping aside to let her in. "Did you find the place okay?"

"It wasn't hard." She looks around the foyer, taking everything in. The house is an older build that was remodeled before my parents bought it, but the people who owned it before left behind things like the molding and some intricate circle medallion thing above the chandelier. I'm sure it has a proper name, but I've never bothered to find out. That's what captures Ophelia's gaze, and she stares up at it studying the tiny details.

"Do you mind studying in the living room?" I gesture to the space to my right.

"That's fine."

"What's the book today?" I point at the one she holds close to her heart, leading her into the living space. She sits down on the edge of the couch, placing her book on the coffee table and her bag on the floor.

She's still busy looking around, and I wonder what this place looks like from her perspective. It's not decorated like your typical bachelor pad, but that's because my mom handled all of that before I moved in freshman year. Everything in here was picked out by her. From the dark leather library sofas, to the thick wood coffee table, and the pillows.

Ophelia shakes her head, physically snapping out of wherever she wandered off to. "W-What did you ask?"

"What book are you reading today?" I could easily look at it now where it sits, but I want to hear her tell me.

"Oh." She leans forward, excitement lighting up her face at my question.

All I fucking did was ask her about her book and she's glowing? And I always thought girls were so hard to please.

"—It's about this F1 driver who falls for his ... I guess you could call him his rival's ... his frenemies ... sister." She rambles and realize I missed the first part of what she was saying. "I started it this morning and I'm almost done. I can't put it down. Thank God there are three more books in the series about the other drivers."

"Where do you fit all these books?" I've only ever seen her read paperbacks, not read on her phone or another device.

Setting her laptop up, she keeps her eyes focused on that almost like she doesn't want to look at me. "I fit them wherever I can. Under my bed. The closet. Shelves. Stacked on the floor. I try to go through them regularly and donate ones I know I won't reread and sometimes I ship some back to my parents so I can make room for new ones I order."

"How many books do you read in a year?"

"Mmm," she purses her lips. "I don't really track it, but I'd guess somewhere between three and five hundred."

"Holy fuck." The words fly out of my mouth. "That's a lot of books."

"There are a lot of lives to live inside pages and not enough time." She brings up her Word document with the essay she's been working on, as well as another with some of the exercises I gave her to work on to help her analyze more clearly. "How many books do you read?"

"Not nearly that many," I admit, pacing the room.

I'm fucking nervous at having her here, in my home, in my space. "Maybe fifty."

"Fifty? That's not a lot."

I gasp in mock offense. "Ophelia, there are people who read zero books a year, and you're telling me fifty isn't a lot?"

"Not compared to how many I read."

She has me there. "Do you want anything to drink before we study?"

"Um ... water's fine. Or Diet Coke if you have it."

"Let me check."

In the kitchen, I take a moment to catch my breath and give myself a much-needed mental pep talk.

I can't believe I'm letting a girl make me lose my cool, but here the fuck we are.

Rifling through the pantry, I grab some snacks—chips, goldfish crackers, and some of those cheap zebra cakes that are so bad but so good—before getting her drink and returning to the room to dump my bounty onto the table.

"Whoa." Her eyes widen. "Snacks too? Five-star service. Where should I leave my review? Will Yelp suffice?"

"Are you sassing me?"

She laughs, picking up her notebook she likes to scribble notes and doodles in. "Maybe a little."

"We could order pizza too … or Chinese … whatever. If you're hungry, that is?"

"I'm okay, right now. I just want to study. Unless you're hungry, then by all means order dinner."

"I'm not hungry yet. Where should we start?"

"You're the tutor, you tell me."

I clear my throat. I'm royally botching this. Playing hockey in a stadium full of screaming fans and scouts watching is no big deal compared to tutoring the girl I've harbored a crush on.

"Let me look over that exercise I gave you last time."

"Sure." She clicks the screen on her laptop and slides it over to me. "I do think it helped, but I still struggle with this kind of stuff. It just feels wrong in my brain to say an author meant a certain thing when we have no real way of knowing if we can't ask them. It's all speculation."

I look up from the screen over to her beside me. "It is in a way, but it's also comprehension. If an author is wanting you to have a certain takeaway from something, then they're going to leave a trail of bread crumbs for you to follow."

"I guess." She bites her lip, pulling her vibrant red hair off the back of her neck and tying it into a ponytail. "It's hard for my brain to grasp that."

"We all have our struggles. Math." I shudder over the one word. "That's my nightmare."

Her nose crinkles. "I have a hard time imagining you struggling with anything. You seem like you have it all put together."

I snort, trying to hide the noise with a cough. "Believe me, I don't. I appreciate you thinking I do."

I look over her answers to the questions I posed, highlighting and making notes in track changes about her analysis. Passing her laptop back over to her she frowns.

"That's a lot of red." A heavy exhale rocks her body, pulling her the tiniest bit closer to me on the couch.

"Sorry."

"Don't be sorry. This is what you're supposed to do. It's just … no wonder I've been failing. I can't grasp the most basic parts of this class, apparently." She rubs her temples like she feels a headache coming on. "Why can't this be easy?"

I don't know what makes me do it, but I reach over plucking her hand from the side of her head and enfold it in mine.

"Don't get worked up about it or you'll shut down. This is why you have me, remember? I'm going to help you through this, Ophelia. By the end of the semester, you'll be a pro at this class."

"You think so?" There's a telltale emotional sniffle in her words.

"I know so." Clearing my throat, I squeeze her hand. "I get the impression you want to be good at everything, and believe me I understand that since I'm the same way, and sometimes we're not great at things, but not being great, doesn't mean you're a failure."

She looks at where my hand holds hers like she's confused on how it got there, but she doesn't pull it away.

"I've always been too hard on myself, I know. My brother is naturally good at everything, insanely smart too. He's my idol, and I've always just wanted to be more like him, but I'm not. I'm just ... me."

"There's nothing wrong with being *you,* and I'm sure your brother would say the same."

She cracked a smile. "He would. He's the best."

"What's your brother's name?" I like getting to know her like this, little pieces, just small morsels of insight into who she is.

"Gus—short for Augustus."

"Where's he at?"

"Boston, finishing up law school." She studies the way our fingers lock together. "He wants me to make more friends. I've never been very good at that. I have Logan, so at least there's that."

"Logan." I bristle at the mention of the guy's name. I have no fucking right to feel territorial but fuck it if I don't want to go caveman over her speaking about some guy that's not her brother. "He your boyfriend?"

What if she says yes?

Fuck, it makes me an asshole, but I know if she does, I wouldn't back down from this.

She laughs, shaking her head. "Do you think I would be sitting here holding your hand if he was?" Fair point. "He's my best friend since, well, forever. I can't remember a time in my life without him. He doesn't go here. It's lonely without him and Gus."

I don't like her talking about being alone. Ophelia isn't the kind of person who should feel like she has to hide.

"What about your roommates?"

"Kenna and Li are great, truly, I couldn't have asked for better and they try ... but..." She shrugs, her eyes distant. "I'm not good at talking to people."

"You talk to me." I point out.

"You're different."

I study the side of her face, the gentle slope of her nose, trying to figure out what she means because she sounds almost distressed by it. "Different how?"

Her throat bobs with a swallow, reluctant hazel eyes

meeting my wanting gaze. "I haven't figured that out yet."

"I hope it's a good different." The confession slips easily off my tongue. I don't know what it is about this girl that makes me loose lipped.

"It seems to be so far. I'll keep you in the loop." She winks at me and seems as surprised by the gesture as I am if how fast she pulls her hand from mine is any indication. "Studying ... I need to ... study." She nods to herself like she's putting herself into work mode.

I need to stop getting distracted around her, but it seems like an impossible feat at this point.

"How far have you gotten on your *Les Mis* paper?"

She frowns, nervously tucking a lock of red hair behind her ear. "Not far enough," she seems to bite out the words through clenched teeth. Her frustration bleeds through her words.

"Has Lindon assigned the next book yet?"

"Books, plural. Well, short stories. We're doing a whole series on Edgar Allen Poe."

"I love me some Poe—the poet and Poe Dameron." I wait for recognition to click into place on her face, but it doesn't happen. "You don't know Poe? Only the greatest X-Wing pilot ever? Star Wars?"

"Never watched it."

I slam a hand to my chest, falling back dramatically

on the couch. "I'm dead. Deceased by this information. Never watched Star Wars? That's a crime, Ophelia."

"Guess you'll have to arrest me then, sorry."

I know she means the comment innocently, but my brain immediately pictures her lying naked in my bed, handcuffs on her wrists, completely at my mercy.

Clearing my throat, I say a silent prayer that I don't get a stiffy. That'd be embarrassing.

"You start working on your paper and make a list of anything you want me to go over with you. I'm going to grab my copy of Poe's stories."

"I have my own."

I tap her nose as I rise from the couch. "I'm sure you do, but I've made highlights and notes in my collection that might help you."

She pulls a disgusted face. "Oh, no. You're one of *those* people."

"One of those…?"

"Yeah, the monsters who write in books."

I throw my head back with laughter. "I'm not a monster. I love my books just right, thank you very much. There's something nice about being able to look back at what parts resonated with me at the time."

"Mmm." She hums thoughtfully, twisting her lips back and forth. "Still not buying it."

I take the stairs two at a time, my soul nearly

leaving my body when I come face to face with Millie at the top of them standing with a little smirk.

"She's pretty."

"Who?" I blurt stupidly like I have no idea who she's talking about.

She rolls her eyes at my dumbness. "The girl you're tutoring. She's pretty."

"Yeah, she is."

She grins at this information and pokes me hard in the side of the ribs. "Does my big bro have a crush?"

"Don't be stupid." I bypass her, swinging my door open. I'm not at all surprised when she follows me inside. "I'm tutoring her, that's all."

"Mhmm." She sits on the end of my bed, eyeing the mess of Legos on my desk. "You keep saying that, but I don't believe you."

"You don't have to believe me." I squat down, looking for the large tome that has all of Poe's work in it. "Ah, there you are." I grab it from the bottom shelf. It's heavy and awkward, but I do think the notes I've made in it will help Ophelia as she reads along.

"I can't help it. It's my job as your little sister to annoy the shit out of you."

"Oh, believe me, I know."

She sticks her tongue out at me. "Don't act like you

148

don't use your big bro privileges to drive me insane too."

I grin because I know she's right. Snapping my fingers to point at her, I ask, "If I order dinner do you want anything?"

She bounces where she sits. Millie has always been full of energy. It's why our parents put her in dance lessons at a young age. She still does ballet and it really surprised me that she wanted to come here instead of pursuing a dance school, but I didn't ask questions. Millie does what Millie wants. As she should.

"I'll never say no to food."

"Should've known."

Millie follows me out of my room and goes back to her while I take the stairs down to Ophelia.

Her eyes widen at the sight of the big book. "Jeez, that thing is huge."

"Thanks, darlin'." I wink. "Best compliment you can give a guy."

"I was talking about the book."

"Sure, you were." I can't help but joke with her.

I set the book on the coffee table, tapping my finger on the hardcover. "It's got everything you need in here, and like I said, I highlighted quotes and made notes in the margins. There are probably sticky notes in there too."

"Will you take a look at what I have for my paper so far?"

"Absolutely." I take her laptop, sitting back down beside her—closer than I was before. Her perfume hits me, something floral and fruity but not overbearing. It suits her. The desire to lean in and taste her nearly overwhelms me. It's been over a year since I got laid, and fuck if my body isn't feeling it.

Pushing those thoughts from my brain, I scroll up the first page of her essay and start reading. It's not bad, in fact I'm a little impressed. I flag some things as I go that I know Professor Lindon will have an issue with and pass it back to her to correct them.

"I'm going to order dinner now. I'm starved." She's already been here over an hour, and my stomach has come to life with a vengeance. If I don't eat soon, I'm going to end up in a bad mood. "Are you hungry yet?"

"A little," she replies in a small voice.

"Mills!" I call upstairs, and Ophelia's head whips in my direction. "I'm ordering Chinese! Do you want the usual?"

"Yes!" She yells back almost instantly, her voice muffled through her closed door.

"Who's Mills?" Ophelia asks, giving me a funny look.

"Oh, that's Millie, my little sister."

"Right, I think you mentioned her before. Is she hiding upstairs because of me? The guys too?"

Instantly, I feel like crap that Ophelia would think I'm … what? Embarrassed of her or something that I'd make my sister hide upstairs while we study?

"What? Fuck no," I curse. "She's doing schoolwork. She's not banned from coming down here, but she knows we're studying and to stay quiet. The guys— Jude and Daire—are out at the bar tonight. No one's hiding."

"Oh." Relief has her shoulders relaxing. "Okay. That's good." She redoes her ponytail and I think it has more to do with wanting to move her hands than needing to fix it.

"So … Chinese. What do you want?"

"Um." She bites her lip. "Sweet and sour chicken and vegetable rice, please. I have some cash I can give you." She sets her laptop aside and reaches for her bag.

"Don't worry about it. I got it."

She continues rifling through her bag in search of her wallet. "I don't need you to buy my dinner. I can—"

I cross in front of her, grabbing her wandering hands so she'll stop looking for her wallet. "I know you can, but you're a guest in my house. I'm buying your dinner."

"I'm not a guest, if anything I'm a pest since you've been suckered into helping me with all of this."

"I hate that you think that."

Her eyes drop. "Well, it's true."

Sighing, I let her hands go. "I'm going to order; you get back to that." I snap my fingers at her computer.

In the kitchen, I pull out the to-go menu for the local place I always order from. Just in case the guys come back early, or want something tomorrow, I order extra food. It's enough to feed an army, but it won't go to waste in a house with two hockey players and a football player.

I'm about to put the number in when Ophelia tiptoes quietly into the kitchen.

"Yes?" I prompt, drawing out the word questioningly since it's barely been two minutes since I left her in the living room.

"Are you sure you're okay getting my dinner? Like I said, I have cash and—"

"Ophelia?"

"Yes?" Pale fingers grip the hem of her shirt.

"Don't worry about the food, okay? I told you, I got it."

"Okay." She looks around the kitchen. "If you're sure."

"I'm sure."

She ducks her head, pressing her lips into a thin line as she turns and goes.

I chuckle to myself, amused by her cute behavior. I place the order and I'm told it's going to be an hour for delivery or thirty if I pick it up. "Hold on a sec," I tell the guy. I find Ophelia back in her spot, pouring over her paper. She looks up when she hears me. "Do you mind if we pick up the food? We'll get it sooner than delivery."

"That's fine."

Putting the phone back to my ear I tell the guy, "I'll pick it up. Mhmm. See you in thirty." Hanging up the phone, I toss it onto one of the chairs. "Whatcha thinking about Daisy? You look stressed." I sit on the coffee table in front of her. She eyes me over the top of her laptop, covered in stickers. There's one of a horse, Hogwarts castle, a Hufflepuff badger, Wanda Maximoff, and — "You like Spiderman?" I grin, pointing at the sticker.

"Spiderman? He's my favorite marvel hero ... well, second favorite. Wanda is first forever and always."

"I love Spiderman." I bite my tongue because I don't need to tell the girl I like that I have fucking Spiderman sheets, she might not let me live it down. "Wanda's great too."

"Why Spiderman?" She closes her laptop, her eyes

lighting with excitement. "I figured guys like you would say Captain America. Or Thor."

My shoulders shake with amusement. "Why would you think they'd be my favorite?"

"I don't know." She sets her laptop beside her, so it doesn't slide off the pillow she's using to prop it up. "I just figured big beefy athletic dudes would also pick the big beefy comic heroes." She shrugs at her explanation. "Not pick the nerdy dorky hero."

My lips tip up on the corners, unable to stop my smile. "You think I'm big and beefy, Daisy?"

She blows air out, puffing up her lips. "That's all you got from that isn't it?"

I chuckle, tapping my finger on her bare ankle. "No, but it was my favorite part."

"So, tell me then, big beefy athlete dude bro—" Her rambling only makes my smile grow. "Why is Spiderman so special to you?"

I rub my hands on my jeans, thinking about my answer. "Because he's normal. Because despite his powers and abilities he's still this dorky teenager who fucks up and is trying to figure things out. He doesn't see himself as this ... this powerful being. He's just Peter. Also," I tap her knee this time, "I was a bit of a dork myself back in the day."

"Back in the day, huh?" She arches her brow. "In what? Preschool?"

Chest shaking with laughter, I manage to compose myself and say, "No."

"He had braces until he was a sophomore in high school." I hang my head as my sister bounces down the last few stairs, carrying an empty can of Sprite. "I have pictures on my phone if you want to see." She's already pulling her phone out of her back pocket as she walks over to Ophelia. "Look at this poser." She shows off whatever embarrassing photo she brought up of me. "This was homecoming his freshman year. He wore orange. What kind of loser wears *orange*?"

"I was trying to stand out," I grumble under my breath.

"And stand out you did." Millie giggles at my discomfort. "Ooh, here's another one. Vacation to Spain. He bought that shell necklace in the airport before we even left the States and wore it the whole time. I'm pretty sure he'd still be wearing it if the ocean hadn't washed it away."

"Ha, ha," I intone, letting my sister have her fun while Ophelia looks at each photo.

"This was also his sophomore year. Halloween. He went as Spiderman every single year. Look at the braces. Hold on, I'll zoom in. The rubber bands are red, blue, and black. I bet the tech wanted to kill him when he asked for that."

My head drops, shaking back and forth. Luckily, I'm used to my little sis terrorizing me. I'm pretty sure it's in the sibling handbook somewhere. Besides, I dish it right back.

"All right, Mills. Ophelia and I have to go pick up dinner."

"Fine." She rolls her eyes, tucking her phone away. "But don't think I'm finished."

"You want me to go with you?" Ophelia looks at me with wide, startled eyes.

"Sure, why not." I hold a hand out to her, and she slips it in mine. The top of her hand is speckled with freckles, her nails painted with some sort of glitter.

"I should probably keep working on my paper." She looks at her laptop, sitting lonesome on the couch.

"Everyone needs a break, we'll go get the food and eat, then get back to it for a little while."

"Are you sure? It's getting late. I don't want to impose."

"I'm sure or I wouldn't have asked."

Grabbing my keys and wallet, I motion for her to follow me into the garage. I open the passenger door of my Bronco and she hops in, admiring the interior.

"I love this car." She rubs the leather seats as I push

the button to raise the garage door, then crank the engine. "I wish my parents would let me have one."

"That's what you said last time," I chuckle. "Or something close to it."

She gives me a funny look, brows knitted as I drive down the street. "Last time?"

"The night we met?" I don't know why it comes out as a question.

"Ah, the night we met," she repeats, nodding along. "Jay ... and Daisy."

I give her a funny look. "You remember, right?"

She scoffs, biting her lip. "Of course, I remember. Why wouldn't I remember? That would be crazy."

She looks out the passenger window, the street-lights reflecting into the car and haloing her in an orange glow. It's getting dark out, but not fully there. In a few more weeks it'll be pitch black at this time of night.

"You okay over there, Daisy?"

She rubs her hands over the top of her jeans. "I'm great."

She seems nervous, more so than usual. "You know, I'm not going to kidnap you."

Her head swivels quickly in my direction but I keep my eyes on the road, my hand on the gear shift.

"I didn't think that before, but now..." She trails off.

Chuckling, I turn onto the street the restaurant is on. "Trust me, I just really want dinner."

"This would be a convenient cover," she muses, back to staring out the window. "But I suppose I trust you somewhat or I wouldn't be in the car with you."

Parallel parking the Bronco, I leave the engine running. "I'll be right back."

"I'm not going anywhere."

Crossing in front of the car, I head inside the restaurant. It's packed with college students and local residents. If their to-go orders are anything like this no wonder he said it would be over an hour.

At the register, I pass my card and wait for the bags of food.

Over my shoulder, I look through the window and can easily see my car with Ophelia inside. I grin to myself when I see her reading her book. I hadn't even noticed she brought it with her.

"Here you go." My card is handed back to me along with the bags of food. I toss in some extra packs of soy sauce.

"Thanks, see ya next time."

When Ophelia sees me coming, she hastily tucks her book away, giving me a good chuckle.

Setting the bags on the floor in the back, I jog around and hop in. My buckle clicks into place while I eye the girl beside me. "You want anything else while we're out?"

She shakes her head rapidly. "No, no. This is enough." She turns around, her mouth falling when she sees how many bags there are. "Are we feeding an army?"

I shrug, pulling back onto the road when it's clear. "I'm starving, there's food for you, my sister, and I went ahead and ordered stuff for my roommates so they can have it whenever."

"That was thoughtful of you." She straightens back up in her seat.

"Eh, more out of self-preservation than anything so they don't eat my leftovers."

She laughs. "Leftovers are nice. Once, my brother ate my leftover macaroni and cheese from this local restaurant. It's *the best* mac n' cheese I've ever had and when I tell you cried when I found out he ate it, I mean I *sobbed*. I also threw a book at his head. Then I cried because his hard head dented my book."

I snort at the visual of Ophelia throwing a book at her brother. "Millie's thrown a shoe at me once … more than once."

"Why do you brothers have to be so annoying?"

"It's in our DNA."

"Apparently so."

"By the way," I clear my throat, turning left onto the road that will take us back to my house, "I wasn't kidding yesterday."

"About what?"

"Taking you to skate. Teaching you. We can do it this weekend if you want. If you don't have plans."

Be cool, Cree. You act like you've never spoken to a girl before.

"Seriously?" Her surprise bothers me for some reason. Does she think I lied about teaching her?

"Yeah, Daisy."

"Oh … all right … yeah, I'm free all weekend. Just let me know what time works best for you."

I glance over at her, finding her fidgeting nervously again with her shirt.

Flashing her my best smile before I return my eyes promptly to the road, I say, "It's a date then."

FOURTEEN

Ophelia

I DON'T KNOW how I accidentally agreed to *two* dates all in the span of a day. I mean … saying yes to Cal wasn't an *accident*, but it wasn't exactly on purpose either. But Cree, I definitely didn't think he meant taking me to skate would be a date.

It put me in the awkward situation of having to tell Cal the next time I saw him that I was busy this weekend since I didn't know when Cree would want to go ice skating.

Friday, after our study session was over, he ended up asking if Saturday at one o'clock would work.

And that's how I find myself now, standing outside my closet absolutely clueless about what to wear. He said to make sure I wear layers since it's not exactly cold outside yet, but I will be on the ice.

Flicking through my wardrobe I pull out a couple of different shirt options—all short sleeve—then rifle in my dresser, past some books I have shoved in there, to my crewnecks. I pull out one with the Hogwarts castle on it that says Welcome Home. I have a feeling Cree will get a kick out of it.

Why do you care if he finds it amusing or not?

I try to ignore my thoughts before I drive myself insane with my constant back and forth.

Yanking open another drawer that houses my jeans, I pull out my favorite pair that's old and faded with rips in the knees. Wiggling out of my red and black plaid pajama bottoms, I yank the jeans on. They're the kind of pair you have to fight to get on, but once you get them on then they loosen up.

Zipping them, I snap the button in place and turn to my tops. I'm sure I look crazy right now standing here with half-brushed hair, a majorly over-sized Tinkerbell pajama top, and my skinny jeans.

Cree said this was a date, but I don't know if he meant that figuratively or literally.

Picking up a cute, cropped olive-green shirt I hold it up and inspect it before sitting it back down and grabbing another, this one a pale blue with a daisy embroidered on the front.

Daisy.

I switch out my Tinkerbell night shirt for that one.

That leaves my mess of hair to try to do something with. Sitting at my desk, I smooth my hairbrush through it, working through the tangled knots. My hair is long, probably too long at this point since when it's down it's nearly to my waist, but getting my haircut has always been one of my least favorite things, so if I can get by snipping the ends off myself, then I do. Much to the horror of my mom who only frequents the very best of salons back home.

Once it's brushed through, I braid it, so it'll stay out of my way on the ice.

I also have an irrational fear of falling and somehow slicing my hair off with a blade … I should probably be more worried about a finger, but I did say it was irrational.

There's an hour before Cree is picking me up, but I wanted to be ready early that so I wouldn't be stressing.

Kenna and Li have both already left today, saying

they were going to the mall with their friend Rory. They invited me along but obviously I declined. I could've told them I was going out with Cree, but instead I said I had to study. It's not a total lie. I will have to study later. I'm not even sure why I wasn't honest about my plans.

Grabbing a granola bar from our kitchenette area, I sit down on the couch with my latest book and drape a blanket over my lap.

When my phone goes off with an alert sound, I nearly fall off the couch in surprise, dropping my book in the process. Catching my breath, I pick it up and find a text from Cree saying he's outside. I reply back, letting him know I'll be down in a minute.

Putting the blanket back, I return my book to my room and grab the crewneck I set out as well as my bag. Making sure no crumbs are stuck to my clothes, I lock up the room behind me.

Taking the elevator down, I burst outside, shocked when I nearly mow Cree down.

"Whoa." He steadies me with a warm gentle hand to my shoulder.

I give myself a moment to take him in. Dark denim jeans, white tee, and a denim button down over top in a much lighter shade than his pants. He smiles that smile of his, the one that shows off his dimples, and I feel myself sway a bit.

"Hi." I blink up at him, my thoughts scattering away like leaves in the wind. He's way too nice to look at. It makes my brain go all funny.

"Hi." His chest shakes with a chuckle. "You okay?"

"I'm … great."

I take a step away from him, and he waits a moment before releasing his hold on me.

"I thought we could go to the rink and then get something to eat if you want?" He starts walking, and I follow him to wherever he parked his car.

"That sounds great."

"Cool." He dips his head, a dark lock of hair falling over his forehead just so. It seems like everything he does, intentional and not, is attractive to me. It's really unfair that someone can look like him and be kind. Where is the flaw? I need to find one stat so I can stop these butterflies in my belly.

His Bronco comes into view, and he heads to the passenger side first, opening the door for me. I can't believe my blunder the other night when we went to get dinner … but then … maybe it wasn't exactly a blunder since he said that's what I said last time, but…

I'm not Daisy.

It's all so confusing.

He has to be mistaken or whoever the real Daisy is said something similar.

Cree hops in the driver's side, strapping his seatbelt on while I do the same. "How's your day been so far?"

I can't exactly tell him I've been a bit freaked out by this ... excursion—I don't want to use the word date—because that would make me look pathetic.

"Good." I pull at one of the frayed edges on the knee of my jeans. "I studied some and read. Not much else. What about you?" I glance over at him and bite my tongue not to groan because even his profile is perfect.

"Went and got breakfast with my roommates and sis. She argued with Jude the whole time. I'm not sure I'm going to survive a whole year living under one roof with the two of them." He brushes his fingers through his hair, mussing it.

"I'm sorry."

"I'll survive it. Somehow."

It's only a few minutes longer when we pull into the lot outside one of the athletics buildings.

"I thought we were going to a rink." I hold onto the seatbelt pressed firmly to my chest as he parks right up front. The lot is mostly empty with it being the weekend.

"We are."

"Here?"

His blue eyes sparkle, his lips twitching as he tries not to laugh. "Yeah, here."

"Are we allowed?"

"Yeah. It's a practice rink so we'll be fine."

He unbuckles his seatbelt, reaching for the door when I gasp.

"I don't have skates!"

"Daisy," he says slowly, like I'm an animal he's terrified of startling into running away, "I have skates for you. They're my sisters. I think they'll fit you, and if they don't there are always spares inside."

"Oh." My cheeks heat with embarrassment at my outburst.

Reaching over, he plucks my hand from where I'm squeezing the seatbelt in a death grip.

"You worry too much. Relax. Enjoy yourself."

"Enjoy myself. I can do that."

"All right." He gives me an encouraging smile. This time he manages to make it out of the vehicle, grabbing a duffel from the backseat.

He opens the passenger door and holds out a hand in case I need it since the Bronco is lifted. I take the offered hand, and even once I'm out and steady on the ground, he keeps a hold on it, curling our fingers together as he leads me to the main doors of the building.

"I guess this is like home away from home for you, huh?"

"Sort of." He leads me through another set of doors then down a long hall. After yet another door, I feel the cold as we enter the area of the rink. Cree leads me right up to where we'll step on and sets his bag down, letting go of my hand for the first time since I got out of the car. "Go ahead and sit down there." He points to a bench. "And take your shoes off. I'll see if these skates work for you." He pulls out a pair that looks practically brand new.

Taking my shoes and socks off, I set them beside me on the bench. I hold my hand out for the skates, but Cree surprises me when he grabs my ankle. So much so a tiny squeak leaves my throat, making icy blue eyes flick up to mine with amusement. He rubs his thumb and forefinger against the back of my foot on the tendon there before slipping the skate on.

"Perfect fit." He grins, balancing my foot and the heavy skate on his thigh. He laces it up nice and tight before doing the same with the other.

"What if I fall on my face?" I bite my bottom lip nervously.

"I'm not going to let you fall."

"You can't promise that."

He chuckles, sitting beside me as he puts his own skates on. "Fine, I'll do my best to not let you fall. Does that suffice?"

"Okay." I look over my shoulder at the rink. "If you didn't play hockey, what do you think you'd do?"

He thinks seriously about my question before he replies. "Maybe lacrosse, but honestly I'm not really that into sports other than hockey. It's my ... well, it's my passion." He stretches his arms above his head, flashing a bit of taut stomach and dark hair leading down from his naval. "So, if I didn't have hockey, I'd probably focus on my other hobbies I already do. Reading and Legos." His cheeks heat like he's shared something really embarrassing.

"You like Legos?" I poke his side. "That's cute."

He groans, covering his face with his hands. "Don't say cute. That's like the kiss of death for guys when it comes to girls."

"What kind of Legos do you build? Any kind or?" I prompt. I really don't know much about Legos, but I know I've seen all different kinds as far as fandoms and other things.

"I like to do buildings and monuments." His cheeks get even redder when he adds, "Spiderman. Star Wars ones too."

"You'll have to show me some time."

He stares at me in surprise. "You ... you want to see my Legos?"

"Sure." I shrug. "Why not?"

"I just ... cool ... yeah ... I'll show you my Legos."

I giggle, impressed I've flustered him since Cree seems unflappable.

He stands and walks over to the entrance onto the ice, making it look way too easy to balance on the blade guards and walk at the same time. "Come on." He crooks a finger, beckoning me to stand and waddle over.

I stand up, take one step, and promptly tip over. I'm only saved from smacking my face into the floor by Cree's quick reflexes.

His body shakes with laughter as he holds me upright and doesn't let go. "You know, I expected you to fall once you got on the ice, not before."

"Be nice!" I lightly punch his arm. "I don't have good balance."

"Where's your sweatshirt?" His eyes narrow, just now realizing I don't have it.

I smack my forehead. "Oh no! I left it in your car." He shakes his head in amusement and has me sit back down on the bench. Shrugging out of his denim shirt he hands it to me. "B-But you need your shirt."

"I'm used to it. I'll be fine."

"But—"

"Put the shirt on, Ophelia."

Oh.

Oh.

I *like* his bossy tone. Probably a little too much.

I slip my arms into the long sleeve shirt. The sleeves are way too long for me, but before I can roll them up myself, he's already doing it for me. His fingers graze my wrist, eyes on me the entire time. He moves to the other sleeve, doing the same.

My breath catches in my throat. I don't think I'm imagining the sexual tension between us. It's practically a visible thing existing in the space of our bodies, vibrating with energy.

Cree is the first to move, clearing his throat he steadies his hands on his thighs and stands back up. "Let's try this again." This time he holds out both his hands. I put mine in them, letting him pull me up. He helps me waddle over to where I need to step onto the ice. "Put your hands here and hold on," he instructs, guiding my hands to the barrier around the rink.

I clasp it so tightly my knuckles turn white.

He slips his blade guards off and then he's on the ice. He skates away like he can't help himself, his infectious laugh filling the air, before he circles back for me.

"All right, I'm going to hold one of your hands to balance you while you remove the guards."

"O-Okay." My voice trembles embarrassingly, but he doesn't seem to notice. Once my guards are off, he helps me onto the ice. "Oh! Oh! This is weird! I don't like this! *Cree!*" I shriek his name.

His laughter booms around us, skating backwards while holding onto me.

He makes it look so easy.

"You're fine. Just breathe."

"I'm gonna fall!"

"I would never let you fall." He sounds hurt that I would think he would.

"Not on purpose!" A scream tears out of my throat when he skates faster. "How are you going so fast? You're going backwards!"

He chuckles, squeezing my hands. "Hockey, remember?"

"Is this where I confess, I've never watched a single game of hockey?"

"Shame." He scolds. "We need to remedy that."

"How?" I keep trying to run my mouth to distract myself from the fact that I'm gliding across ice on what's practically razor-sharp knives.

"You'll come to one of my games. They haven't started yet, but when they do, I'll get you a ticket."

Crowds. Screaming fans. Buzzers.

"No thank you."

"No?" He arches an amused brow.

"I'd rather watch from the comfort of my bed."

"But it's so much better in person," he argues passionately. "You get to see every bit of action and be in the midst of things."

"That's okay. I don't like people-ing."

"Well," he grins at me, "at least you're honest."

"But I would like to watch sometime," I admit quietly.

His dimples pop out. "You can watch from your bed … and maybe if you feel like sorta people-ing you can come see a practice."

"I would be allowed to do that?"

"I'd ask Coach beforehand, but I don't think he'd say no."

"Oh … okay. That could be fun." It really would be interesting to see in person since I have no idea what really goes on with hockey.

"Want to try on your own?" He questions, arching a brow.

"No!" I panic, gripping onto his hands even tighter. "Don't you dare let me go!"

"I won't. Not until you're ready." He seems sincere, so I hope that means he's not going to try to pull a dad move and let me go anyway.

The skates feel funny on my feet—tight and heavy. It's also a strange sensation gliding over the ice, but not unpleasant either. Cold seeps up from the ice and I'm thankful Cree offered me the extra layer of his shirt since I left my sweatshirt behind in the car. Despite that, I still feel sweat forming under my arms, but I think that's more from nerves than actual physical exertion.

Cree pulls me around the entire rink for several laps before I finally get brave enough to try on my own.

"You can let go."

His eyes widen with surprise. "Are you sure?"

I bite my lip, double checking with myself that I'm not going to majorly regret this and nod. "I'm ready."

"I'll be right here." His assurance makes me smile. There's an edge to Cree, one I'm not sure other people notice, but I see it from time to time. However, he really is sweet. He cares. It's more than I can say about a lot of other people.

Slowly, finger by finger, he releases me. He stays close in case I lose my balance. My arms go out to my sides, and by some miracle, I manage to stay upright. Moving forward on my own isn't easy, and I'm far from graceful, but it doesn't matter because I'm *doing it*.

Tears prick my eyes, and I hope Cree doesn't notice because I don't want to explain why I'm emotional.

He lets out an excited scream and claps his hands. "Fuck, yes! Look at you go!"

My smile grows larger with his praise. I manage a

few more feet before I get wobbly. "Grab me! Grab me, please!" I cry in panic.

His hands are right there, grabbing onto me immediately without any sort of hesitation. He pulls me closer to him than I was before, until his arms are wrapped firmly around my body.

"You did it." His eyes crinkle at the corners with how big his smile is.

"I did it," I echo.

My breath catches when he kisses the end of my nose. Our eyes connect, and the moment seems to stretch out endlessly. I think he might kiss me, really kiss me, on the lips, but then he looks away, and the moment is gone.

Clearing his throat, he says, "Let's grab something to eat. I'm starving."

THE CAFE CREE brings me to is a few blocks from campus, in walking distance but he drives us. It's small, but cute with a moon and stars aesthetic. Handmade paper stars dangle from the ceiling on fishing wire.

Menus sit in the middle of the blue tiled table. I pick one up, perusing it while Cree already seems to know what he wants.

"Do you know what you'd like?" he asks when I put the menu away.

"I was going to get the avocado toast."

"I'll go place our order." He jumps up, heading to the register. He's not there long when he returns with a numbered card.

"How'd you find this place?" I look around at the various art prints of constellations.

He shrugs. "I was on a run one day and doing my cool down. I saw they sold coffee and came in. The rest is, as they say, history. It's usually quiet in here and the food's great. Coffee too."

"Clearly, I need to get out more."

He fiddles with the pepper shaker, like he finds the need to keep his hands busy. "I can help with that."

Resting my elbow on the table, I lay my head in my hand. "Thank you for taking me ice skating. It meant a lot to me."

"Any time. Is there anything else you've never done before that you want to?"

Twisting my lips together, I think before answering. "It's silly."

"I would never think that anything you want to do is silly."

"I've always wanted to sleep under the stars. Being

in here reminded me of that." I point to the ceiling full of stars.

"Like camping?"

"I guess or even just the backyard. It doesn't have to be some big deal."

"Tell me something else you want to do." He seems almost desperate for information.

"I don't know … lots of things." I scoot back when I see the girl approach with our plates of food. "Thank you."

She smiles, so I return the gesture.

"Thanks, Cindy," Cree says over his shoulder since she's already walking away.

My avocado toast looks amazing. I dig in immediately. Apparently ice-skating gives you quite the appetite.

Across from me, Cree takes a bite of the flatbread pizza he ordered.

"Thank you for lunch." I point down at my plate. "I can—"

"If you say you can pay me back, I might lose my shit."

"Oh, well in that case I can't pay you back."

"Good girl." He winks, my stomach dipping with the gesture.

I didn't know a wink could be sexy, but Cree just

proved it. It makes me think about him kissing the tip of my nose and how I thought he might kiss me for real.

Do I want him to kiss me?

I don't think I'd mind it if he did.

Clearing my throat and forcing thoughts of Cree's lips from my brain, I ask, "What made you want to major in English?"

Cringing after I've asked it, I silently scold myself. I should've asked him something better even if I am curious about where this jock got his love for reading and writing.

He finishes chewing a bite of pizza, wiping his fingers on a napkin before answering. "I don't know. I always loved reading, and nothing else excited me. I didn't want to go into business or financing." He makes a face as if the idea alone makes him ill. "English seemed like the best fit especially since I figured my future was with hockey."

"And now you're not sure?"

He twists his lips back and forth. "I love hockey. It's my passion. But it's a hard, rough sport. Injuries are common. I guess, I worry about my body taking so much beating long term, but will I be happy going another route? That's what I'm trying to figure out. What's your plan post-college?"

I laugh humorlessly. "That's a loaded question, one I

desperately need to figure out."

"It hard to decide what you want to do the rest of your life. It's a lot of pressure."

"You're telling me." I finish my toast, pushing my plate to the end of the table. "I thought maybe a teacher, but I'm not so sure anymore. I just want to be happy with whatever I do."

"You have time. You'll get it figured out."

"I hope so."

Cree finishes up as well and tells me to sit tight. I watch him with narrowed eyes when he heads back to the counter to order something else. He waits there for whatever it is and I practically bounce of my seat when he carries over a frozen coffee for me, a coffee for himself and—

"These brownies are even better than the ones on campus. No sprinkles, but you'll have to trust me." He sets the small plate between us on the table.

I reach forward and pull off a corner, popping it into my mouth. "Mmm. That's incredible." He grins in amusement as I reach for another piece. "Aren't you going to have some?"

"Nah, I'm enjoying watching you too much."

"Say no more." I pull the plate all the way to my side, thoroughly enjoying my brownie. "I have to get another one of those to take home with me."

He produces a small paper bag I somehow missed and slides it across the table to me. "Already ahead of you."

"Wow, keep treating me this good, and I might ask you to marry me."

He laughs, his eyes glittering with amusement. He looks me over, those dimples popping back out. "I wouldn't say no."

My breath catches—which makes me nearly choke on brownie. Somehow, I manage to recover before I make a fool of myself and need the Heimlich maneuver in the middle of the café.

Brushing crumbs off my lap, Cree and I stand to leave.

We're quiet on the drive back to school. I'm surprised when he parks at my dorm and hops out, coming around to open my door. He walks with me up to the entrance and pauses.

"You gonna go on another date with me, Daisy?"

This was a real date!

"Um ... do you want to?"

He bites his lip, trying to hide his smile. "I wouldn't ask if I didn't."

"Then ... yeah. If you're sure you're not sick of me with all the tutoring and stuff."

Ophelia, stop trying to convince the hot guy not to go out with you!

"I'd never get sick of you."

A startled breath escapes me when his warm fingers brush gently over my cheek. He leans in, and I'm certain this time that he's actually going to kiss me. I brace myself for it and everything.

But then he clears his throat and takes a step back.

"You might eventually."

And isn't that my biggest fear? That the people I love and care about will get sick of me, and I'll be left alone? It's why I do everything I can to not be a burden.

"I promise you, that's not going to happen." His Adam's apple bobs, a curse flying out of his throat. "Fuck it."

In the blink of an eye, the span of one single second, his big hands are on my face nearly swallowing it in his grasp. Then his lips are on mine.

His.

Lips.

Are.

On.

Mine.

My body folds in on itself. No, not on itself, but into him. Like he's the sun and I'm a flower absorbing his warmth. On their own accord, my arms go around his neck, pressing into him like I think I can sink inside. He groans low in his throat, his body vibrating with pleasure. The kiss deepens, his tongue sweeping inside my mouth.

More. I want more.

His hands are firm on my face, but not hurting me. It's like he's afraid I'll turn to mist and slip away.

Something inside me awakens, a tiny sound escaping me.

Cree swallows that sound with one of his own.

We're making out in front of my dorm.

Normally, that thought would scare me enough that I'd stop this. I hate attention and don't like making a scene. But I can't bring myself to break this.

I want it too much.

My lips are sore when he pulls back slightly, his mouth hovering over mine. Our breaths are heavier than normal, my heart beating a whole new song.

Alive.

I was living before, but now I feel alive—like something inside me has woken up and said *this* is what life is about. *This* is what all those books I've read were telling me. I thought it wasn't real. Just words on a paper. Something I was incapable of feeling.

But it's there, existing in the space of our bodies, this new awareness.

Of him.

Of myself.

Tears prick my eyes because I realize I never thought I'd feel desire. It was just a word. One I knew the definition of, guessed the feeling of, but it didn't exist to me.

Now, it does.

Looking up into his icy blue eyes I decide a lot of new words might exist for me with his help.

I've kissed other guys. Had sex. Even had a few short-term boyfriends in high school.

But it was just a thing I did because I thought I was supposed to, that it was what was normal and expected of me, not because I had feelings for them.

I grip onto his arm, his skin warm beneath my hands.

"You have no idea how long I've been waiting to kiss you."

I blink up at him, unable to keep the surprise from my face. "Really?"

His thumb rubs over my bottom lip. "It's all I could think about." He presses a small, quick kiss to my mouth again.

My thoughts are a whirlwind I can't even begin to decipher. All I can focus on is the emotions planting inside me. Taking root. Growing.

And that's not to say I've never felt certain things, I have. I love my parents, my brother, Logan too.

But when it comes to things of the romantic nature it's like any emotion involving that was turned off and didn't exist. I was wrong, though. They were there, just waiting for the right person.

His tongue slides out, wetting his lips. "I have to go, but I can see you tomorrow to study if you want?"

I nod, it's the only thing I can make myself do in that moment.

He laughs like he knows. "You can come over to my place again."

Another nod.

His grin is brilliant, clearly pleased with his kissing skills. So cocky. But that doesn't even bother me, because he has every right to be cocky when he can kiss that good.

My hands shake the tiniest bit from adrenaline when I tuck my hair behind my ear.

"Thank you for today," I call after him, not letting any passing glances from people walking by bother me.

Cree tips his head. "You're welcome." He starts walking backwards, back in the direction of his car. "See you tomorrow, Daisy."

I smile, rocking back on the balls of my feet as excitement floods me. "Tomorrow."

FIFTEEN

CREE

I'M grateful the house is empty. Jude's out with his football buddies, Daire went with Bowie to some sort of truck rally, and Millie's working on a project at the student center.

The doorbell rings right on time, and I open it—probably way too quickly—to Ophelia standing there looking not nearly as awkward as she did the other day. There's a new confidence in her, this glow, and yeah, it's fucking selfish, but I like to think it's because of me.

"Did you have a good night?" I step aside to let her in.

"Yes." Her hazel eyes are more green than gold today. She takes off her backpack, sitting it down by her feet. "It was made even better by the extra brownie. Thank you again."

"No problem." I lock up the door. "Do you want to study in the living room or my room?"

The question comes out before I can stop it. Keeping her in the living room is the safest bet. There's no bed nearby—not that you can't fuck on the couch— but especially because if she goes into my room, she's going to see my explosion of nerdy stuff.

She spins around, her hair flowing out behind her. "I kind of want to see your room. I think bedrooms say so much about a person, what they surround them- selves with when they sleep." Her cheeks turn a shade of red at her admission, her eyes darting down to the ground.

I clear my throat, nodding at the stairs. "All right, up you go." I scoop her backpack up before she can and follow her upstairs. "First door on your right there."

She peeks at me over her shoulder with a smile that seems more like the Ophelia I met a year ago than the one I see now. She was still shy then, but there was a freeness to her that night.

She walks right into my room, stopping in the middle so she can spin it around and take it all in.

Shelves of books, Legos, and trophies.

My bed made but it's ruffled since I was laying on top of it earlier.

The chair in the corner with a basket on top of freshly washed clothes I haven't bothered to fold. At least they're clean. I deserve some credit for that fact.

There's a Spiderman poster—one my parents had custom made for me from this really cool artist—hanging above the chair. I notice her lips twitch with amusement, her eyes circling back to the bed. The covers are folded back, exposing my Spiderman sheets.

"You really are a fan of Spiderman." I shrug. There's no use in denying it. "And you weren't kidding about the Legos."

I do cringe at that because there's an embarrassing amount of completed ones around my whole room, and this doesn't even include the ones at my parents' house. The one I've been working on is spread out on my desk.

She walks over there now, picking up a random Lego from one of my sorted piles. Turning to face me, she holds it up. "Would you ever let me help you?"

"You…" I stare at her, absorbing what she asked. "You want to help me put together my Legos?"

"Sure. It looks fun. Besides, I need to get a new

hobby other than reading. Not that reading is bad, it's not, but I need other things to occupy my time. I tried embroidery but I kept stabbing myself with the needle. Then it was crochet, but I got bored with it."

"Um ... yeah. After we study you can help if you want."

"Sounds fun." She sets the Lego back in the pile I had it in. "The Legos, not the studying. Not that studying is bad, just tedious."

I chuckle at her rambling. "You wanna sit on the bed? I can pull the chair up."

She rolls her eyes at me. "We're both adults. I think we can sit on the bed together."

Something comes over me, and I stalk over to where she is. I stop beside her, lowering my lips to her ear. "Roll your eyes at me again and I'll spank you."

Her breath catches, eyes dilating, and I grin, because I know she doesn't mind the idea of that at all.

But now isn't the time for that. We really do have to study. I pass Ophelia her bag, and she sits down on my bed, adjusting the pillows behind her.

"Are you feeling any better about this class?"

She sighs, unzipping her bag. "Yes and no. I feel like I'm understanding the material better, but I won't know for sure until I get my grades back from Professor Lindon. Because while I think I'm getting it, he could completely obliterate that if he doesn't like the things I've turned in recently."

Besides the essay she's been working on, there was an extensive worksheet on the last book they focused on.

"You'll have to let me know what he says."

"Oh, I will." She pulls her hair back, securing it with an elastic. When her hair is back from her face, she pats the space beside her on the bed. "I don't bite."

I chuckle. "But what if I do?"

Her cheeks turn a vibrant pink, making her freckles even more prominent.

"Be good," she warns. "I can't fail this class again."

"I'll be on my best behavior. For now."

A COUPLE of hours later Ophelia's done all the studying I think her brain can handle, and her essay is almost done. I read over it again, point out a couple of things I think she should change and explain why before telling her to email it to me tomorrow, and I'll give it a final read.

"I'm ordering pizza." I roll off the bed, searching for my phone. I find it on the floor, halfway under the edge of the rug. "I'm starving. What kind do you like?"

"Hawaiian." She packs up her stuff, seeming relieved to be done.

I do a slow turn in her direction, giving her a dramatic look. "Not the fruit pizza."

She points a finger at me. "Don't you dare judge me! It's delicious and everyone that's a hater hasn't tried it."

It's difficult to hide my amusement. I love those moments when Ophelia sparks to life, her personality shining through.

"Fine, I'll withhold judgement."

She wiggles her finger, pointing at me. "Lies! The judgement is all over your face right now, sir."

"Sir, huh?" I smirk, scrolling through my phone where I have the number saved. "I like the sound of that."

"You … you're … *Oh my God.*"

"I bet I can make you say oh my God again." I look her up and down with the phone pressed to my ear, letting her know with my eyes exactly what I mean.

"You're dangerous."

"You have no idea, babe."

They pick up on the other end, and I place our order. Tossing my phone on the bed, I watch Ophelia. She's looking at some of the trophies on my bookshelf. I stuffed most of them in my closet at my parents', but there are some that are more special to me that I chose to display here.

She turns around like she can sense the feel of my eyes on her back. "You must be really good at hockey."

I shrug, the picture of nonchalance. "I'm okay."

"Don't lie," she scolds playfully. "The NFL wouldn't be interested in you if you weren't amazing."

Laughing, I close the distance between us, placing my hands on her hips. I dip my head, brushing my nose lightly against hers. "It's the N*H*L, babe."

"You've called me babe twice in the span of a few minutes.

"Do you not like it?"

"I *do* like it, that's the problem." Her eyes drift closed.

"How's that a problem?"

Her eyes pop on. "Because you scare me."

My brows furrow, offense tightening my shoulders. "You're scared of me?"

She tugs on the bottom of her t-shirt with a faded print of the Deathly Hallows symbol on it.

"I didn't say I was scared *of* you." Relief floods me with that declaration. "Just that you scare me. This." She wags a finger between us. "Whatever this is, scares me. It's intense, right?"

I nod, because she's not kidding. I still think about

that night we first met. It's not like I looked at her and two seconds later thought *damn that's the girl I'm going to marry,* but I knew she was someone I wanted to get to know, and the more I do, the more I like her.

That tension builds between us again, my eyes going to her lips, thinking about the kiss outside her dorm yesterday. I'd be lying if I didn't say it turned me on and made me want more.

"It is," I finally answer her, my words rough with want.

"I shouldn't … you're my tutor … I can't … I don't want to ruin things."

I shake my head roughly. "We won't. It won't ruin things. I won't let it."

"You can't promise that." Her hands form into fists at her sides, her nails digging into her palms.

I cross the short distance between us in just a few steps. My right hand delves into the soft locks of her hair, now freed from her ponytail, my other hand going to her hip. "I can and I will. It doesn't have to be complicated."

"What are you saying? Just sex?"

I shake my head. "I'm not sure I can have just sex with you, Ophelia."

"W-What does that mean?" Her breath puffs against my chin.

"It means ... if you want this." I press into her, and she gasps. "We figure it out as we go."

Her eyes dart up to mine, the green now nearly swallowed by gold. Her lips are redder than normal from rubbing them together. A tiny sound leaves her throat as she sways into me.

I don't know who breaks first, but suddenly her mouth is on mine, and I'm picking her up, her legs wrapping around my waist. She gasps when her center lines up with mine, feeling me hard and ready. I can't help it. I'm half-hard any time she's near me.

Her hands are on my cheeks, and I'm thankful as fuck that I shaved before she came over. Now I don't have to worry about marking up her skin.

For someone who's quiet and fairly reserved, Ophelia sure knows how to kiss and isn't shy about expressing herself with tiny sounds and subtle move-ments. I turn us around, lowering her back to the bed and following her so my body is a cocoon around her. Our tongues tangle together, one of her legs pressing into my back and forcing my body even closer to hers.

She tastes like the peppermint she sucked on earlier. Her fingers delve into my hair, tugging roughly.

Breaking the kiss, I gaze down at her. She's panting to catch her breath. I'm winded too.

No words pass between us, but she gives the tiniest

nod and it's all I need. I dive back in, capturing her lips with mine. My hand is on her cheek, guiding her head back. Then I'm kissing my way down her neck.

She fists my shirt, yanking at it with desperation.

"You wanna feel my bare skin?" I murmur into her neck, feeling her nod. "Greedy little thing, aren't you?" I kiss the spot my mouth is near. "I like that." My teeth bite into her flesh and she cries out, not in pain but pleasure. "Cat got your tongue, sweetheart?" I grip her face in my hand, my hold firm and commanding. "Use your words or I won't give you what you want."

With a tiny little gasp, she says, "Take your shirt off."

"Don't forget the please." I growl, biting her shoulder.

"Please."

I hook my fingers into the back of my shirt and yank it off. It settles on the bed somewhere to my right. Her greedy little hands eat up my flesh, tracing every dip and curve of my abdominals. Every fucking hour I've put into honing my body is worth it for the way she touches me so reverently.

Gripping her neck, I angle her head back and kiss down the slope, over her collarbone. I need more of her.

"This okay?" I twist my fingers into the bottom of her shirt. She nods so fast I'm surprised she doesn't get whiplash. "I like that," I confess, nipping her chin. "How eager you are. How badly you want me." I don't take her shirt off completely, not yet, but I do ease it up her stomach kissing the smooth skin there. She shivers, her hips rocking off the mattress. "You don't even have to tell me you want me. I see it, Ophelia. I feel it." With my hand on her stomach, I feel the vibrations in her body. The hum of energy. "But that doesn't mean I don't like to hear it."

"Cree. Please."

"Mmm, that's more like it." I move fast, shoving her shirt up over her breasts and then arms, using it to secure her hands together. "Look at you." My eyes take her in, her small breasts straining with each breath behind the cage of her tiny pink lace bra. "I'm going to mark every inch of your skin so you never forget this. Never forget *me*." A tiny whimper escapes her lips. "If," I kiss the skin above her naval, "you want me to stop, or you're not comfortable with something. Like this." I tug on her shirt wrapped firmly around her slender wrists. "Then I want you to use a safe word. You have to pick it, and it has to be something you wouldn't say accidentally during sex. Specific. It has to be specific. Do you understand?"

She nods jerkily, her throat contracting with a swallow. She whispers something I can't hear.

"Louder, sweetheart." I stroke my finger over her cheek, down around her chin.

"O-Otter."

"Otter?" My lips quirk in amusement. "Like the animal?"

Another nod. "I-It was the first thing that popped in my head."

"I don't care what it is, as long as you remember."

"Will you?"

"I won't forget." I dip my head, kissing the swell of her breast. Her hands jerk like she wants to touch me, but with them bound she can't. It's not that I don't want her to touch me, it's just so much more fun this way. "Things aren't going to get too crazy this time," I speak into the skin between her breasts, grinning when goose-bumps pimple her skin. "But I still want you to have a safe word."

She swallows thickly, dipping her head in a nod. "Can you please just…"

"What, Ophelia? Tell me what you want." I lick a trail between her breasts, down to her stomach. She wiggles, tiny little noises escaping her throat. "I can't give you what you want if you don't ask for it."

Glancing up at her, I find her eyes hooded, her top teeth digging into her bottom lip.

"Y-Your mouth?"

"My mouth." I grin, her body flushing. "Where do you want my mouth?"

"Don't make me say it?"

My smile grows. "Oh, darling, that's not how this goes, and you know it."

She gives a tiny whimper. Flipping her over, she squeals at the sudden movement when she lands on her stomach. I jerk her hips up and slap my hand over her jean clad ass. She cries out in surprise, her tied hands splayed out in front of her. She uses her arms to support her weight. She looks back at me, her mouth round with surprise.

"If you don't do what I ask, I'm going to spank you. When I tell you to tell me what you want, you better listen." I squeeze her ass. Her eyes flash that molten golden color I'm learning mean she's turned on. "Now tell me, where do you want my mouth?"

She doesn't hesitate this time, there's a confidence that comes over her, and I fucking love seeing it. "I want your mouth on my pussy."

"Hmm," I hum, rubbing her ass. "I can do that."

I flip her back around, eliciting another little scream from her. I get rid of her shoes, dropping them to the floor. When my fingers go to the button on her jeans, her gaze is rapt on every movement I make. The button pops, then I take the zipper between my two fingers sliding it down slowly—oh so fucking slowly, teasing both of us. My dick is so fucking hard pressed against my own jeans, but this isn't about me. Not yet.

My breath is hot against her skin, and I can't help but kiss the top of her pubic bone.

She lifts her hips when I wiggle her jeans down and off her body.

"No panties?" I practically pant, surprised to find her already bare.

She shakes her head. "I don't like them. They feel too tight against me." My eyes close and I count to ten, trying to calm down. "Cree?"

"I'm okay." I wrap my arms around her thighs, laying down on my stomach. "Fuck, your pussy is wet. That's all for me isn't it, sweetheart? I like that. I like that a lot."

She opens her mouth to say something, but whatever it is turns into a moan when my tongue swipes out, licking along her seam.

I lick and suck, learning what she likes and doesn't, from the sounds and movements she makes. Sucking her clit into my mouth, I slide two fingers inside her and hook them. Her thighs start to shake, then she starts begging.

"Oh, God. Cree. Don't stop. Please. I'm almost there." That's when I stop, sliding my fingers out and sitting up. "What are you doing?" she cries desperately. "I said don't stop."

I move up her body, bracing my hands beside her head I hold myself up. "You don't tell me what to do, Ophelia. You'll learn that real quick. But don't worry, I'll make it worth your while."

Sliding off the bed I undo my belt and jeans, sliding my boxer-briefs off with them all in one movement.

Ophelia sits up slightly, her eyes widening as she stares at my cock.

I take it in my hand, pumping once. Twice. I roll my wrist around the head. "You like what you see?" Her cheeks pinken at being caught. "Don't be embarrassed. I like you looking."

I grab a condom, ripping the foil open. I roll it down my length, grinning the whole time at the way she watches me. She cries out in surprise again when I grab her legs and pull her to the end of the bed where I stand.

"You ready?"

"*God, yes.*"

I guide my cock to her entrance. "Just the tip," I joke. When she starts to smile, I slam all the way inside her, whole body rocking upward with the movement.

"*Oh my God.*"

"God's not listening, sweetheart. It's all me. Say *my*

name." My fingers dig into her hips. She'll probably have bruises, but she doesn't seem to mind my tight grip.

Her fingers wiggle, desperate to touch me and I like seeing that but knowing she can't. Next time. Next time she can touch me all she wants. But I'm being selfish this round.

Her bra is still on, but I want to see her. All of her. I grab roughly at the lace yanking it down past her breasts, the straps settling around her arms.

"Fuck." I grip one of her breasts in my hand, squeezing. I circle my thumb around her tiny pert pink nipple. "You're perfect."

And she is. It's like she was fucking made for me.

She moves her hips, meeting my thrusts. Rubbing my thumb on her clit, her pussy squeezes my dick. Perspiration clings to my chest, and there's sweat dotting her brow. I can tell she's close to an orgasm. I don't even have to ask. It's only our second time, but I already feel like I know her body backwards and forwards.

"Cree!" She screams my name as she comes, her pussy squeezing my dick.

"Fuck, yes, baby." My head falls back, my eyes closing. *"Fuck."*

I pull out of her body and rip the condom off, fisting

myself in my hand. My hand pumps my cock as I come all over her abdomen.

She lies there, eyes half-lidded as she watches. I untie her shirt from around her wrists, gently massaging them.

"Let me clean you up," I murmur, heading into the bathroom.

Returning a minute later with a wet cloth I wipe her up, my eyes feasting on her. She's so fucking sexy and doesn't even realize it.

When she's clean, she finally speaks. "When can we do that again?"

Laughter explodes out of me, and I look down at my dick, already starting to get hard again. "Don't worry, babe. I'm almost ready to go." But then the doorbell rings and I curse. "Fucking pizza," I mutter. "You wait here."

I grab my jeans and yank them on, jogging downstairs to grab the two pies.

I've never wanted pizza less in my life.

Carrying them back up the stairs, I find Ophelia sitting up, her legs curled behind her. She's still completely naked and not at all shy about it.

"I don't want the pizza," she says as I close my door behind me.

"I don't either."

Setting the boxes down on my desk chair, I stalk over to her. When I get close, she rises up on her knees, her hand going behind my head, tugging my mouth to hers.

My body falls over hers, and we forget the pizza and studying and Legos.

This is all about us.

SIXTEEN

Ophelia

"I DID A BAD THING." The words are the first thing out of my mouth when Logan answers my Facetime call.

"Um…" Logan's eyes widen. "You're going to have to be more specific than that."

"Ugh." I cover my face with my other hand. I'm speed-walking around campus like a complete and utter maniac, but after what happened yesterday with Cree, I'm full of restless energy and can't stop thinking about it. It doesn't help that every time I move, I feel traces of it in the soreness of my muscles. "Don't make me say it out loud."

"Filly, why'd you call me then if not to tell me this really bad thing that you did?"

I frown, looking around to see if anyone's eavesdropping. They're not. No one cares what I did except me.

"I slept with my tutor."

Logan gapes at me in astonishment. "You did what?"

"I know!" I cringe. "I told you it was bad! *Three* times."

"This happened three times and you're just now telling me?"

"All of it happened yesterday."

Logan shakes his head, sitting inside his car. A coffee comes into view, and he takes a long sip. "Three times, huh? Dude must have some serious stamina."

"Be serious, Lo!"

"I am!"

"He's a hockey player," I end up saying by way of explanation.

"I think I need to take up hockey."

"You're not helping. What do I do?"

"I think you're a bit late asking that, don't you? You already did the deed with the guy."

"Logan," I hiss. "I called you for real advice."

"Do you like this guy?"

I only hesitate for a few seconds before I give a tiny nod. "Yeah, I think I do. He's funny and nice, smart too. He likes to read, and he makes me laugh. Not to mention he's hot and the sex—"

"Filly," he cuts me off, "I love you, but I don't want to hear about the sex."

"Right." I blush.

"Who gives a fuck if he's your tutor? Have some fun. That's what college is all about. Don't put pressure on yourself."

"Logan," I hiss, pinching the bridge of my nose. "You're supposed to talk me out of this!"

He grins. "No can do. I'm the devil on your shoulder remember?"

I have called him that once or twice or a hundred times.

"So, you don't think this is bad idea?"

"I didn't say that, but no one knows the outcome of certain things, and you have to find out for yourself. That's why I say have fun."

"Fun," I repeat. "Right. I can do that."

He chuckles, his laughter reminding me of younger days spent running around each other's houses, eating sweets, and falling into a sugar coma.

"I want you to be happy. That's all that matters."

"I am happy. Happier than I've been."

"Good. I gotta head into class, but I miss you."

"All right. I miss you, too."

"Later, Filly." He winks, ending the call.

I tuck my phone into my back pocket. My next class isn't for another hour, and I don't feel like heading back to my dorm, so I go to the library instead. I'm caught up on everything, so I end up finding one of the big leather chairs in a secluded corner to sit and read.

I don't think I'll ever forget the first time I picked up a book.

At first, I wasn't all that excited. Pages and pages of *words*. Nothing about that seemed so great. But then my eyes took in the words, my brain formed the images, and I fell into worlds beyond my wildest dreams all created with a variation of the same twenty-six letters.

After that first book, I never stopped reading. I read everything I could get my grubby little hands on, and my parents were more than happy to indulge me.

Setting my alarm on my phone so I don't get so lost in my book that I forget to go to class, I crack open the spine and start reading.

Sure enough, my alarm goes off and I nearly jump out of my skin at the interruption. I quickly silence it and stuff everything back into my bag before throwing my backpack over my shoulder and hauling ass out of the building.

Pushing the door open to exit the library, I nearly mow someone down in the process.

"So sorry," I mutter, ready to scurry on my way.

"Ophelia?"

I turn, taking in the girl who is immediately recognizable as my roommate.

"Oh, hi Kenna. I'm really sorry about that. I have to get to class."

"I'm glad I caught you." She hesitates outside the door, clutching a book to her chest. Shuffling my feet, I fight all my instincts to run off since I don't want to be late to class. "Li and I are going out to dinner tonight with Rory. It'll be really lowkey, promise. We want you to come."

I hesitate, my thoughts ping-ponging around inside my head. "Where are you having dinner?"

"It's the place Rory waitresses. It's Italian. A tad bit fancy but you don't have to dress up, and it's pretty quiet. Not overly crowded."

Rubbing my lips together, I nod. "Okay. I can go."

"Great! The three of us can go over together from the dorm. See you later." She waves excitedly and rushes into the library.

Hurrying down the steps, I make a mad dash for my

next class, sliding into a seat just in time since the Professor is a stickler on tardiness.

I can't believe I agreed to dinner with the girls, but it's been a while since I've done anything with them. I think this will be good for me. I hope, at least.

LI AND KENNA giggle as they get ready, dancing and singing along to a song about kissing other people.

I'm much more subdued in my bedroom, scouring my closet for something to wear. My go-to tends to be a t-shirt and jeans, but I feel like putting on something a little nicer tonight.

Deep in the back I find a lavender dress with white flowers on it. I don't remember purchasing it. More than likely my mom thought it was cute and slipped it in there. Right now, I'm feeling pretty thankful for that.

Putting the dress on, I peek at my appearance in the mirror beside my desk. My red hair hangs down in its loose natural waves. I'm sure it would look better if I curled some of the pieces, but I don't care. I haven't bothered with makeup other than mascara and some pink gloss but looking at my reflection I feel pretty.

Opening the door, I peek out and spot Kenna and Li in Kenna's room.

"Is this okay?" I ask, tugging at the bottom of the dress. Both girls turn to me, twin O's forming on their mouths. "Oh no." My eyes widen in horror. "Is it really that bad?"

"No!" Kenna gasps, setting down the tube of red lipstick clasped in her hand. "You look gorgeous! That color is amazing on you."

Heat rushes to my cheeks. "Really?"

"You're so pretty, Ophelia." Li gives me a reassuring smile. "The dress looks great on you."

I let out a breath I didn't even realize I'd been holding. "Thank you for inviting me out tonight."

Kenna crosses the distance between us, squeezing my elbow. "You're always welcome to hang out with us."

I know Kenna always extends invites to me, and I appreciate it so much, but … I have a hard time believing people truly want my company and it's not out of pity. Social anxiety can be crippling. But when someone keeps reaching out their hand, eventually you decide to grab it.

Clearing my throat, I smooth my hands down the bodice. "So, this is okay?"

"It's great," Kenna assures me, taking a step back.

She's dressed in a cute black dress, fitted to her body and ending just above her knees. Li on the other hand has on a pair of leather pants—at least they look leather—and a white wrap top. I don't think I could pull off something like that, but Li makes it look effortless.

"We're almost ready." Li picks up a mascara tube. "We'll head out in a few."

"I can drive," I volunteer, raising my hand like I'm in class. I lower it awkwardly when I realize what I've done. Both girls look at me in surprise. "That way if you guys want to drink you can … I won't. I don't really like the taste of alcohol all that much."

They exchange a look and Kenna nods with a smile. "That would be great. Thanks, Ophelia."

I let them finish getting ready, leaving the door to my room open behind me. Swiping my phone from my dresser, I can't help the stupid giddy smile that appears when I see a text from Cree.

Cree: Sorry I couldn't tutor tonight. I'll make it up to you. If it's any consolation, I can't stop thinking about you.

He had some sort of hockey obligation he wasn't sure how late it would run, and frankly I needed a break today from studying. If I cram too much information down, it'll get lost.

Me: I suppose that does make me feel a bit better. ;)

Cree: What are you up to tonight? Reading?

Me: Actually, I'm going out with the girls.

Cree: Going out? Where?

Me: I don't know the name of the place. Kenna said it's the restaurant her friend Rory works at.

Cree: I know Rory.

Me: You do?

Is that jealousy flaring in my chest?

Cree: She's dating a friend of mine.

And my jealousy melts away.

Cree: Enjoy your night with the girls.

Me: I'll try to, thanks.

"Hey, are you ready?" Li pokes her head into my room.

"Yeah, give me one second." I put my phone away, grab my bag and keys.

The girls follow me out to my car and pile inside. I take a deep breath as the engine starts and smile to myself.

I'm putting myself out there. Logan and Gus will be proud of me. *I'm* proud of me.

THE RESTAURANT IS DECORATED in warm tones with low lighting. It's pleasing, and like Kenna said it's nice but not too fancy. My eyes scan the room, taking in every detail. Skimming over the bar, my eyes swing back, stopping on a familiar form.

Icy blue eyes take me in, a glass of something I can't identify clasped in his hand. The smirk on his lips when he knows I've spotted him sends a shiver down my spine. The ghostly caress of his fingers on my skin, the memories of yesterday, invade my mind.

Did he come here because of me?

It seems like such a selfish thought, but I can't think of any other explanation.

The hostess leads us to a booth, Kenna and Li taking one side while I sit on the other. I eye the empty space beside me, silently worried that Rory won't want to sit by me. It's not like we *know* each other. I've only met her a handful of times.

Kenna must notice my expression because she smiles gently. "Rory's running a little late but she's so excited you decided to join us."

I nod, looking over the leather-bound menu that was placed in front of me.

Choices extend down the page in an almost over-whelming number. Heat sears the side of my face, and I peek over at the bar, catching Cree watching me. I never knew someone's eyes on your body could feel like a physical caress, but his does.

A few minutes later, Rory arrives apologizing profusely and with her beside me, it blocks my view of Cree and his of me.

"I'm so sorry, guys. I lost track of time, and I was chilling in my sweats, so I had to change, and it's just been one of *those* days you know? Where everything that can go wrong does?"

"I know exactly what you mean," Li pipes in. "We haven't been here long. We don't even have drinks."

"That makes me feel a little better." Rory huffs out a sigh, turning her attention to me. Her cheeks are flushed with color like she's been running around. "It's good to see you, Ophelia. How have you been?"

"Oh." I set my menu down. "I'm good. Just busy studying. The usual."

"I feel that. This year is kicking my butt. Mascen is sitting back laughing at me since he graduated and doesn't have to deal with this anymore. Jerk."

Despite her calling him a jerk, I get the impression she means it playfully.

A waiter interrupts then for our drink order. The other girls all get wine while I stick with water. It isn't long before he's back with them and a basket of bread—bless him—and takes our food order.

When he's gone, I swipe a piece of bread, slathering it in butter. My stomach seems to have come to life, reminding me I haven't eaten enough today.

The other girls chat about this and that, doing their best to include me, but I'm not the best at conversating and tend to only give a few words in reply.

It reminds me of how easily words seem to flow around Cree. I don't know what it is about him that has me running my mouth so much.

When our food is placed before us, my appetite is subdued thanks to gorging myself on the bread.

"What is it you're studying again?" Rory asks me, pushing her glasses back up her nose. "I know we've talked about this before, but I can't remember."

I chew and swallow my bite of pasta. "I'm an English major."

"That's right." She snaps her fingers. "Do you like it?"

I shrug, pushing noodles around my plate. "I like books and writing, so it seemed fitting."

"Are you going to the football game this weekend?" Kenna asks Rory, thankfully taking the conversation away from me.

I eat about half my plate before I can't put another bite in my mouth and know I'll need a to-go box. My bladder also reminds me I've downed three glasses of water since we've been here.

"I'm so sorry, Rory. I need to use the restroom. Do you mind scooting out?"

"Of course not!" She stands up, stepping aside to give me space to get out.

Sliding from the booth, I stand up and smooth my skirt down—paranoid it might be sticking up in the back and I don't want to give anyone a free show.

The heat returns and I'm not surprised when I look up to Cree still at the bar. He has what looks like a glass of water now sitting beside him. His arms are crossed on the wooden top, eyes so intense it sends a shiver straight down my spine.

Forcing myself away from that intensity, I head to the back where there's a sign for the bathrooms. Pushing the door open into the restroom, I find a long counter with several sinks and then toilets closed off into individual spaces with actual doors. Way better than the normal stalls with massive cracks.

Closing and locking a door behind me, I quickly pee and wash my hands.

I barely open the door to leave when suddenly a big body is pushing his way through. My first instinct is to scream, and he must realize that because his hand goes over my mouth. At the same moment I recognize the smell of his cologne, and I'm able to take him in fully.

Cree.

He pushes me into the first open stall and slams the door closed behind us, twisting the lock. His hand is still on my mouth, and he lowers it slowly.

"What are you—"

"You have no idea what you in this little dress is doing to me," he growls, his hand warm on the outside of my thigh. "I promised myself I was going to be good. That I was going to let you have your girls night. But *fuck*, Ophelia," his lips skim my jaw, "I can't do that."

"Cree—"

"Shh," he hushes me, his hand going around my throat. He doesn't squeeze, just uses it to hold my head against the wall. "Ever since I saw you walk in wearing that dress, I've been sitting there wondering if you're wearing panties or not. Don't answer," he adds when he sees my lips move, "will you let me find out for myself?"

I give a tiny, jerky nod.

"Good girl." He grins. "You're so good for me." His fingers on my thigh grip tighter before the pressure releases and they skim over to the inner part. I spread my legs, giving him better access. His smile broadens. "Eager, aren't you? I like that. I like it a lot." He kisses my neck. Up his fingers go, grazing ever so lightly until he comes to my center. "You are wearing them this time."

The pressure on my throat eases and I know that

means he wants me to speak. "I hate them, but I can't not wear them with a dress."

"That's right," he murmurs, using his teeth to graze my chin before he gives me a forceful kiss. "This is my pussy now, isn't it? I can't have you showing it to anyone else." I gasp when he slides my panties to the side, rubbing his fingers over my folds. "Mmm, you're getting wet already. Naughty, girl. Do you like this? Hmm? Do you like that I cornered you? Do you like my hand on your throat?"

"Yes," I gasp, arching into his touch.

"I like this side of you." His voice is gruff, his fingers flexing against my throat. "Is this the real you? Are you afraid people won't like your wild side?" He doesn't wait for my answer, pushing his fingers inside me. I cry out, the sound barely audible thanks to his hand on my throat. "You need to stop worrying so much about other people. You hear me, baby? Let yourself live a little."

My head lolls to the side, pleasure rocking through my body. I'd say I'm living a little right now, considering he's fingering me in a women's restroom.

Burying his face into my neck he murmurs more things to me, some reaching my brain, most falling useless to the floor because I can't focus on words right now.

He pumps his fingers harder, faster. Mine dig into

his shoulders, squeezing tight but he doesn't need to notice.

My eyes start to drift close, and he growls out, "Don't you dare shut your eyes. You look at me when you come. I want you to remember who's giving you pleasure."

"You," I barely utter through parted lips.

"That's right, baby." His eyes are intense, the blue even more impossibly vibrant than normal. "This is me making you feel so good."

My legs start to shake, and it's only the weight of his body pressing into me that keeps me upright.

When he notices the cry on my lips, he kisses me forcefully, swallowing any sound I might make as I come.

I feel wobbly and light-headed as I come down from the high. He supports me easily with his body. The hand that was around my throat now caresses my hair gently.

"You're so beautiful," he murmurs. "Such a good girl. Yesterday wasn't enough. This isn't enough. More. I need so much more of you."

When I've fully recovered, he straightens my dress and steps back as far as he can in the space, which isn't much. If I take a big enough breath our chests will touch. He looks me over, that smirk of his fully in place. One dimple winks playfully at me.

"You look thoroughly fucked, Ophelia. Enjoy the rest of your dinner with your friends."

I watch with rapt attention as he brings his fingers to his lips, the ones that were inside me moments ago, and licks them clean.

Then, he slips the door open, and he's gone.

Leaning against the wall it takes me a bit to recover. Cleaning myself up, I rewash my hands before going back to the booth.

"There you are." Rory smiles, sliding out to let me back in. "We were getting worried. You were gone a while. Everything okay?"

"Y-Yeah. I'm fine. Just … started my period," I lie.

"Oh, I hate when that happens."

"Do you need a tampon?" Kenna asks across the table.

"No, no. I got it all taken care of."

Leaning around Rory, I search the bar, but Cree's gone and a part of me wonders if the entire thing was a figment of my imagination.

SEVENTEEN

CREE

COVERED IN SWEAT, I get off the bench and towel the perspiration off my face. Wiping down the equipment I head upstairs for a shower. I don't normally work out this late, but I had a hell of a lot of pent-up energy after what happened with Ophelia in the restaurant bathroom. I didn't intend for that to happen, but I can't say I'm sorry that it did. I don't know what made me go to the restaurant or follow her into the bathroom but watching her fall apart on my fingers was ... well, let's just say I'll be replaying that image over and over tonight while I go to sleep.

"What are doing down there so late?" Daire's voice interrupts my thoughts.

I close the basement door behind me. "Just felt like getting another workout in."

I try to edge around him, but he blocks my way. "You never work out this late."

It's not like I can lie, considering I'm drenched in sweat right now. "I needed the distraction." It's partially the truth. Daire shakes his head, laughing humorlessly. "What?" I prompt, feeling my hackles rise.

He rolls his tongue in his mouth, glancing to the side. "I just don't get it."

"Get what?"

"You're acting so weird." He tosses his arms in the air. "We've only had one party this year, you never want to go out much anymore. You're so fucking wrapped up in this chick you can't even see straight."

"This has nothing to do with her."

"Are you really going to stand there and lie to me? I'm not blind. Not stupid either. It's obvious what the difference is. I thought we were going to go all out this year. It's our last and you don't seem to fucking care. College is going to be over. Real life is about to start."

"This is real life," I argue. I don't feel like doing this

with him right now. It feels like lately my best friend isn't my friend at all. "I'm allowed to date if I want."

"It's not about dating, and you know it."

I narrow my eyes on him. "If I had never told you about looking for the girl I hooked up with last year, would you still feel this way?" He opens his mouth but I plow on, otherwise I might punch him in the face. "I spent all last year searching for her. Pining, if you will. And you never fucking noticed. So no, Ophelia isn't the only factor in this equation. It's the fact I told you."

"It just doesn't make any sense to me!" He throws his arms in the air. "I don't get it. At all."

"You don't have to. Let me live my life. I'm having fun."

"Fun," he laughs humorlessly. "All right. Call it that if you want."

"What's that supposed to mean?"

"Haven't you already married this girl in your mind? You seem pretty delusional to me."

I have no fucking clue who pissed in his Cheerios, but Daire is typically easy-going. He's the kind of friend who always has your back.

"No, I haven't," I snap back. "You wouldn't get it. And I'm not stupid either, Daire. There's something going on with you that you don't want to talk about. That's fine. But don't take your anger out on me."

Not bothering to give him a chance to respond, I jog up the stairs to my room, locking the door behind me. I shower, spending longer in there than normal trying to get rid of my frustration. It works ... somewhat.

Stretching out in bed, I swipe my phone off the side table and unplug it from the charger.

I shouldn't do it, but I send a text to Ophelia.

Me: I hope I didn't come across too strong tonight. I don't want to scare you.

Me: I know I can be intense.

I have to wait a few painstaking minutes, not even Tom Holland's Spiderman playing on my TV can distract me, until I hear back from her.

Ophelia: You didn't.

Ophelia: I didn't say otter, did I?

Me: You remembered?

Ophelia: You told me not to forget.

I grin at my phone screen.

Me: I did, didn't I?

Ophelia: I'm kind of glad you texted. I was starting to think it was all in my imagination. You left so fast.

Me: I didn't want to sit at the bar with a boner.

It's another minute before I get a response.

Ophelia: I could've taken care of that.

Me: Nah. It was about you. Not me. Can't help getting turned on though.

Ophelia: I'm turning off my lights and going to bed. Have a goodnight.

Me: Sweet dreams, Daisy.

Ophelia: Back at you, Jay.

I set my phone back on the table, and before I can roll back over, it starts ringing. I grin, thinking it's Ophelia, but instead it's Teddy's name on the screen. My brows furrow, curious why I'm hearing from him. We text some, but not often. He's been busy getting settled in New York City with his girlfriend.

"Hello?" I answer.

"Cree, my man. I need a favor. Huge. I'll owe you a kidney."

"Um ... what did you do?" With Teddy you never know what kind of shit he's gotten into. Sure, he settled down last year, and his girlfriend Vanessa has definitely helped him chill out, but at the end of the day, he's still Teddy.

He chuckles at my question. "I didn't do anything. Why do you all always assume it's me?"

"Because it usually is."

"Anyway," he plows on, "I might need to crash at your place with my mom for a day or two. Friday and Saturday night."

"With your mom?"

He clears his throat, getting serious. "Yeah, I finally convinced her to leave my dad, but she's scared of staying in a hotel in case he tracks her down, so I told her I'd come help move her out this weekend and see if I could find us a place to crash. I know my dad wouldn't think of your place."

"Wow, yeah, of course. Your mom can take my room, and I'll crash on the couch. You'll have to sleep on the other couch."

Teddy confessed to us last year what an abusive asshole his dad is, so I'm fucking glad as hell he's finally been able to get his mom to leave that dick.

"Sleepover! Fucking fantastic! Thanks, Cree."

I shake my head. "Any time, bro. Is there anything else I can do to help?"

"Nah, this is more than enough. I have movers scheduled to help too, but I know my mom is freaking out, so I want to be there to support her in person through this transition. I told her she could live with Vanessa and me for a bit, but she doesn't want to do that."

"Does she have a place figured out?"

"She's going to stay in an apartment in Manhattan for a bit until the divorce is over. I'm paying for it so my sperm donor of a father can't say shit about it. He's getting served the papers Friday afternoon, so that's why I figured it would be safer for her to be somewhere else for a bit before going to the apartment since I'm sure he'll find out it's in my name. I'm still hoping I can convince her to stay with us for a week or two. I'd feel better if I could keep an eye on her." I'm not sure he takes a breath through his entire speech.

"That's harsh, dude."

"It is what it is. All that matters is she's leaving his ass."

"I guess so. Seriously, let me know if there's anything I can do. I'm sure the other guys would be happy to help too."

"I appreciate it. Mascen is going to the house with me. I figure that motherfucker has one intimidating looking scowl that scares most people. But my dad shouldn't be there anyway since he's in California on business. He gets to the airport Friday afternoon, so that's when they plan to serve him, when he's leaving there."

"I'll see you Friday."

"Thanks, again. I appreciate it." The sincerity in Teddy's voice gives me pause. He's so rarely serious, but I know this is a huge deal for him. He didn't tell us about his abuse for a long time.

"Of course. Stay out of trouble. Say hi to Vanessa for me."

We end the call and I plug my phone back in.

Teddy's mom and Teddy himself under my roof for a weekend? This is bound to be interesting.

EIGHTEEN

Ophelia

"HEY! WAIT UP! OPHELIA!"

Callahan's voice echoes behind me, and I slow my steps out of the barn. "Hey, sorry. How are you?"

"I texted you." He comes to a stop in front of me, his chest rising and falling rapidly, trying to catch his breath from his jog after me. "You didn't respond."

"I didn't? I don't remember getting anything." I rack my brain, trying to recall ignoring a text message.

"Maybe it was the wrong number," he reasons easily, using the bottom of his shirt to wipe sweat from his brow. "I wanted to see if you were free to go out this weekend?"

"Out?" I mimic.

"Yeah…" His smile falls the tiniest bit. "On a date? With me?"

"Oh!" I shriek, probably a little too enthusiastically. "That's right! A … date. Um…" Panic seizes my chest, fire burning my cheeks. I feel awful that I completely and totally forgot about Cal.

It's ironic that I agreed in the first place in the hopes that maybe something with him would be better than my feelings for Cree since that's so intense. I guess I was wrong, intensity can be good and if there's no spark there's no … well, there's nothing.

But because I'm the kind of person I am, I can't stomach the thought of saying no after I already agreed.

"Did you forget?" He cocks his head to the side, studying me.

"No!" I scoff. "Of course not!"

His lips press into a thin line. "I thought we could go to a karaoke bar." I don't think I'm able to hide the look of disgust on my face based on the frown he gives. "Or not."

Karaoke means horrible singing. A bar means obnoxious loud drunk people.

But I still don't want to say no, because then I'll

invariably be asked why, and I don't want to explain that large crowds and loud noises make me anxious.

"That'll be ... great." There's not one single hint of enthusiasm in my voice.

Cal either doesn't notice or doesn't care. "Cool." He smiles. "Does Friday night work?"

"Yep." I don't have plans. I never have plans. I can't even study with Cree because one of his friends that graduated is visiting.

"Are you staying for dinner?" He falls into step beside me, leaving the barn behind us.

"I wasn't going to."

"You should." He bumps his arm playfully into mine. "Grandma is making her famous roasted chicken."

"That's okay. I have a lot of studying to do."

I'm supposed to meet Cree at the coffee shop in less than an hour, so I don't have much time to linger.

"All right, well maybe next time." He stops beside my car, stepping out of the way when I swing the door open. "Oh, let me make sure I have your number right. I can text you the address for Friday, or I can pick you up if you want."

"The address is fine." If I need to escape, I'd like to have my own car. "What time?"

"Seven?"

"Okay." I make sure he has my number correct, and sure enough it was a digit off. "I'll see you later, Cal."

He grins, and it's a nice smile. Nothing wrong with it at all. But there aren't any butterflies or happy feelings. "See you, Ophelia."

CREE IS SITTING at the exact same table he was at the first night we met—well, second night according to him. I smile when I see he already has a frozen coffee and brownie waiting in my spot.

Scurrying over, I set my backpack in an empty chair and sit down across from him.

"Hi." I sound way too happy to see my tutor turned … fuck buddy?

Oh, God. Are we fuck buddies?

"Hey." He grins, closing the book he's reading and sliding it over. I scan the title, smiling to myself when it's one I recognize. "How was your day?"

"Good, but long." He leans forward and I'm questioning why when he presses his lips gently to mine. "Oh." I say a bit shocked. "Hi."

He chuckles, leaning back in his seat. He's the epitome of cool and casual. "Hi."

Nervous, I tuck a piece of damp hair behind my ear and pull out my laptop, setting it up on the table.

"I made some worksheets for you to fill out. I'm sure the last thing you want is more homework, but it'll help me to see your analysis on these questions."

Cree slides me a few pieces of printed paper stapled together. "You really take this tutoring thing seriously," I joke, pulling out a pen to begin answering them.

He clears his throat awkwardly. "Of course, I do."

I take a bite of brownie and read the first question. Cree chuckles when I wrinkle my nose in disgust. He's doing his job, though, giving me questions Professor Lindon would. The kind that makes my brain hurt because the answer seems obvious in my brain, but I know it's not the one he wants.

Closing my eyes, I think over the question and everything Cree has taught me the past few weeks. Taking a deep breath, I start scribbling my answer to the first prompt. Across from me, Cree opens his laptop, probably working on his own school stuff since I'm occupied for the moment.

In the time it takes for me to finish the brownie and drink my coffee I manage to answer three of the prompts, but I have three more to go. My hand cramps, forcing me to release my tight grip on my pen.

I don't know what makes me blurt it—impulse

control issues, maybe—but suddenly I'm saying, "I have a date Friday night."

Cree's eyes narrow on me, his gaze sharp. His jaw muscle twitches with anger, and I could smack myself for saying something. It's not important.

"You have a date?" He enunciates every single word carefully and slowly.

"Yeah." My lips flatten. Heat rises to my face, and I wish I had some of my coffee left to cool me down.

"Why?"

Biting my lip, I tear a corner off the piece of paper in front of me and roll it into a ball between my fingers. "Um … he asked before … before you and I did anything, and I felt bad to say no."

"You felt bad to say no?"

"Y-Yes. I mean, he's a nice guy and we work together. I didn't want to hurt his feelings."

"So, you're telling me that before we even hooked up you didn't want to go out with this guy, but you said yes anyway?"

"Exactly." He scrubs a hand over his face, looking pissed, frustrated, and hurt at the same time. "Listen, I'm not good at this kind of thing," I confess, stretching my fingers out nervously.

"Dates?"

"Feelings."

"Do you have feelings for him?" His nostrils flare with the question.

"No." The answer comes easy enough. "I like him as a person but that's it."

"Do you have feelings for me?"

So many. A whole explosion. A riot of color that blinds me.

"Yes." I draw a random shape on the table. "I'm not inexperienced, but for the sake of being honest you're the first guy who's ever made me feel anything."

Excited. Slightly nauseated. Butterflies in my tummy.

"Then cancel."

I cringe at the idea of backing out on Cal. "I can't. That's rude."

"Where's he even taking you?"

"A karaoke bar." I rattle off the name. Cree's lips turn down and he looks annoyed, but more than anything it's the hurt in his eyes and set of his shoulders that makes me feel like shit.

"You're doing this then?"

"I don't want to hurt him," I mutter.

"But it's okay if you hurt me?" He scoffs, gathering up his things.

"Where are you going?" I hate that I sound like I'm begging, but I don't want him to go. I don't want to fight either. I want him to understand why this is complicated for me. I don't like disappointing people—

so much so that I go out of my way time and time again to please others even when it makes me miserable enough to throw up.

"I think that's enough studying for tonight."

"Cree!" I call after him as he rushes out of the shop, the few people inside at this late hour stare at me, and I feel incredibly small beneath their eyes.

Sitting back down, the chair feels ten times more uncomfortable than it was before. I hate this. I hate how I never seem to do the right thing even though that's all I'm trying to do. It's all so confusing.

A tear slides down my cheek, and I wipe it away hastily. Now's not the time to get upset, and I have to stop beating myself up.

Yes, I slept with Cree, but I don't owe him anything.

But it makes me sick to think maybe I've thrown away the potential of something great, just to spare someone else's feelings that I don't even care about.

NINETEEN

CREE

DAYS HAVE PASSED since I saw Ophelia in the coffee shop, and my anger hasn't lessened. I'm not even angry at her, if I'm being perfectly honest. I'm mad at myself for not having an honest conversation with her about what I want. Now she's going on a date with a guy she admitted herself she doesn't feel anything for, but she's more concerned about hurting his feelings by canceling than hurting mine by going.

Frustration has my fists curling together. It's Friday evening which means she's going to be in a bar with some dude I don't even know. The worst part is, I *know* the last place Ophelia wants to be is a place like that.

Stepping away from my bed, the sheets changed, I grab the shit I'll need tonight and make my way downstairs. Teddy is supposed to be here with his mom any minute. I gave Millie and the guys a heads up about what's going on. Jude already knows about Teddy's past, but I felt like Daire and Millie deserved an explanation.

"Who's making dinner tonight?" Daire asks from the living room, his feet kicked up on the table and a game playing on the TV.

"It's Jude's turn," I mutter, dropping my stuff on the armchair in the corner.

"You sound annoyed." His brows furrow, watching me.

"That's because I am, dipshit."

"Hey, what did I do?" He holds his hands up, flashing an easy smile. He seems a little more like himself tonight.

"Nothing." I sit back on the couch, crossing my arms over my chest.

"Dude, spit it out. It's not cute when you play coy."

Groaning, I tug at my hair. I seriously need to get a haircut soon. "Ophelia's going on a date tonight"

The fucking traitor bursts out laughing. "Oh, that's

amazing. I think I love this chick now." He claps his hands loudly.

"What's going on?" Jude walks into the room from the kitchen, clutching a beer.

Daire looks at him over the back of the couch. "Ophelia, the girl that has this one so moony," he tosses a thumb in my direction, "is going on a date tonight."

Jude cringes. "Shit, dude, I'm sorry."

I throw my hands up. "At least someone feels sorry for me."

Jude takes a swig of beer. "Hope you fuckers are okay with grilled chicken and salad because that's what I'm making."

"Sounds healthy," Daire grumbles. We all eat right for the most part. As athletes we have to take care of our bodies. "I mean, delicious," he adds when Jude glares at him.

"We can't eat so much junk," Jude reasons, heading back into the kitchen. He already tossed out a bag of Daire's favorite Doritos right in front of him the other day.

I get a text from Teddy telling me they're almost here, so I force myself up and open the garage door so they can bring anything in that way, and if Teddy wants to park his car inside, he can. I'll have to move mine out, but it's no biggie.

Standing outside a minute or so passes when headlights appear and the car swings into the driveway. I'm kind of surprised to see Teddy's still driving his Porsche. I know he loves that car, but I figured he'd ditch it since his dad bought it.

Teddy hops out, grinning from ear to ear. "Thanks so much, man." He claps me on the back.

"Do you want to park in the garage?"

"Um…" He thinks, while his mom gets out of the passenger side looking wary and utterly exhausted. "Maybe I should. If he would remember this place and drive by and see my car … well, that would tell him everything he needs to know."

"Hi." His mom approaches, extending her hand. "I assume you're Cree." I give a nod and she adds, "It's nice to meet you. I wish it was under better circumstances."

"It's nice to meet you too, ma'am. If you want to shower or rest, whatever, you'll be staying in the first room on the right up the stairs. If you're hungry Jude's making chicken and salad for dinner."

"Thank you." With a small bag clutched to her chest, she heads inside through the garage.

"Seriously, dude, I can't thank you enough for this." He hugs me.

"Stop thanking me." I shove him away jokingly. "It's no big deal."

"Trust me," he clears his throat, seeming to get a bit choked up, "all of this is a huge deal."

We switch out the cars and head inside together.

"My man, Teddy!" Daire calls out, lifting a beer up in greeting from the couch.

"Hey, Daire." Teddy bumps his fist against his extended hand.

Jude pokes his head out of the kitchen and grins when he sees his former roommate. "Didn't think I'd be seeing you around these parts any time soon."

"Eh, you know how it goes with family."

Jude chuckles. "Oh, I do. How's Vanessa?"

"She's good." Teddy shoves his hands in his jean pockets, looking around. "She gives me hell but man," he shakes his head with a grin, "I love that girl. She's the best thing that ever happened to me."

Before I can stop him, Daire launches into telling Teddy all about Ophelia. I can tell my best friend thinks Teddy's going to be on his side with this and believe I'm crazy. But after Daire finishes his soliloquy, Teddy shakes his head, chuckling.

"The love bug got you good too, didn't it?"

"I wouldn't say love," I argue, but Teddy cuts me off.

"When you know, you know. It's instinctual. Primal. You feel it in here." He slams a fist against his chest. "It doesn't always happen the first time you look at someone, all that love at first sight shit, but it can build. Start out as a low rumble and *bam* the next thing you know it's this big thing. That was me with Vanessa."

Daire makes a disgusted face and turns back to the TV. "I hate y'all."

"She's on a date tonight," I mutter under my breath.

"Your girl's on a date, and you're standing around with us sorry fucks?" Teddy looks at me like I've lost my mind. Maybe I have. "Get your ass out of here and go get her."

"You think?"

He taps the side of his head. "I know."

I PULL into the lot of the bar Ophelia said she'd be at with her date, scanning the cars to see if I spot her Mercedes. When I see it, I let out a breath of relief. She drove herself. That's a good sign.

I park as close to her car as I can get and head inside.

As far as plans go, mine is non-existent. I'm winging this shit.

Inside, someone sings a horrible rendition of Britney Spears' Toxic. I'm not too much of a man to admit I recognize the song.

My eyes scan the tables, searching for vibrant red hair. It isn't long until I spot her, and it takes everything in me to fight my instinct to march over there and pull her away from the guy beside her who's grinning at something. I've never wanted to punch a guy more. Not even on the ice.

Something holds me back, reminding me that even though Ophelia said she didn't have feelings for this guy, she could be having fun, and I'd be real prick if I pulled her away like some neanderthal, so I choose to get a table where I can watch inconspicuously and see how things go.

I'll give it fifteen minutes. If she's enjoying herself, I'll leave. If she's not ... I'm still leaving but she's coming with me.

I order a Diet Coke and a basket of fries since I'm taking up space at a table, but don't plan on touching either. My eyes stay glued on the couple a few tables down from me. The guy seems decent enough, not pushy or gross, but Ophelia appears lost. Her eyes look around the room, never landing on any particular thing. Her shoulders curl up to her ears like she's trying to roll into a ball and escape. She doesn't look miserable per se, but she doesn't appear to be having fun either.

I smile at the waitress when she sets my stuff down on the table and go ahead and ask for my ticket since I won't be here much longer. When she comes back with that, I slip her a twenty and make my move. I've seen enough.

Stalking over to the table, people who are standing move out of my way as if they can sense I'm not to be messed with.

Approaching the table, Ophelia spots me first. She can't stop the smile that overtakes her, shoulders flattening from their hunched turtle position. Her date notices her change in demeanor, and I can tell he thinks it's about him at first, but he quickly realizes she's not looking at him. His gaze swings my way, his lips turning down in a frown.

"Can I help you with something?" His tone isn't unkind, but it's not exactly friendly either.

"No, but she can."

"She...?" He glances at Ophelia and back to me, eyes turning to slits. "What's going on here?"

"Well, you see," I begin, leaning against the table, "Ophelia here felt bad to cancel on you, and I respect her need to be nice, even if it may have pissed me off at first. But now, she's fulfilled her duties, and I've come to collect my girlfriend."

"Girlfriend?" The guy blurts, looking back at Ophelia. "I didn't know you had a boyfriend."

"I didn't know either," she says softly.

"You wanna be my girlfriend, Daisy?"

She blinks at me, blinks again. Then she shocks me, and I think herself too, when she practically leaps out of her chair and launches herself at me. With a laugh, I catch her, holding her tight against my chest.

She leans back, hands on my cheeks. "Maybe."

"Maybe?" I laugh, incredulously. "That looked like more than a maybe to me with that reaction."

"Yeah, maybe." Her smile lights up her eyes. "I have to keep you on your toes." She sticks her tongue out playfully.

"Good point." I rub my nose against hers, then skim my lips over her cheek stopping at her ear. "But it doesn't mean you're not mine."

"I can't believe this," the guy says, looking between the two of us.

Ophelia lays her head on my chest. "I'm really sorry, Cal. Seriously, so sorry." She looks up at me, her eyes bright with happiness. It's so different from when I first saw her this fall in the coffee shop. Then, her eyes were sheltered, wary. All of that is gone now. There's a confidence growing in her. I don't know if she sees it, but I do.

"Can we get out of here?" I ask, nuzzling my head into her neck. I feel her nod. "Sorry, dude," I say to the guy, but let's be real I'm not sorry at all.

Leaving my arm around Ophelia, we head outside and over to her car. "I can't believe you busted my date." She laughs, shaking her head. "You're something."

"I was jealous." There's no point not admitting it since it was pretty obvious.

"I could tell." She leans her back against the driver's side of her door with a little self-satisfied smirk.

I can't help it when I lean in and kiss her. A groan rumbles in my throat, and I deepen the kiss, my tongue tangling with hers.

It doesn't last long, she gives me a little nudge and I break away. She's a tiny bit out of breath, and I can't help but feel satisfied at that fact.

"Us kissing is dangerous."

"And why is that?" I prompt, rubbing my lips with my thumb. It's not enough to get rid of the taste of her.

"Because we end up having sex."

My shoulders shake with laughter. She's not wrong. "That's true."

"And since you ruined my date—" She pokes my stomach. "I think you owe me one."

I grab her waist, tugging her close until I can rest my forehead on hers. "I guess so."

"You better make it a good one," she jokes. "I only expect the best from my very own Gatsby. You know, if you're going to be my boyfriend and all."

"I like that challenge."

"Mhmm," she hums, standing on her tiptoes to press a quick kiss to my lips. "I'm going back to my dorm now."

Pressing my hips into her so she feels how turned on I am, I groan, "That's unfair."

She places her hand over my jeans, rubbing the outline of my dick. "You'll get over it." Her hand is gone in an instant, and she opens her car door. "Goodnight, Cree."

I shake my head. "You little…" Hands on my hips I grin. "Text me when you get to your dorm."

"I will." She closes the door, and the car rumbles to life. I step back, watching her leave before I get in my car and drive back home.

When I walk in, it looks like everyone's already eaten and headed to their rooms. Teddy's hanging in the living room since we'll both be crashing on the couches.

He mutes the TV when I walk in, sitting up curiously. "How'd it go?"

"Well, I got the girl, so mission accomplished."

"Excellent." He nods excitedly, holding his fist out for mine to bump. "Do you know what the fuck is up with Daire?" His sudden question takes me by surprise since I thought I was the only one dealing with his attitude. "Dude acts like something crawled up his ass."

I shake my head. "No, I don't know."

Teddy gets up from the couch, following me into the kitchen where I grab a bowl of salad from the fridge that either Jude or Millie set aside for me and dig in. I'm starving.

He sits down across from me at the table looking exhausted.

"How'd it go today packing up your mom's stuff and getting her out of there?"

He taps his fingers of the table. Bags are forming under his eyes. I don't think I can recall a time when I've ever seen Teddy as what I'd describe as tired.

"It was rough." He plays with the pepper shaker on the table. It's a pig with wings, an addition from my sister. "She cried a lot. Changed her mind almost thirty different times. She's scared, and I understand that, but I promised to protect her. I won't let her down, not with this. I think I got her to see that she has to trust me more than she fears him."

"She's strong for leaving."

He sighs wearily, scratching the back of his head. "She is. She'll see that in time."

"I'm glad you didn't give up on getting her to leave."

He tips the chair on its back legs. "This adulting shit is hard. Whatever you do, don't grow up and graduate. Shit's for the birds."

I chuckle, chewing an overfull bite of chicken. "Too late. I graduate in the spring."

He smiles back at me, and I can tell from the dullness in his eyes that he's exhausted. It's a rare sight on Teddy McCallister. Dude normally has the energy of a golden retriever puppy. In other words, he's nonstop bouncing off the walls.

"Eh. I shouldn't complain. It's mostly pretty great. No dad to deal with, my own place, and living with the love of my life in Brooklyn. Yeah, forget what I said before."

I laugh, shaking my head. Rinsing out the bowl, I stick it in the dishwasher. "I don't know about you, but I'm ready to crash."

"Pining for a woman will do that to you." He winks, the chair almost tipping over with him in it. He quickly recovers, righting it. "It's worth it. When you find the right one."

Bracing my hands on the kitchen island, I ask him, "When'd you know? When did you know Vanessa was the one?"

He taps his fingers on top of the table. "There wasn't one specific moment. It was a bunch of little moments all added together. When I realized this girl made my life better and I couldn't imagine her not in it. She sure as hell took a lot of convincing, but I didn't care, because at the end of the day I wanted her to know I was serious. She wasn't some whim, she's everything."

"Do you believe in love at first sight? I'm not sure I do, but dude," I shake my head, my shoulders tense, "the first time I saw her it's like something came over me and I haven't been able to shake it since."

"No," he says in a definitive tone, "I think love at first sight is bullshit, honestly. Connection at first sight? That's real. To me that's instinct based, less emotional. Sometimes it leads to something and sometimes it doesn't. Now," he stands up, walking to the pantry, "do you have any hot chocolate and mini-marshmallows so we can kick off this slumber party?"

TWENTY

Ophelia

I DRAG myself out of my car, nervous to see Cal after our disastrous date, but I felt the need to come to the farm in the hopes of catching him so I can apologize.

Trudging toward the barn I'm not surprised when I run into Mary, bustling about with the energy of someone half her age. I hope I can remain as active as she has when I'm at that point in my life.

"Ophelia?" She blurts my name in surprise, giving me a funny look. "What are you doing here? You don't normally work weekends."

"I know." I fiddle nervously with the end of the braid I styled my hair with this morning. "I ... uh ... I'm actually looking for Cal."

"Callahan is out riding. I'm not sure when he'll be back."

Rocking back on my heels, I shove my hands in pockets. "Do you mind if I take Calliope out and see if I can find him?"

She shrugs, moving some bins around. "I don't mind, dear."

"Thanks." I squeeze her arm as I pass by, and she smiles.

I have no idea if she knows Cal and I went on a date last night or not. I certainly didn't say anything to her, and I don't know how open Callahan is about that part of his life with his grandparents.

It takes some time to get Calliope ready, but once I swing my legs over and settle into the saddle, I give myself a moment to breathe, to let peace settle inside me.

While the farm isn't huge, not compared to how massive some operations are, that doesn't mean it's little by any means. He's not in the first two places I check, and I don't have too much time to look for him since I need to catch up on homework, and I'm having a movie night with Kenna and Li. Normally, I hang in my room and read when they have one but not this time. I'm realizing *I've* sheltered myself. I kept myself from doing things because I've been afraid people are being nice because they feel they have to, not because they want to hang out with me. My eyes are being opened, and I'm realizing that was never the case, just something my anxiety convinced me to believe.

Third time's the charm when I approach the clearing with a small natural pond. The same one we kissed at a year ago. Cal sits on the ground, his personal horse Finley, grazing nearby. He looks over his shoulder when he hears my approach, and even from a distance, I don't miss the way he winces.

Slowing Calliope, I come to a stop and hop down keeping her reins in my hand. Calliope can be a bit of a wild card, and I don't need her taking off.

"Hi, Cal," I say softly as I approach, like I'm not trying to spook him.

"Hi." His voice is glum as I come to a stop beside him. He pulls a tall blade of grass loose from the earth, wrapping it around his finger. Squinting from the sun, he tilts his head back to peer up at me. "Why didn't you tell me?"

"Tell you what?"

"That you were interested in someone else. I'm a big boy, Ophelia. I don't need a pity date." Removing his baseball cap, he shakes out his sandy hair before replacing it.

"It wasn't pity." He makes a noise like he doubts that. "Listen, I agreed to our date before anything happened with Cree, and I wanted to keep my word—give you a chance, but it was wrong of me because I already knew my feelings for Cree are strong. I'm really sorry. I know that doesn't make it okay, and it was a shitty thing, and I'd be a thousand times more upset than you are if roles were reversed. I can't make this up to you or make it right. I really wish I could."

He sighs, one that rattles his whole body. "It's okay. *I'm* okay. My ego is a bit bruised," he rips the blade of grass into tiny pieces, "but I'll get over it."

"Are we okay?" I point between the two of us. I don't want there to be unnecessary tension between the two of us. I'm not always the best at resolving issues but I'm trying, so hopefully that counts for something.

Cal holds out his fist for me to bump mine against. "We're good. Now get out of here, Ophelia. It's the weekend. Go enjoy yourself."

"You're a good guy, Callahan."

He mock winces, swatting his hand over his head. "Ah, not the kiss of death."

I laugh, getting ready to mount Calliope. "The kiss of death?"

"When a girl tells a guy he's a good guy, it means he's good, but not for her."

I pause, rubbing my lips together as I think. "You'll find your person, but I'm not her."

"I know," he says, and seems sincere about it. "Now seriously, go enjoy your weekend with your boyfriend. Don't worry about my feelings. I'm a big boy."

I shake my head, stifling a laugh. "You're my friend, Cal. Of course, I worry."

Settling onto the saddle, Calliope quickly accelerates from a trot to a gallop.

~

"What movie are we watching?"

I've showered and changed out of my clothes into a pair of sweatpants and an oversized shirt with our school logo on it.

I watched a movie with the girls maybe two to three times last year. One of those times Rory and her friend Zoey came too. They usually stick with historical romances, or sappy rom-coms. Not that I'm complaining. But if someone says it's going to be a horror movie, I'll be hiding under our small couch.

Over the sound of popping popcorn, Kenna says, "We haven't decided yet, do you have any suggestions?"

"I'm sure whatever you want to watch is fine." I settle on the couch, tucking my legs beneath me.

Kenna cocks her head to the side, studying me. "Ophelia, your opinion is valid, and we want your input. Surely there are movies you love."

I move my hair behind my shoulders. "I love *The Hunger Games* movies."

"Ooh, those are good! Liam Hemsworth is a hottie!"

"I personally prefer Peeta."

She gives a small smile at that, removing the popcorn from the microwave and dumping it into a bowl. There's also a smorgasbord of snacks, candy, drink choices—some alcoholic, some not—and pizza.

The bathroom door opens, letting out a cloud of steam. Li pulls her hair up and off her neck, tying the damp black strands into a low bun. "Did you pick a movie yet?"

"Are you cool with *The Hunger Games*?" Kenna asks her, adding more butter and salt to the popcorn.

"Ooh, yes. I haven't seen those in forever." Smiling at me, she adds, "I'm so glad you decided to watch with us tonight."

"Me too."

And I mean it. I never wanted to impose on Kenna and Li and the friendship they formed with each other and Rory before I became their roommate, but I see now that I've kept them from truly getting to know me because I was protecting myself, not them. I've always had this fear that if I let people get too close, they won't like what they see. Logan got through my walls, slowly but surely when we were children. Cree on the other hand blasted right through them like they'd never existed at all. And because of him I'm finding it easier to let other people in too.

"We like hanging out with you." Li plops down on the couch beside me.

Kenna brings the popcorn over in a massive bowl, setting it on the table. "What would you ladies like to drink?"

"Oh, I can grab something." I start to get up, but she waves me back down on the couch. "No, nope. I'll get it. I'm already up."

"I'll just have some Dr. Pepper." I know I saw plenty of cans in the fridge.

"Same for me, girl." Li smiles up at Kenna. "Thanks."

"Thank you," I add, embarrassed I didn't say that already.

After she spreads the pizza and other snacks on the table, Kenna grabs the drinks and joins us on the couch. It's a small sofa so we end up all cozied together. I put the movie on and since Li is in the middle, she's the designated popcorn bowl holder.

I told Cree I was hanging out with the girls, and I could tell he was disappointed I wouldn't be seeing him tonight, but at the same time glad that I'm making an effort. Logan too, was happy when I told him. He said something along the lines of, "It's about fucking time, Ophelia. You need to stop sheltering yourself so much. You're a fucking amazing person. Start showing the real you."

Having social anxiety, on top of my autism, has been a major hinderance in my life. But I'm growing. I'm learning. I'm accepting myself.

We watch the entire first movie and then put the second on. It's late by the time it finishes, my eyes heavy with tiredness. We all agree to call it a night and that we'll watch the final two another night. Somehow, all three of us in a zombie like state, manage to clean up our mess before heading our separate ways to bed.

Climbing beneath my covers, I glance at the book I'm reading that rests on my nightstand.

A grin I can't control breaks over my face.

I didn't pick up my book once today because I was too busy with friends.

I fall asleep with a smile still on my face.

TWENTY-ONE

CREE

THE WHOLE WEEK drags by with classes and practice. I do get together with Ophelia a couple times to study, but that's all we do. I don't even kiss her because I'm trying to be on my best behavior, and I know if I kiss her that chances are we'll both get carried away, and I want to give her a proper date first. Sure, I count our ice skating and lunch as a date, but I want something a little less casual and more special.

And I might've spent my entire week planning it.

I knew taking her to dinner wouldn't be enough. Is

it a proper date? Sure. But I want to do something different for Ophelia, something unexpected that she'll never forget.

It took me a little while to get my thoughts in order, but now everything is set up and ready.

I just have to pick up the girl.

Jogging down the stairs, I swipe my keys from the table I always drop them on when I come in.

"You look nice, where are you going?" Millie peers at me over the back of the couch with narrowed eyes.

"A date."

"Ooh, with the girl you're tutoring?" She wags her brows.

"Yes. Be good tonight." I point a warning finger at her.

She rolls her eyes, fighting a smile. "Yes, dad."

"Where's Jude?" I know Daire is out, but I thought Jude was still here.

"Right here, dude." He sits up from where he was laying on the couch and I couldn't see him.

I hesitate in the foyer. "Are you guys hanging out?"

Jude pales, but my sister snorts. "We're watching Vampire Diaries. This dude got sucked into it with me." She points at said dude.

I know I can't grumble too much if that's truly all they're doing, but a big part of me doesn't trust Jude with my little sister. I know he'd never mistreat her, but he's a manwhore, so the last thing I want is him him screwing around with her.

"Don't you have a date?" Jude prompts when I linger too long.

I narrow my eyes on my friend. "Be good."

He raises his hands as if he's showing me, he's keeping them to himself. Millie tosses a throw pillow at me that I dodge easily.

I can't afford to get hung up on thoughts of Jude and my sister, not tonight.

Pushing the button for the garage, I hop in my Bronco and crank the engine. The drive over to campus takes longer than I'd like since it's a busy hour, but eventually I'm parking outside of Ophelia's dorm.

I shoot her a text that I'm on my way up, and she replies with a heart emoji.

Taking the stairs up to her dorm, not in the mood to wait around for the elevators, I knock on the door of the room she gave me.

It opens not much later, and Kenna pokes her head out. "Hi, Cree. She's almost ready. You can wait in here." She steps aside and lets me in, pointing to the couch for me to sit.

"You're helping her get ready?" I ask, surprised.

Ophelia's mentioned a few times her lack of friends

and trouble making them, even with her roommates who she says are always nice. And since I know Kenna and Li fairly well, I know she isn't lying, and they're some of the nicest chicks.

"I'm on hair and makeup and Li is on dress duty. I was so excited when she asked us for help with her date, and *very* surprised when I learned it was with you." She pokes my shoulder. "You little hussies have been holding out on all of us."

I chuckle. "It's pretty new. No secrets, I swear."

"Mhmm," she hums doubtfully, giving me another playful shove. "She'll be ready in five minutes."

She opens the door to what I assume is Ophelia's room but makes sure I don't get a peek inside.

Sitting down on the couch, I rub my hands nervously over my jeans.

I don't think my palms have sweated once in my life. But tonight, they're damp with perspiration.

Keep it together, man. It's just a date with a girl you've already been seeing. Chill out.

Easier said than done.

Even though Kenna said five minutes, I fully expected to wait longer, so I'm surprised when the door to Ophelia's room opens and it's her that steps out, fully taking my breath away.

Holy shit she's fucking gorgeous. Goddamn, how is she real? How am I so lucky that she wants me?

Her red hair is curled in waves, hanging halfway down her back. Some sort of little clip thing with tiny pearls holds her hair back on the right side. I don't know anything about makeup, but I know she's glowing, her skin shimmering a pale gold color where the light hits her.

My eyes move to her body, taking in the pale purple dress she wears. It's silky looking, the straps thin on her shoulders showing off every delectable freckle.

"Wow." I struggle to find the oxygen to form more words. "You ... you look stunning. I mean, you're always beautiful, but wow."

She ducks her head shyly, giving me the tiniest barely-there smile. "Thank you. You don't look too bad yourself."

I look down at my dark wash jeans and the light blue button down I put on.

"You look way better, babe. Believe me."

Somehow, I get my feet to move and cross the distance between us. Placing my hand on her waist, I duck down but suddenly Kenna's there pushing me away.

"Nuh-uh, Romeo. Save the kissing for later. Don't ruin her lipstick."

"But I really want to kiss her," I protest, Ophelia giggling at my admission.

"Save it," Kenna bosses.

"You heard the woman, save it." Ophelia pokes my chest lightly. "I can't thank you guys enough." She turns to her roommates.

"Girl, it was so much fun. You have nothing to thank us for. We love hanging out with you." Li comes forward, giving her a hug and an air kiss on each cheek.

Kenna does the same, saying, "Have fun tonight."

Grabbing my girl's hand, I lead her out of the dorm, this time taking the elevator to save her feet in the heels she's wearing. They're not super tall, but since I've never seen her wear anything other than sneakers, I have a feeling she's not that comfortable in them.

Opening the passenger door for her to get in, I let out a curse at the sunflowers sitting on the seat.

"I was supposed to bring these up with me," I explain, handing them to her.

She gives them a sniff, even though I'm pretty sure they don't smell like anything. "Thank you." A blush that I don't think is from the makeup stains her cheeks. "That was sweet of you."

"You're welcome." I offer her a hand to get into the vehicle. She takes it, shooting me a grateful smile.

"What exactly are we doing on this date? Do I get

to know yet?" The question pours out of her the second I'm behind the wheel.

Cranking the engine, I grin over at her. "Nah, I'm going to make you suffer a little longer."

She pouts her delectable lips. "That's a little unfair."

"Don't worry, I think you're going to love it."

At least I hope she does. I put a lot of thought and time into it, wanting to do something special and unforgettable.

The drive takes about forty minutes, and I purposely park at the back of the building so she can't see where we are. She eyes the brick building, ivy growing along the side. It's small, nothing special. But like most things, people, books, it's the inside that matters.

"We're here," I announce, undoing my belt.

"Where is here, exactly?"

"It's … you just have to see for yourself."

She frowns, brow furrowed with puzzlement. She doesn't question me any further, unbuckling her seatbelt. I meet her at the passenger side, helping her out.

"This isn't going to be anything like karaoke, right?" She hisses under her breath.

I throw my head back and laugh. "No, nothing like that."

This place took a lot of searching for. I knew I

wanted to do something that would encompass our love of books and that Ophelia would enjoy. When this old book binding business popped up, I knew it was exactly what I was looking for. I contacted the owner, explained what I wanted, and she was more than happy to help me out.

Holding the back door open for Ophelia, I let her go inside first. The place has muted lighting and smells like paper.

The door shuts behind me, and Ophelia looks around the backroom we've come through. I came by already when I met with the owner, so I'm familiar with the layout. Back here is mostly storage and odds and ends that don't make much sense to people like us who don't understand this process.

Taking her hand, I lead her through another door into the open main space. As promised, the owner has set up a table, and the meal I had delivered sits waiting in takeout boxes. Sure, takeout boxes probably aren't the best look, but it's everything else that matters more.

"Oh my God." Ophelia lets go of my hand, spinning around to take in the piles and piles of books, stacked on shelves, the floor, tables, every available surface. In the middle of the room are printers and binding machines. "Is this an old-fashioned printer?"

"Sure is." I shove my hands in my pockets, watching

the look of pure joy on her face, knowing I made the right choice bringing her here.

She continues to spin until she stops right in front of me. Her teeth dig slightly into her bottom lip, trying to contain her smile.

"This is *so* much better than a karaoke bar."

Laughter escapes me, and I'd feel bad for the other dude if he hadn't been encroaching on my girl.

"I'm glad you think so. Let's eat and then the owner, Betty, is going to show us how to bind a book."

"Are you serious?" Her hazel eyes glow.

"I don't joke about books."

"Which book do we get to do?"

"Guess." I rock back on my heels. It's hard to contain my excitement.

"Um…" She taps her bottom lip, thinking. "I really have no idea. I'm too happy to think straight."

I grin, pleased by her enthusiasm. *"The Great Gatsby."*

Her smile turns to a quick frown, then quickly back to a smile again. Her reaction confuses me, but I don't call her out on it.

"That's so cool." She claps her hands, vibrating with excitement.

"I thought so." I guide her over to the table. "Let's eat before it gets too cold."

Pulling out a chair for her, she sits, and I scoot her in. Taking my place across from her, I start opening the boxes. I checked out the menus of restaurants nearby the printer before settling on one.

There's everything we'll need, drinks, utensils, and napkins. Ophelia peeks inside the open boxes at what I got for us. I chose a little of everything so she'd have a choice and figured if she wanted, she could try different things.

"This looks delicious." She eyes the spread of food. "But who's going to eat all of this?"

"Us, sweetheart," I joke, passing her a set of utensils. "Eat what you want. It doesn't matter."

Picking up a homemade mozzarella stick, she dips it into marinara. "I'm starving," she admits, before taking a huge bite. "I hope I don't drop anything on my dress."

"You won't. But if you do, I can afford dry cleaning."

"So can I," she says with a soft laugh. "I have to admit all of this…" She pauses, looking around again. "I can't imagine a better date, Cree. Truly. This is so thoughtful."

"I'm glad you think so. I wanted it to be unforgettable."

"Trust me, there's no forgetting this." She gets a forkful of salad next, smiling after she's chewed and swallowed. "One bite of salad totally cancels out the mozzarella stick, right?"

"Absolutely." I take a bite of salad too.

We chat about anything and everything as we eat, things we haven't talked about yet, and expounding on things we have. Again and again, Ophelia tells me she's not normally this chatty with people, like she's somehow embarrassed by that fact, but I fucking love that I bring out her words. I've only really known her almost two months now, but the change in her has been obvious. I know I can't take credit for all it, because this is who she's always been, she's just kept it hidden away. Now she's finally breaking free of the confines she put herself in for some reason I can't fathom.

After we've eaten, I clean up all the boxes and stack the ones that still have food over by the door, so we don't leave without them.

Knocking on the office door where Betty told me she'd be, she comes out and introduces herself to Ophelia before showing us how all the machines work and letting us both help until at the end of the night, we leave with one specially bound copy of *The Great Gatsby*.

Ophelia clutches it against her chest on the way out to my car like it's the most precious gift she's ever been given. It fills me with a selfish sort of pride seeing that.

Starting up the car, Ophelia rests her head back and turns to look at me with a wistful smile.

"Cree, I don't have the proper words for what tonight was but I'm going to go with magical. Pure and utter magic."

"I'm glad you loved it, baby."

"Best date ever, that's all I have to say." She smiles reverently at the book lying in her lap.

I grin the whole drive back to campus, chatting with her about first one thing and then another. Conversation is so easy with her.

Walking her back to her room, I pause outside the door and give her a tender kiss on her lips. Her fingers curl behind my neck, her body angling into mine.

I promised myself I'd be on my best behavior tonight, but she's making it very difficult with the way her hands explore my chest.

Then she says, "Kenna and Li aren't here tonight. They're staying with Rory."

I look into her eyes, reading what she doesn't say aloud there. "You want me to come in?"

She gives a tiny nod and a small gasping, "Yes."

She unlocks the door to her dorm suite and with surprising strength tugs me inside. I close the door and lock it behind me.

"Where do you want me, Ophelia?" I want to give

her as much control this time as I can. She deserves to feel her own power.

She tugs her bottom lip between her teeth. "Couch."

I sit down and she pulls her dress up her thighs before straddling me. "Where do you want my hands?" Right now, I have them firmly pressed against the fabric of the couch. It's a struggle not to put them all over her body, but I think it's important to give her a chance to call the shots.

She doesn't answer with words, instead grabbing my hands and placing them on her waist. My fingers splay onto her ass, and she rolls her hips against me. She captures my mouth, kissing me like I've been craving to do since the moment I saw her tonight.

"You make me lose my mind," she murmurs into the skin of my neck, kissing her way down. Her fingers find the first button of my shirt, and she undoes them quickly with my help. I'm fucking greedy to feel her hands on my bare skin.

She shoves my shirt over my shoulders, and I sit up, yanking it off and tossing it onto the chair.

She traces down my stomach with a single finger, circling my naval.

Then she's climbing off of me, and before I can beg her to come back, she's sliding my belt off and reaching for my button and zipper. I kick my shoes from my feet, and she yanks my jeans all the way down, leaving me in just my boxer-briefs.

Watching me through hooded eyes, she rubs her hands over my hardened cock but makes no move to pull me out.

"Don't tease me, Ophelia," I growl. "My restrain only lasts so long."

She pouts. "But I haven't even gotten to the fun part yet."

"You can have your fun a little longer," I warn, holding her chin in my hand. "And then it's my turn." She gives a coy smile, palming me some more before pulling my cock out. I shove my underwear down my legs, unable to take my eyes off the image of her kneeling before me, my cock in her hand. "You have me where you want me. Now, what are you going to do about it?"

She wraps her mouth around my cock, and my head drops back against the couch. *"Fuck,"* I groan, losing my breath. She works her mouth up and down my cock, swirling her tongue around the tip. She uses her hand on the base, gripping me tight. Her eyes are hooded, but her gaze never strays from mine the entire time. It's fucking hot. "God, look at you on your knees."

She hums and I feel the sound in my dick. It makes

my hips thrust, my cock pushing harder into her mouth. She takes it, tears pooling in her eyes.

"Ophelia," I groan out her name, "if you don't stop, I'm going to come in that pretty little mouth, and I'm not done having my fun with you."

She lets my cock go and I reach down, wiping her saliva off her mouth. She's still wearing her dress and heels as I help her to her feet. She kicks them off and I stand up, towering over her. I curl my hand behind her neck, holding on tight. She looks up at me with wide, trusting hazel eyes.

"You're fucking beautiful."

She glows under my praise. I'll keep telling her over and over again until she realizes that she's the most gorgeous person I've ever met. Inside and out.

I ease one of the straps of her dress off her shoulder, kissing the skin exposed there. A tiny gasp escapes her throat, and her head falls back exposing more of her neck to my greedy mouth. I suck the skin there and have no doubt a mark will be left behind. It makes me selfishly happy to think about her walking around campus with my mark on her neck.

I have this insane need to claim her.

Every pulse of blood through my veins seems to say, *mine, mine, mine.*

She makes me lose my ever-loving mind.

"This dress ... you have no idea how much I love you in this dress."

Her body bows into mine. "I'd love this dress even more if it was on the floor."

I chuckle, nipping her jaw. "Say no more."

I find the zipper and ease it down. The other strap falls down her shoulder, and she gives a tiny shimmy, letting the dress fall slowly down her body.

She's almost entirely naked—no bra, and just the skimpiest thong.

"Fuck." I cup her small breasts in my hands. "You're so beautiful." I dip my head down, capturing her lips in a deep kiss. Guiding her to the end of the couch, I position her and command in a low growl, "Bend over."

She does as I demand with no protest. She tilts her head so she can look back at me as I caress her ass.

"Dammit, I need a condom," I curse, swiping up my pants and getting one from my wallet.

I waste no time putting it on. My fingers find her center and she's soaking wet, totally ready for me.

"Cree," she begs, one of the first words she's uttered in a while. "Please."

"Please, what?" I taunt with a wicked grin.

"I want you to fuck me."

"Ask nicely." I smack her ass, and she rocks forward, her fingers gripping the couch cushions.

"Fuck me, *please*."

That's more like it. I massage the ass cheek I smacked and plunge inside her. She gasps, the sound quickly turning into a moan.

Holding onto her hips, I fuck her hard and fast. I don't have it in me to take this slow, or to even have some fun. This is all about getting us both to a hasty release.

Reaching between us, I rub her clit. Her pussy squeezes me tight, and the need to come is almost too much, but I want her to orgasm first.

"Come on, baby." I press my lips against her back. "You're almost there. I can feel it."

"Yes, yes," she pants, "I'm so close. I'm—"

She falls apart and I let go, moaning as I come. Spent, I collapse over her, holding her against me and bracing my other hand on the couch so I don't crush her. I press a tender kiss to the smooth skin of her back.

"You were fucking made for me. You hear me?" She gives a nod. "Me and me alone."

Pulling out of her, I get rid of the condom, and she goes to the bathroom.

We settle in her bed, her naked body wrapped around mine.

Pressing my lips to the top of her head, she sighs dreamily already drifting off to sleep.

TWENTY-TWO

Ophelia

SITTING in the stands near the ice, watching Cree's hockey practice is vastly different than I expected.

Honestly, I don't know what I expected since I have no knowledge of hockey beyond there being ice, skates, and a puck, and some weird sword looking thing they bat the puck around with. It kind of reminds of a cat playing with a mouse. I have a feeling Cree will lose his mind if I tell him any of my thoughts.

The text from him this morning about going to the rink was unexpected. To be honest, I'd forgotten about his mention of watching a practice, but I guess he finally got it okayed by his coach. It surprises me that he's so understanding about my desire to avoid certain things, like a game and the chaos that includes. He doesn't ask questions, he just respects me.

Except for sometimes.

Despite the chill in the air, I feel blood rush to my cheeks with the memory of a few days ago after we finished studying and he tied me to his bed, having his way with me.

Forcing thoughts of that evening from my mind, I focus on the guys zooming back and forth on the ice. I keep my eyes on Cree's number, thirty-six. He skates so fast it looks like he's flying.

I never realized what an aggressive game hockey is, and this is only practice. I have to imagine it's even worse with a real opponent.

I wince when Cree takes a particularly brutal hit from a player, but he brushes it off like nothing happened whereas if something like that happened to me I would no doubt struggle to catch my breath for a good five minutes and then feel like my body had been put through a meat grinder.

Practice is long, but I don't lose interest the entire time which surprises the hell out of me.

Wait until I tell Gus and Logan, I watched a hockey practice.

Almost as soon as I have that thought, I think about the fact if I share this with them, they're inevitably going to ask why. Logan knows I had sex with my tutor, but he doesn't know that we're kind of sort of together now. Both my brother and best friend are going to be pissed at me for not letting them know. Not that my brother wants to know about the sex part, but he'll definitely be hurt that I haven't told him I'm in a relationship.

By the time the guys are pouring off the ice, the sudden change jolts me from my wandering thoughts. Cree showed me where to wait for him once practice is over, so I gather my stuff up and head that way. It's a long hall, brightly lit. The walls are white but there are large posters of each player. I find Cree's, smiling up at it. He's in his uniform, his ... sword, or whatever it is, is clasped in his hand. His bright eyes, shimmer with mischief. His smile doesn't show his dimples, but it seems genuine enough.

After walking up and down the hall, I sit down on the floor and pull out my current read from my bag, flipping the book open and pulling out my bookmark of the moment—a paperclip.

When guys start leaving the locker room I get a few

peculiar looks, one guy even glares, and then Cree walks out, duffel bag slung over his shoulder. He grins when he sees me, the dimples that were missing in the photo flashing at me.

"What'd you think, Daisy?" He holds out a hand to help me up after I've finished tucking my book away.

"It was interesting."

"Interesting?" He chuckles, like he expected me to say more.

"Exciting, too," I supply.

He shakes his head, laughing. With long fingers he sweeps his damp hair out of his eyes. I don't know how he makes something simple look so fucking hot.

His hand in mine is warm, despite the chilly hall. Tipping his head down, he smiles at me like I'm ... well, like I'm the most special thing he's ever laid his eyes on. The look sends butterflies in my belly taking flight.

"Do you mind if we get something to eat before hitting the coffee shop to study?"

"Please," I practically beg, letting him lead me toward the exit where it's nearly dark already. The days have grown so much shorter. "I'm starving."

We hit up the dining hall for dinner. Cree gets fish and veggies, while I opt for mac n' cheese. Lately, it's been one of my go-to foods. I get these random cravings for things and eat them often until I'm sick of it. It's an endless cycle of mine I doubt I'll ever grow out of. Last month I had peanut butter and banana sandwiches every day for lunch.

"I'm always starving after practice," Cree explains, piercing a piece of sweet potato with his fork.

"I just like food." I point at the mac n' cheese. "The cheesier the better."

"Can't argue with that." Cree eyes my dish like he'd enjoy nothing more than swiping it out from under me, but he takes a bite of fish instead. "How was class today?"

He knows I had my Critical Approaches to Literature class today.

"Better than it used to be. I actually participated in the discussion because I felt confident enough to engage in it."

His eyes light up with pride. "That's fucking amazing." He holds out his fist for me to bump. "I'm so proud of you."

I beam beneath his praise. It means more to me than he'll ever know. I've come so far with his help, learning how to get past those hang ups in my brain and analyze the way Professor Lindon wants and expects from his students.

"It's all thanks to you."

He guffaws. "You understand the material, Ophelia.

You just needed a little extra help to see it in a different light, that's it."

I bow my head, grateful for his words. I doubt myself way too much. I grew up with my brother excelling at every little thing he does, and then there was me. I struggled with school, with socializing, with so many other little things growing up. I know my parents worried endlessly about me. Why wasn't I like my brother? Or their friends kids? Why was I so different?

I didn't get my diagnosis of autism until I was almost sixteen.

It was a relief to my parents, I think. Finally, a label that explained why I was ... *me*.

For me, it felt like a label I didn't want. There's nothing wrong with being autistic. I like who I am, and I don't care, but that doesn't mean that other people don't hear that word and automatically assume something, and that's not fair. It's why I keep closed-lipped about it. I haven't even told Cree. Do I think he'd care? No. I truly don't. But that doesn't mean that tiny kernel of fear doesn't hold me back. I wish I could silence that little voice that whispers at me, but I haven't learned how yet.

"What are you thinking about?" Cree brings me back to reality.

"Nothing. Just drifted off," I lie.

He cocks his head to the side. "Ophelia, I know when you're lying to me. Out with it."

I swallow past the lump in my throat. I hate that there's a part of me that's terrified he'll be mad or run screaming from the building. If he did, that would say way more about him than it does me.

Wetting my lips, I open my mouth and decide to put it out there. There's no sense in keeping it a secret. That's stupid. Everything always has a way of coming to light eventually.

"There's something I haven't told you." I bite my lip nervously.

He arches a brow, his fingers stilling on the table like he knows this is serious. "What is it?" He sounds hesitant.

"The reason I needed a tutor … why I have trouble with some things and social settings can be awkward…"

"Out with it," he begs when I trail off. "You're worrying me."

I brace my shoulders, holding my chin high.

Autism is nothing to be ashamed of. It makes me a little more special than others, and that's never a bad thing.

With that thought in my mind, I say without a single waver to my voice, "I'm autistic."

His brows furrow deeply. "Okay?"

It comes out as a question, and now I'm the one looking at him funny.

"Okay?" I repeat back to him.

"That's it? That's what you were worried to tell me?"

"Um..." My shoulders relax from their stiff posture. "Yeah." I tuck my hair nervously behind my ear.

"Ophelia." His face softens. "You thought I'd care about something like that?"

I shrug, looking away. "It's a big deal to some people. A big enough issue that some might—"

"Might what?" He prompts, trying to force me to make eye contact. "Break up with you? Do you think I'm that much of an asshole?"

"No!" I rush to say. "I don't. It's just something I've always kind of kept to myself for the most part."

He watches me for a long moment. "It doesn't bother me. But it does make me sad that you'd think it would make any difference."

"I told you that's not it."

"Well, it has to be some of it," he argues, "or you would've told me sooner and not acted so stressed to tell me."

"It's not you, I promise. It's me. It's an insecurity of mine. Growing up I felt like I could never measure up to what my parents wanted or expected. Even though they never said it, I felt like I was a disappointment to them."

He wets his lips, shaking his head lightly. "I don't think you could ever be a disappointment to anyone, least of all me." His words bring tears to my eyes. "Fuck, Ophelia. Please, don't cry." He's around the table in a blink, wrapping me into the warmest hug anyone's ever given me.

"You're too good for me."

He chuckles. "I don't know about that." He presses a tender kiss to the side of my forehead. "Are you sure you're up for studying tonight?"

"Yeah." I can't afford to miss out on any extra studying.

I have this irrational fear that if I go too many days without his help that my brain will mass delete everything he's taught me. I've come too far to regress.

"If you're sure."

I nod quickly, not wanting to give him a chance to back out. "Besides, I need my brownie." It's not a lie, either. I've been looking forward to my chocolate brownie with rainbow sprinkles all day, and after this talk, I need it more than ever.

He chuckles, finishing the last of his veggies. "I should've known. It's really the brownie that's most important here, right?" He winks, letting me go so he can return to his previous spot.

"Absolutely," I joke, sticking out my tongue at him.

Finishing up our dinner, we dump our trays and dishes in the designated areas and head outside walking to the coffee shop. During our walk, Cree tosses his arm over my shoulders, tugging me close to him.

Holding the door open, Cree says, "You grab a table. I'll get drinks and dessert."

I pick a table in the quietest corner and set everything up. I figure if we get in a good hour of studying, then I'll feel like we accomplished something.

Cree approaches the table a few minutes later. "For milady." He sets the frozen coffee beside me along with a brownie. Pulling out the chair across from me he sits down with his own coffee, something hot, and brownie. "What do they put in these brownies to make them so good?" He swallows a bite, staring at the dessert like it holds all the answers in the world.

"It's the sprinkles," I reason. "Rainbow sprinkles make everything better. Ice cream, cake, and definitely brownies."

"I think you have a point." Reaching across the table, he swipes the corner of my mouth, coming away with a bright blue sprinkle. He sticks it in his mouth, humming. "Mmm."

"You stole my sprinkle."

He grins, dimple flashing. "You'll get over it."

He's right. It's impossible to be peeved with him over anything. It's annoying, really. He's too cute for his own good. Cree has this wholesome, sweetness to him, but then there's this other side of him, the one that comes out in the bedroom, that is impossibly dirty and sexy.

He sobers, growing serious, but doesn't say anything.

"Is something wrong?" I put my hand on top of his on the table.

"No, I just wanted to ask you something." He clears his throat, sitting up straight. He flips his hand over beneath mine, holding on. "My parents are coming to visit."

"Okay?" I prompt when he doesn't say anything more for a few beats.

"I'd like to introduce you to them. As my girlfriend." He looks at me beneath long lashes, his blue eyes questioning like he thinks his question might send me running. And maybe it used to would have, but not today.

"That would be…" I pause, searching for the right word. "Nice."

"Are you sure?" He squeezes my hand lightly. "I

don't want to do anything you aren't comfortable with."

"I'd like to meet them." I mean it, too. Cree speaks often of his family and obviously I've met Millie several times. "When are they coming?"

"This weekend."

That's perfect for me. It doesn't give me too much time to overthink and stress about it.

"Can't wait." I smile and he returns the gesture.

When I sit back, and we start going over the material, I realize I am actually excited to meet his parents. I can't help but feel a tiny bit proud of myself for that fact.

TWENTY-THREE

CREE

I WASN'T surprised when my mom called to tell me that she and my dad had decided to come visit and attend my first game of the season. I didn't think they'd be able to hold out until the holidays to see us. I'm not complaining. I know Millie and I are incredibly lucky to have parents who care so much and are involved in our lives.

Pulling up outside Ophelia's dorm, she's already walking out the door in a green sweater dress and brown boots. Her hair is loose but tucked behind her ears so she can't hide behind it.

Millie leans up from the back between the two front seats. "Your girlfriend is so freaking cute. I don't know what she sees in you."

I put my hand on her face and shove her into the back. "Shut up, Mills." Ophelia opens the passenger door before I have a chance to hop out and get it. "I was going to get the door for you, babe."

"Babe? You call her babe? Aww," Millie taunts, and I turn around to give her my best brotherly death glare.

Ophelia climbs in, shutting the door. With a small laugh she looks back at Millie. "Hey, Millie."

"Hi, Ophelia," she replies back. "I was just telling my idiot brother here that I don't know how he landed you."

Ophelia's lips turn down. "What do you mean?"

"Just that you're way better than him, clearly." Millie rolls her eyes, but her tone is entirely joking.

"Ignore her," I tell Ophelia, reversing out of the parking space. "She's in rare form today."

Our parents are staying in a hotel downtown with a nice restaurant, so that's where we're meeting them for dinner.

"Do you think your parents will like me?" Ophelia's question is soft, barely uttered, at my side.

Millie snorts from the back. "Are you kidding me? They'll love you. You're kind, sweet, smart, and beautiful. Like I said, way too good for this one."

"She was asking me," I gripe at my little sister.

She huffs from the back. "Are you telling me my answer is wrong?"

"No, but—"

"That's what I thought."

Ophelia laughs, shaking her head. "You two bicker like I do with my brother."

"I can't help it," Millie leans forward again, "I've been stuck with him for my entire life."

"Right back at ya, Millicent."

"Bleh." She pretends to gag. "Cut the Millicent crap. Only Mom and Dad call me that sometimes, and our grandparents always. It makes me sound like an old lady who owns a million cats."

I shake my head, trying not to laugh at my sister. Steering the conversation in a different direction, I ask Ophelia, "What are you reading lately?"

"I need to start a new book. I didn't finish the last one I read after the hero said he hoped her birth control failed and he could knock her up." She gags over the idea. "Forced pregnancy is not sexy to me. It ruins the fantasy of it all. Nope. No way." She shakes her head rapidly. "That is not my kink."

Millie giggle-snorts from the back. "What is your kink then?" Then she gags. "Oh, God, forget I asked. You're dating my brother. I don't wanna know. Why did I ask that? I hate myself. Ew. Cree, take me home. I feel dirty. I need a shower. One hot enough to melt my skin off."

"Can you stop being dramatic for five seconds?" I practically beg.

We have at least ten more minutes before I get to the hotel. I'd like to endure it without crashing my car when I decide to strangle my sister. And I'd preferably not like to take out Ophelia along with the two of us.

"Me? Dramatic?" She mock gasps. "Do you hear this slander, Ophelia? I'm never dramatic. I'm hurt that you'd think so, brother."

This time I'm the one rolling my eyes. I turn up the volume on the radio, drowning out my sister's nagging.

The hotel doesn't have any public parking, which means I'm shelling out a ridiculous amount to be able to park in the garage on site. Not that it hurts my wallet, but it's the point of it.

Grabbing Ophelia's hand, she glances up at me with a nervous smile. I lower my head to her ear. "You have nothing to worry about." Giving her hand a tiny squeeze, we start for the elevator where Millie is already waiting.

"Come on you two love birds, time is a ticking."

Shaking my head, we step onto the elevator, and I push the button for the ground floor where the restaurant is.

When I told my mom I was bringing my girlfriend I'm pretty sure she might've peed her pants with glee. I've spoken to her about Ophelia, she's no secret, but I'd never used the label before, and I know it made her happy.

Combing my fingers through my hair, I brace myself for my mom's inevitable excitement the moment she lays her eyes on Ophelia. I guess it's a good thing that I already know she'll love her. Neither of my parents are the kind that would ever judge who we love. They've never cared about any of that shit as long as we're happy. More parents should be that way. Part of loving your child is accepting everything about them.

Unless they're a murderer. Don't accept them then.

The elevator gives a happy ding when we reach the correct floor.

Millie hops out, a skip to her step. Immediately spotting our parents waiting in the lobby. She runs over and hugs them both, giving them obnoxiously loud kisses smacked on their cheeks. Even though we've spent all day with them, she acts like she hasn't seen them in years.

"You have nothing to worry about." I assure Ophelia one last time as we approach my parents.

My mom lights up immediately. Her body vibrates with giddy excitement.

"Mom," I practically beg her not to embarrass me with that one single word. "Dad," I nod at my father, "I'd like you guys to meet my girlfriend, Ophelia. Ophelia, this is my mom, Hillary, and my dad, Grant."

"Hi," Ophelia says, and I don't miss the slight shake in her voice. "It's nice to meet you both."

She extends her hand for a handshake, but my mom dismisses it. "None of that nonsense. Give me a hug."

Ophelia hesitates, looking at me as my mom reaches for her. I tell her with my eyes she doesn't have to hug her if she doesn't want to, and that seems to reassure her. She accepts the hug and even initiates one with my dad.

"Are you kids hungry?" He rubs his stomach, signaling that he's hungry and wants to move this along.

"Starved." I haven't had anything since I scarfed down a protein bar after my workout.

He leads the way, ushering all of us on, even my mother, and gives the hostess our last name before being led to a private table.

"This place is beautiful." Ophelia's eyes dart around the inside of the restaurant. It's like a lux ocean theme. There's even a massive aquarium in the center.

"Isn't it gorgeous?" My mom smooths the back of her dress before sitting down. Ophelia and I sit across from my parents, putting Millie on the end which I feel sort of bad for, but she doesn't seem to mind. "It reminds me of you," she says to Ophelia.

"Me?" She points at herself. "Why me?"

My mom hesitates. "Oh, I just…" Her cheeks color. "You remind me of The Little Mermaid. Ariel. With the red hair." She tugs on her own strands of hair. "I'm embarrassing myself. I'll stop."

Ophelia tosses a small smile her way. "It's okay. I get that a lot. I'm not going to lie; thanks to the movie I was certain I would sprout a fin as soon as my legs touched the water. I spent months afraid of a bath or shower. It was a nightmare for my parents. It doesn't help that my brother would leave sand around my bed and try to convince me I was in the ocean every night in my sleep."

My parents laugh, exchanging a look with each other that I know means they already love her. Beside me, Ophelia glances up at me for reassurance, and I dip my head in a nod. She's doing great. There's nothing for her to worry about.

We order dinner, and dig in. Conversation is easy,

my parents asking her about school and her dreams of the future. At the end of the evening, we say goodnight to my parents with them heading up to their suite.

We've hardly pulled out of the parking garage when a soft snore comes from the back of the car. I glance back briefly to see Millie with her head pressed against the glass, snoozing away.

Ophelia turns to me with a happy smile, and I'm so fucking relieved that tonight went so well. I knew it would, but that doesn't mean there wasn't some stress involved.

"Your parents are great."

"Yeah?" I turn out of the garage.

"Mhmm. It was really nice meeting them. I see why you're so great."

I chuckle, amused. "Careful. Keep complimenting me and it'll go to my head."

"Ha, ha," she mocks.

"Back to your dorm or?" I let her finish the thought.

"You want me to stay over?"

I shrug. "Why not?"

She thinks for a moment. "I'll stay with you."

I try—and fail—not to show how pleased her answer makes me. "Good."

TWENTY-FOUR

Ophelia

THERE'S something different about standing in the center of Cree's bedroom knowing I'm staying the night and not here to study. There's a new Lego project spread on his desk that looks distinctly Harry Potter related.

I pick up one of the pieces, turning it over in my fingers before replacing it in the exact spot I found it.

Cree bounds into the room with bottles of water, kicking the door shut behind him. It bangs closed and he mutters, "Shit," at the loud sound, clicking the lock in place. He passes me a bottle of water. "Thought you might be thirsty."

"Thanks." I untwist the cap and take a couple of sips. "Do you mind if I shower?"

"Sure, yeah. Go ahead."

"Are you nervous about me staying the night?" I've never seen Cree so unsure of himself, and I kind of like it because it means he's affected by me as much as I am by him.

"No," he scoffs, rubbing the back of his head. "Maybe a little. But what if I kick you in my sleep? I've woken up to the covers shoved off the bed more than once."

"Then I'll kick you right back."

He laughs, relief flooding him. "I'm worrying for nothing. I know." He leans in, pressing a tender kiss to the corner of my mouth. "Let me grab you something to change into."

Rifling through his dresser, he procures a t-shirt and passes it to me. It's a hockey shirt with Aldridge University Hockey on the front and his last name and number on the back.

"Admit it, you just wanted to get your name on me."

"Guilty." He picks a Lego off the floor, looks at it, then the piles, before putting it where it belongs. Thankfully it's not the one I checked out earlier.

With his shirt in hand, I lock myself in the bathroom because I truly just want to shower. Kenna did my makeup again and while it looks amazing, I'm still not used to the feel of wearing so much and want more than anything to scrub my face clean.

When I get out of the shower, the mirror is fogged over with steam. I wipe it away and use some of Cree's toothpaste on my finger to swipe over my teeth, rinsing my mouth out with water. I slip his shirt over my body and find that it hangs to the middle of my thighs. Folding up my clothes, I open the door and find Cree lying on top of the bed in nothing put a pair of sweatpants, one arm behind his head, the other cradling a paperback. I don't think I've ever seen something so hot in my entire life. I couldn't have even conjured something so perfect from my mind if I'd bothered to try.

I set my clothes down on top of his dresser and head for his bed, pulling the sheets back.

"Are you sleepy?" He slips a bookmark—a real one—into his book and closes it before setting it on the bedside table.

"A little."

"Only a little." He smirks, reaching over to trace a circle on the side of my bare knee.

"A very, very little."

His chuckle is husky and warm, full of promise. "Good. I haven't had my dessert yet."

I squeal when he flips over suddenly so he's on top of me. "Hi." My voice is a tiny squeak.

"Hi," he repeats with a laugh. "I want to try something. Are you game?"

"Try what?"

"Nothing too crazy."

"I won't need a safe word?"

"You *always* need a safe word—in my humble opinion even with vanilla sex, that way you always know if someone's comfortable or not. But I'm trying to ease you in over here."

"Ease me into what?"

"The kinkier stuff."

"Kinkier than tying me up?"

"Eventually, yes." I love how he says it like it's a definite and honestly, the way my thighs clench together, I'm not opposed. "I'd like to handcuff you." He rubs my wrists as if to drive home his point. "Gag you. Bring you to the edge over and over again until you cry begging for me to let you come." He kisses my neck as I moan. "That's just the tip of the iceberg, baby. Now," he eases off of me, "for what I want tonight. You need a book."

"A-A book?" I stutter in surprise, missing the loss of his body heat when he gets off the bed.

"Mhmm," he hums, crossing the room to his book-cases. "Something dirty, I think." He crouches down, scanning the spines. "Aha." He pulls one out, flips through it. A smirk forms on his full lips. "This will do."

He crosses the room and extends the book to me. I don't see the cover or title, he hands it to me already open to a page. My eyes drop down, my teeth digging into my bottom lip when I see he's already getting hard, and we haven't even done anything yet.

"Start reading," he commands in a bossy tone.

"W-What?" I stutter, a tiny scream flying out of my throat when he yanks me further down the bed and fits his body between my legs. He uses his shoulders to nudge my legs open. A satisfied grin meets his lips when he finds that I'm not wearing underwear.

"Start. Reading." His tone brooks no room for argument. I drop my eyes to the page and read the first sentence. He pinches my hip and I yelp. "Out loud, love."

Wetting my dry lips, I do as he asks. *His hands are on her hips tight enough to bruise. She can feel him —* oh my God." My back bows off the bed as the feel of Cree's tongue against my folds.

His eyes flick up, meeting mine beneath the book

I'm struggling to hold on to. "Every time you stop reading, I stop licking your pussy. *Keep. Reading.*"

I gulp, jerking my head in a nod. He waits for me to start up again. *"She can feel him everywhere and nowhere at the same time."* Cree swirls his tongue around my clit, his eyes peeking up at me in warning. *"Elis presses his lips to the swell of her breasts, smiling when she gasps in response. His tongue—* Cree!*"* I nearly drop the book on my face, overcome with the feelings of pleasure stirring inside me, not to mention how fucking hot it is to see him between my legs beneath the book.

I'll never look at paperbacks the same way again.

His chuckle vibrates against my core, and the orgasm that was so close flutters away. I whimper in annoyance, and he slaps the inside of my thigh. "What did I tell you?"

Biting my lip, I give a tiny nod and search for my voice. *"His tongue swirls around her nipple, sucking the bud between his lips. Casper comes up behind her, his body a thick wall of heat. He steadies her body when she grows weak with lust. Elizabeth didn't dare dream of this moment, of both men taking her, but if she had—"*

My orgasm hits me forcefully, my legs desperate to clamp closed, but Cree holds them open. He keeps going, licking and sucking while his fingers work in and out of me. It makes my orgasm that much more intense, and I feel like it'll never stop. Afraid *he* might stop, with a shaky voice I force myself to keep reading.

"*—but if she had, it couldn't have been as good as the reality. Both men, warriors, are strong and brutal, yet their touch is gentle, reverent when it comes to her. Casper picks her up, holding her naked body to his chest and spreading her legs for his friend. She can feel his cock, large and proud—*"

I come a second time; the orgasm so forceful I see literal stars. I didn't even know that was possible, but pinpoints of light flash behind my closed lids and the book falls from my limp hands, thankfully to the bed because it doesn't hit me and there's no yelp from Cree.

When I finally recover, my entire body is limp, and my thighs shake uncontrollably. Slowly, I blink my eyes open and find Cree watching me with a proud smile.

"Don't look so smug," I gripe, but there's hardly any bite to my voice. I feel too good to access any anger. Licking his lips, he sits up and grabs the book. He climbs off the bed and returns it to where it was. "Hey, I was reading that."

Laughter rumbles through his chest. "You're done for the night." He pulls back the covers, climbing in.

"But it was just getting to the good part." I pout, poking his side when he gets in bed.

"I'm aware."

"And what about you?" I slip my hand beneath the

sheets, but he captures the wandering limb before I reach his cock.

"Tonight, was about your pleasure. Not mine."

"But—"

"No, buts."

I'm a tiny bit sad I don't get to return the favor, but it's sexy as hell that he cares about my pleasure so much.

When I slip beneath the covers, he immediately pulls my body over to his. I lay my head on his chest, hearing the rapid beat of his heart against my ear.

Exhaustion slips into my limbs, and I drift off to sleep.

TWENTY-FIVE

CREE

THE FIRST GAME of the year has me on a fucking high. It's the final period and we're up by two. The team has been working together flawlessly, and even though Daire has been a pain in my ass during practice, he hasn't brought that same attitude to the real thing.

My parents are somewhere in the crowd with Millie. I extended an invite to Ophelia, but I wasn't surprised when she turned it down. It didn't take long to figure out that she doesn't like loud spaces or lots of people, and a hockey game is definitely both of those things.

When the buzzer sounds, I let out a whoop of joy at our first win of the season.

Daire skates up to me, and I'm shocked as hell when he tosses an arm over my shoulder and shouts, "We fucking did it, man!"

The whole team is on a high from our win as we pile into the locker room. But Coach doesn't let us celebrate for long. Before we head for the showers, he comes in, hands on his hips and starts off telling us everything we can do better next time, but he finishes his speech with, "You did good boys, you could do better, but good is better than bad. This is a strong team. A good unit. Let's make this our best season yet." He gives me a significant look and I know what he's communicating.

I need to be on top of my game. The NHL is watching me. I've been unsure going into this season if I wanted to enter the draft. The sport is hard on your body and oftentimes players don't last long. But fuck, I think I'd regret it for the rest of my life if I didn't try.

"Madison, come talk to me after your shower."

"All right, Coach."

Stripping off my gear, I head to the showers. It feels good to wash away the sweat clinging to my body after the vigorous game. Exhaustion is starting to slip in, but I have to keep going. I need to talk to Coach and then meet my parents for dinner since they're leaving early in the morning.

I yank on a pair of jeans and pull on a sweatshirt, telling my boys I'll see them later. Coach's office is down the hall, so I head there, giving a short knock on the door.

His gruff response to come in is immediate. I let myself inside, shutting the door behind me.

"Hey, Coach."

Coach Rogers is in his early fifties, almost entirely gray now, and looks like a chill guy. But looks can fool you, because he's anything but chill when he thinks we're fucking up. He lives and breathes hockey.

Folding his fingers together, he leans over his desk. "I hope to fuck you've made up your mind on what you plan to do, kid. Now's not the time to fool around and bullshit things. You need a solid goal to work toward whether that's professional hockey or not. It'd be a shame to waste your kind of talent on the ice —"

"Coach," I cut him off and he looks ready to throttle me for that fact, "I was unsure if going pro was for me, but I know if I don't at least try to get drafted, I'll regret it for the rest of my life."

The sigh of relief he releases shakes his whole body. "Thank fuck, Madison. You had me worried. I hate seeing talented players walk away. I know the professional world isn't for everyone, but it would've been a shame if you didn't go for it."

I chuckle. "Of course, sir."

"Well, I guess I don't need to go with the rest of my speech then." He gives a solid belly laugh. "If you see Anders out there still, will you send him in?"

"Yeah, of course." I push myself up from the chair.

"Oh, and Madison?" He calls back just as I reach the door.

I look over my shoulder at him. "Mhmm?"

"I've enjoyed coaching you."

I laugh. "Thanks, sir. This year isn't over it yet."

"Keep playing like you did tonight, and it's going to be our best year yet."

I dip my chin in acknowledgement and slip into the hall. I check the locker room for Daire but don't see him, so I shoot him a text that Coach wants to talk to him. It shows he's read my text almost immediately, but he doesn't acknowledge it. I try not to let it bother me, but the sting lingers. I shoot off another text to my parents asking where they are.

Mom: We're in the parking lot. Do you want to ride with us or meet us at the restaurant? Is Ophelia coming? We'd love to see her again before we leave!

I mentioned dinner to Ophelia earlier today, and she wasn't sure if she'd be able to or not.

Me: I'll meet you guys there. I'll call Ophelia and see if she's free.

Ophelia answers after only a few rings. I'm helpless to stop my grin at the sound of her voice when she answers.

"Hey, I'm walking out of the arena now to meet my parents for dinner. Do you want to go or are you studying?"

"Ugh, I can't study another second. What are you guys getting for dinner?"

"Burgers," I reply, heading toward my car in the distance. "It's my favorite place to go after a game."

"How can you think about a burger after a game?" She sounds absolutely disgusted.

"I burn a lot of calories. I'm starving. But I wouldn't be opposed to burning some more off with you."

"Cree!" She admonishes and I know if I could see her in person she would be blushing.

"It's true." I unlock my car and slip inside. "So, what do you say?"

She hums, thinking. "I would like to see your parents before they leave. It was nice having dinner with them last night."

"Then it's settled. I'll swing by and get you."

"I'm in my pajamas!"

"You better hurry then, I'll be there in five minutes."

She hangs up without saying goodbye and I chuckle, tossing my phone onto the passenger seat.

Pulling up outside her dorm, I chuckle when I see her running toward the doors. She's tossed her long hair up in a ponytail, and she's wearing a fitted pair of jeans that make her ass look amazing and an oversized sweatshirt with Winnie the Pooh on it.

She dashes out the door and heads straight for the car. She swings open the passenger door, asking, "Are your parents going to think less of me dressed like this?"

I look at her like she's lost her mind, because clearly, she has. "My parents don't give a shit what you're wearing. They just want to see you."

She hesitates for a second longer before getting in the car. I shoot a text to my mom letting her know I have Ophelia and we're on our way to the restaurant. Restaurant is probably too nice of a word for the hole in the wall burger joint if I'm being honest.

Ophelia bites her lip, wringing her hands together. I reach over, prying her hands apart when I notice. "Were you parents annoyed I didn't come to your game?"

I snort. "Why would they be annoyed about that?"

"Because your girlfriend is probably supposed to be there. I mean, that would be the *normal* thing, but I really don't like loud places and all those people." She shudders. "I mean, I wish I could be there, but it's just…"

"You don't have to explain anything to me or to them. It's not a big deal, I swear. Honestly, when I'm playing, the crowd is the last thing on my mind. As long as I know I've got you to come back to, that's all the matters, and my parents don't care either, babe. A game is a small aspect of my life compared to everything else."

"Well, when you put it like that." She laughs lightly.

It doesn't take me long to get there, and I park on the street in front of the place. My parents' car is down the way, and I assume Millie's with them.

Inside, the place is shotgun style, narrow and extending straight back. My family has already snagged a table and waves us over.

"Ophelia, I'm so happy you could come." My mom stands and opens her arms for a hug. After a brief hesitation, Ophelia wraps her arms around her.

"Thank you for asking me to come."

"Of course, sweetie." My mom slides back into her seat, while Ophelia and I take our own. "We wanted to see you again before we leave."

"Hey, Loser." Millie pokes my arm. "Good game."

"Thanks." I poke her back.

"Hi, y'all what can I get ya to drink?" The waitress asks, notepad in hand.

We all call out our drink orders one at a time, and she goes off to fill them.

Ophelia scans the menu, pursing her lips and crinkling her nose as she reads off items. I already know what I want, just your basic classic cheeseburger, so I don't even bother looking at the menu.

Dad asks me how I felt about the game. Just because you win doesn't always mean it's a good time. And Mom chats Ophelia's ear off with Millie joining them in conversation.

The waitress carries our drinks out on a tray and manages to get each in front of the right person. I might be able to fly across the ice on thin blades, but I don't think I'd be able to balance a tray of drinks or food, and definitely not manage to get it to who it belongs to.

When the last drink is set down, she tucks the tray under her arm and pulls out her notepad again, taking everyone's order.

"It won't be too long, and I'll have those out for y'all." She heads to another table. There are only a few empty tables, and it seems like she's the only waitress. Teddy's girlfriend worked at a diner in town last year. I don't know how she balanced having to work as much as she could on top of her schoolwork. Sure, I have hockey and that's plenty time consuming, but I feel like there's a difference in choosing to do something versus working because you have to pay bills.

"I have to run to the restroom," Millie excuses herself. "I'll be right back."

"Me too!" Ophelia cries, practically leaping out of her chair and running after my sister.

My mom smiles across the table at me, her eyes glittering with happiness. "I *love* her. Where did you find her?"

I chuckle at her question. I'm not about to tell her about the night we met. "She's great, isn't she?"

"Cree, if I could've conjured a woman, she wouldn't have come close to how perfect she is for you. I'm so happy you've found someone who compliments you so well. She's a little shy, but there's so much soul in her and the way she looks at you? I couldn't have asked for more. Now, I just need Millie to find someone."

Both my father and I bristle, none too pleased at the idea of my little sister with someone. I don't think I'll ever stop being overprotective of her. It's my job as her brother.

"Millie's young. She doesn't need to be tied down." My dad tries to rein her in.

My mom shrugs. "You're right. She is. She should have all the fun she can first."

I nearly choke on my sip of soda. "Mom!"

"What? Your sister is allowed to explore her sexuality."

"Oh, for the love of God." My dad covers his face.

"Mom, please, just shut up," I practically beg.

"All I'm saying is, women are allowed to express their sexual desires as much as men are. It shouldn't be so taboo."

"What shouldn't be so taboo?" Millie takes her seat and Ophelia's right behind her.

Ophelia snaps her fingers. "Student teacher romance books? I love those. Taboo books are the best." Her cheeks color when we all stare at her. "Were we not talking about books? Oops."

I cover my face in my hands, trying to hide my laughter, but I fail when my dad snorts. Suddenly we're all laughing and when I lower my hands Ophelia looks around at all of us in shock, wondering what the hell is going on.

"What did I say?"

TWENTY-SIX

Ophelia

THE LIBRARY IS SUBDUED, few people are studying and most of the tables are empty. I guess it makes sense, being a Friday night and all. I'm sure a lot of people aren't like me and have social plans and parties to attend.

I follow Cree through stacks of books, navigating our way back to a secluded table tucked away in a corner. Despite all the open tables I guess he decided he wanted us to hide away.

Setting my bag down on the table, I pull out a chair

and collapse into it. It's been an exhausting week. Finals are approaching quickly. It feels like time is on super-speed and the professors are really laying on the extra work. It's a lot to keep up with, and I'm worried about passing Professor Lindon's class. So far, my grade is passing, but I can't afford for something to happen and fail it again. I would be devastated, and I can't stand the thought of telling my parents what a screw up I am. It makes me feel physically nauseous. I know my brother would tell me I'm being overly sensitive, and I make a silent vow to call him soon. He always has a way of talking me back down when I get too worked up in my head.

"I'm scared," I admit to Cree, the words scraping my throat raw. I hate divulging that tidbit of information, even to him.

"Scared?" He repeats, flicking hair out of his eyes. "Of what?"

I draw my finger around a whorl in the wood table. "Failing this class … *again*."

He blinks across at me, those blue eyes of his seeing too much. "I'm not going to let you fail."

"I hate to inform you," I tuck a piece of hair behind my ear, keeping my eyes on the screen of my computer and away from him, "that when it comes down to it, you don't have much say. What if I panic and bomb my final?"

"We've still got a few more weeks until that, so try to get it off your mind." He stretches his arms above his head, his sweatshirt lifting enough to give me a tantalizing peek at his abdominal muscles and the trail of hair from his naval that disappears into his jeans.

I bite my lip, looking away. I can't afford to let myself get turned on right now. Cree has turned me into a sexual fiend, but I do need to study.

He passes me a printed sheet of paper with questions Professor Lindon will likely give us on our latest study of the classic play *Romeo and Juliet*. I've never quite understood the world's fascination with that story. Maybe it's because I'm obsessed with love stories and happy endings, but I just don't find myself enjoying such a pointless tragedy. Two young deaths that could've easily been prevented if their families hadn't been so blinded by some stupid rivalry. Not to mention, how quickly Romeo fell head over heels in lust with Juliet when he'd been at the party looking for her cousin. I personally didn't find anything appealing about the tale, which makes answering the questions Cree gave me even more difficult.

While I go over those, he reads what I had written of my analysis so far.

He closes my laptop, the lid snapping shut with a tiny clicking noise.

I look up from the sheet of paper, setting my pen down. "Is it horrible?" My nose twitches with the fear that I'll have to start my paper completely over. I have the time since I started it early, but I'd rather not have to scrap the whole thing. He stares at me with a blank expression, blinking slowly. "Just hurry up and tell me if I need to start over or not," I plead, sliding my laptop over to me.

"You don't need to start over."

I narrow my eyes on him. "Then why are you staring at me like that?"

"Because it's good, Ophelia. Great even. It's what Lindon will want to see, and I'm so fucking proud at how far you've come."

I glow beneath his praise. "Really?"

After struggling with this class for the second year in a row, it feels amazing to hear him say that. All I've wanted is to grasp the material and understand what Professor Lindon expects. I'm grateful he suggested a tutor so early in the semester.

"I wouldn't lie to you, Daisy. What you have here is great." He taps a finger against the closed laptop lid.

Luckily, he doesn't seem to notice that I wince when he calls me Daisy. I know he uses it as a term of endearment, but I hate it, because it's a constant reminder that he thinks I'm someone else. I need to tell him, but I haven't been able to bring myself to admit it. I used the situation to my advantage, figuring if he thought I was that girl he'd be more likely to help.

I never thought I'd fall for him in the process.

That's scary to think about, the way this guy has stolen my heart. If I'm being honest, he didn't even steal it. I gratefully handed over piece after piece to him like his beloved Legos, letting him have them and make his own creation.

And how can I possibly tell him I love him with this big lie hanging over my head?

"Hey," he lowers his head, getting in my field of vision, "the paper is turning out great. Stop stressing. I'm serious, you know me, I would tell you if you needed to improve it."

I nod my head like that's exactly what I'm worried about.

We work for another hour—well, I work, and he offers advice here and there when I ask questions, but mostly he reads. I pack my things away, and we start to head out. We don't make it far when he tugs me into an abandoned stack of books.

"What are you—"

He silences my impending question with a kiss. It's

annoying how my worries melt away at the touch of his lips.

His lips part from mine, and he gazes at me through lowered lashes. "I can tell you're in your head." He presses a gentle kiss to my jaw, skimming his lips up to my ear. "Get outta there. Whatever's on your mind, it isn't worth it." My eyes close, hiding the water pooling there. "Focus on me," he murmurs, tugging my bottom lip between his teeth. "Nothing else matters."

"We're in the—"

Another soul-stealing kiss to my lips.

"No one's around. Relax." Somehow, without breaking the kiss, he eases my backpack off my shoulders and gently sets it on the ground. His hands cup my cheeks, practically swallowing them whole in his grasp. "Are you okay with this?" I give the tiniest nod, and he kisses me with a smile. "Such a good girl. Always up for anything."

A gasp flies out of my throat when he picks me up, my legs winding around his waist. He holds me steady, my back against the shelves of books. Part of me is in the moment, the other part of me is worried about someone stumbling upon us. But I realize Cree *likes* this. He gets off on the idea of being caught. It's such a contrast to his good guy personality. He's so sweet, and adorable, but there's this side of him he reserves only for me, and I love that it's our shared little secret. And frankly, I love having this side of me brought out. I've always wondered, what it would be like to be adventurous in my sex life, but I never went there, didn't trust my previous partners enough to even try. But with Cree, I know I'm safe. I know he'll take care of me. And he always puts my pleasure first.

His mouth glides down the side of my neck in teasing little kisses. "It's so fucking unfair how I always want you," he growls lowly. "Do you have any idea how crazy I am for you?"

"I think I can tell." I roll my hips against his hard cock, pressing against his jeans where he rubs against me.

"No." He stops what he's doing, holding me captive with a hand on my chin. He makes sure I'm looking at him, listening, when he says, "I'm not talking about sex, Ophelia. It's fucking great with you, yeah, but I'm crazy about *you*. I love your kindness, the way you read more books than anyone I know. I love how you smile when you think no one's looking at you. I love that you're shy but there's this fire in you anyway and when you let it out? Fuck, baby, it's everything." He pauses, swallowing, his eyes still glued to mine. "I love when you're feeling sassy or playful and stick your tongue out at me. I love..." He wets his lips, his chest moving rapidly with every breath. "I love *you*."

"You love me?"

"Yeah." He nods. "I do."

I grab the back of his head and kiss him with every ounce of passion I have in my body. "I love you, too," I murmur against his lips.

I've fallen fast, so fast, for him but it's been the greatest fall I've ever experienced. This isn't a defeat, it's a conquering. Of us. Of myself. Because I haven't just fallen in love with him, I've fallen in love with myself too.

Cree has opened my eyes to a special kind of love, one I thought only existed through twenty-six letters on the pages of novels. I thought it was something that existed in words, not feelings, but I was so wrong.

"I love you," he says, because he wants to, because he can.

"I love you," I say, because I want to, because I can.

"I love you."

"I love you."

"I love you."

"*I love you.*"

We sink to the floor, and in the middle of the library between stacks of books and numerous worlds, we show each other the magic of that love with the language of our bodies.

"WHAT THE FUCK?" Cree curses, turning onto his street that's parked up with cars everywhere, some even on the lawn of his house.

"What's going on?"

"I have no idea." He parks in the first free spot he finds, shutting off the engine. People spill out his house into the yard. There's a beer pong table set up outside, and despite the chilly weather, the girls gathered around it are barely clothed. Alcohol seems to be flowing freely if the red Solo cups are any indication. "What the fuck?" Cree repeats, looking around in confusion.

We hop out and he takes my hand, heading inside. He spots someone he knows pretty quickly.

"Bowie, what's going on?" he asks a tall, broad guy I've never met before.

"What do you mean, dude? It's a party."

"I can see that. But who threw it?" Impatience bleeds into his tone of voice.

"You didn't?" The guy named Bowie responds with a raised brow. "I thought it was you. I mean, you threw parties all last year. I thought it was weird you only did it once this year before now, so I figured when Daire said there was a party tonight that they were back on." He takes a swig from the cup in his hand.

"Fucking Daire," Cree curses, his hand flexing in mine. "What the fuck is up with this asshole?"

I don't think his question is meant for me or Bowie, because he doesn't wait for an answer before tugging me through the downstairs of the house in search of his friend. We find him in the living room, the furniture all shoved against the wall. He sits in one of the chairs with a girl draped in his lap nursing a beer. His eyes are bloodshot, and he looks … sad, maybe a little scared and stressed too. I don't know him very well, I've only had a few encounters with him, and I've gotten the impression he doesn't like me. I don't understand why he feels that way since he doesn't know me.

"What the hell is this, dude?" Cree shouts at him, smacking the cup out of his hand. It goes flying, the full cup soaking people around us before landing on the floor where the rest spills out.

"What the fuck does it look like, Creature? It's a party. Mellow out. You've had a stick up your ass ever since you got shackled."

"Shackled?" Cree repeats with a snort. "Do you hear yourself? You've had an issue almost this entire semester, and I've been your friend long enough to know something else is up, and you're being an ass because that's what you do. You take your anger out on everyone around you instead of dealing with it like a man."

"Like a man?" Daire screams, jumping up. The girl who was on his lap tumbles to the floor, but he doesn't even notice. She literally crawls away, and I give her a sympathetic look which she returns with a glare. I don't understand why she's pissed at me. I'm not the one who dropped her on the floor. Daire shoves at Cree, and he stumbles back. "What about you, huh?"

"Me?" Cree laughs at him, but I can see the pain in his eyes as he looks at his friend.

Why is it always the ones we care about the most that hurt us the most?

"Oh, come on," Daire tosses his arms out wide in a mocking manner, "I highly doubt you've told her the truth." He looks at me and my brows furrow in confusion. Is he insinuating Cree hasn't told me something? "I guess it doesn't really matter, does it? At the end of the day, we're *all* liars. Me, you, Jude, Millie, and I bet even your girl there has lied about something." Daire spins in a circle, hands cupped around his mouth. "I bet everyone in this fucking room is a goddamn liar!"

"Dude," Jude appears from out of nowhere, tugging

on Daire's arm. "You're drunk. Shut up, you'll regret this in the morning."

Someone's arm brushes against mine, and I turn to see Millie beside me, arms crossed over her chest. She looks pale, worried.

"Are you okay?" I whisper to her—and I realize that the room has gone so silent that I *do* have to whisper if I don't want to be heard. The music has been turned down, and everyone is tuned into what's going on. "Are you sick?"

She gives a tiny shake of her head, and when she spares me a brief glance, I see the panic on her face, the tears in her eyes.

"Don't tell me what to do, fucker!" Daire pulls away from Jude, nearly tripping over his own drunken feet. I thought stuff like this only happened in movies. I never thought I'd bear witness to such a public melt-down. "Are you all listening?" Daire spins again, wanting to make sure everyone in the room is looking at him. In the process, he steals a cup from some guy's hand and makes a big show of gulping the liquid down before dropping the empty cup to the ground. "I think it's time for some lies to come to light. You wanna know why I've been such an asshole?" He slurs at Cree, poking him roughly in the chest. "Because all you care about is your little girlfriend." He tosses a look my way before refocusing his hazy eyes on Cree. "And I needed you. Turns out, your boy is a dad." He laughs obnoxiously, but there's real pain behind the sound. "Had no fucking clue until I saw the kid, and then I just knew he was mine." The whole room gasps at his admission, but he keeps going. "Oh, and guess what? I'm fucking hitched now." He shoves his hand in his pocket, rifling around until he pulls out a ring and slips it on his finger —not even the correct finger at that. "And no, not to the baby mama. She's a professor and a real bitch because she didn't tell me she was pregnant. She really thought she could keep him from me, but I won't let her. No, sir." He beats a hand on his chest, and actual tears escape his eyes. "So, now I'm married to Rosie— yeah, you know that girl I can't fucking stand— because ... well, that's not important." His hands fall to his sides. "Oh, but guess what, there's more." He tosses an arm over Cree's shoulders, swinging him toward Jude.

Jude shakes his head. "Don't do this, man."

Daire laughs loudly like Jude just told him the funniest joke he's ever heard. "But why not? It's so fun!" He squeezes Cree even tighter. Cree glances in my direction with confused eyes. "Are you listening, buddy?" Daire's mouth is practically on Cree's cheek. "This is a big one. Are you ready?" Cree shoves him away, but Daire only laughs. He's crazed, totally wasted.

A pin could drop in the room, that's how silent it is.

"What?" Cree's question is a hushed whisper. It's directed at Daire, then his eyes slide to Jude questioningly. "Well, what is it?"

Daire's eyes slide to Jude, and he must think better of what he was going to say. "It's not important."

"I think it must be for you to be putting on this whole fucking debacle." Cree tosses his arms out at his sides.

Jude dips his head, looking at his shoes.

"Oh, don't be so quick to jump to conclusions, my dude. It's not like you're some holy saint. Nah, you like to think you're a good guy, but you're a liar just like the rest of us—and here's another little secret—*good guys don't lie*. Your sins might not be as shitty as the rest of us, but a lie is a lie *is a lie*."

I wet my dry lips with my tongue. My heart pounds in my ears, and I feel faint.

This night started off good, great even, and I feel like everything is going to hell.

Daire's drunken eyes meet mine, and he smiles, but there's nothing kind in that expression. "Good ole boy Cree here wasn't supposed to be your tutor. Bet you didn't know that? Nah, he's spent a year looking for you, and apparently, you mistook him for your tutor, and this fucker used that situation to his advantage."

"Shut up!" Cree shoves his friend. "Just shut your fucking mouth, dude!"

"You need to sober up." Jude tries to grab Daire, but he darts away, surprisingly light on his feet for a drunk guy. He giggles, actually giggles like a little girl. He's so completely amused by this whole thing, by dropping his friends' truth bombs and his own as well.

He doesn't care that he's imploding people's entire worlds right now.

But something tells me he'll regret this in the morning. He's being a dick right now, but I know Cree, and he'd never be friends with someone who's always this way.

"Seriously?" Daire shoves Jude away from him. "You're going to act like *I'm* the bad guy right now? That's all you."

Cree looks like he doesn't know who he should be mad at.

And I'm standing there thinking about the fact that he was never supposed to be my tutor.

He wasn't supposed to be my tutor, and the only reason he stepped in is because he thinks I'm this Daisy chick. Oh, God. I think I might be sick.

He lied.

I lied.

Daire's been lying.

It seems like Jude and Millie are hiding something.

We're all a bunch of fucking liars.

Every last one of us.

And how can anything, like Cree and me, continue to exist on such a rocky foundation? Neither of us are who we really thought we were.

My God.

I turn away from the chaos in front of me.

I leave behind Cree, who's so focused on his friends he doesn't even notice me slipping away.

Wrapping my arms around myself I walk outside, and down the street.

I don't make it far when I hear Cree yelling after me.

"Ophelia! Ophelia! Wait up! Please, wait!"

I turn around to face him, my arms still firmly wrapped around my form that feels ready to fall to pieces.

He stops in front of me, not even slightly winded from jogging.

Stupid hockey player endurance.

He doesn't say anything.

Neither do I.

We just stand there, the silence stretching between

us endlessly.

I decide to be the first to break it.

"While we're on the topic of secrets and lies — I'm not Daisy."

He laughs — *laughs at me.* "Ophelia, come on. Yes, you are. We might not have given each other our real names that night, but it was you."

"It wasn't." Tears burn my eyes, but I refuse to hold them in. "So, we both lied. You pretended to be my tutor to get close to Daisy, and I pretended to be Daisy because I needed a tutor. Turns out, you weren't actually supposed to be my tutor, and I'm not actually Daisy, so it all evens out." I throw my arms out at my sides, letting them fall back down.

"Ophelia." He cocks his head to the side, giving me a funny look. "You … you don't remember the night we met, do you?"

"I met you at the coffee shop. That was the first time I met you, because I'm not Daisy."

Why can't he understand that?

He takes a step closer to me, brow wrinkled. "We met at the start of school last year, at the bonfire party. You were by yourself, and I approached you. We talked and ended up leaving together and we hooked up. How do you not remember?"

I shake my head rapidly back and forth. "I didn't … I don't … are you not listening? It wasn't me."

"It was Ophelia. Unless you have an identical twin sister I don't know about."

"N-No. No, sister," I stutter out, racking my brain for any memories of a bonfire. "It wasn't me, Cree. It couldn't have been me."

He grips my hand, eyes pleading. "Are you okay? Did you hit your head? You're scaring me."

I pull from his grasp, covering my face with my hands. "This is too much." He reaches for my hands, trying to pull them from my face. "Don't touch me!" I scream, his hands immediately disappearing from my body.

Confusion floods my veins.

How is it possible I'm really Daisy and I don't remember?

A sprinkle hits the bridge of my nose. Another my cheek. I tilt my head back as the sky opens up upon us, drenching us in a cold autumn rain.

"Ophelia, come back inside," he begs. "We can talk. Or I'll take you back to your dorm. Whatever you want." He has to raise his voice to be heard above the downpour.

I wrap my arms around myself, hair plastered to my

head already. Shaking my head back and forth, I take a step away from him, then another.

"You lied to me."

"I know."

"I lied too."

"You didn't—"

"I need space to think. I need ... I need to figure things out." I press a hand to my suddenly throbbing head.

"Let me take you to your dorm."

He just won't stop!

"Cree." I look him in straight in the eyes. "Otter."

His lips part in surprise, and I see slight amusement in his gaze that quickly turns to horror when he realizes what I'm really saying. That he needs to let it go. Let *me* go. Ignoring his distraught expression, I turn my back on him and walk away.

TWENTY-SEVEN

CREE

WATCHING Ophelia walk away from me in the rain is single-handedly the hardest thing I've ever had to do. It kills me to let her go, but I know it's what I have to do.

Lacing my fingers together behind my head, I yell into the night, *"Fuck!"*

Soaked to the bone, I walk down the street back to my house.

Inside, the party has started back up but not with the same energy or loudness as before.

My voice booms as I call out the order, "Party's

over! Get the fuck out of my house, now!" A few people turn to me with a questioning look but go on dancing and drinking. Storming through the house I find the main Bluetooth speaker in the kitchen and turn it off, the music cuts off and there's a chorus of disappointed sounds through the house. Cupping my hands around my mouth, I shout again, "Party's over! Grab your shit and get out now!"

It takes way too long to get everyone out and when I do, I'm left with a drunk Daire passed out on the floor of the living room and Jude and Millie are nowhere to be seen. They could be upstairs, but I have no idea. I'm pissed off and exhausted. This night started off so good and ended in disaster.

Collapsing onto a chair, I eye my drunk friend. I kick his booted foot, and he doesn't even move, just gives a loud snore in response.

I don't even know what to feel, what to focus on.

So many truth bombs were dropped tonight. I can't even wrap my head around them.

Only the band still on Daire's finger—the wrong finger—serves as a reminder that all this shit really did take place.

Apparently Daire has a kid and married Rosie of all people. I have no fucking clue why he had to get married and what that has to do with the kid ... *the kid*.

I can't stop thinking about what Ophelia said—that she lied too, and she's not Daisy.

But she *is*. I'm not crazy. It was her that night.

So how is it possible that night meant so much to me, but she doesn't remember?

My BODY IS stiff when I crack my eyes open and find myself still in the chair I sat down in the night before. Cracking my neck, I lift my arms over my head and stretch. Daire's still on the floor, snoring and completely unbothered. He's going to be bothered soon, though, when I wake his ass up.

Forcing myself up from the chair, my body screams in protest.

It doesn't matter how good of shape you're in, sleeping in a chair all night is good for no one. My clothes are stuck to my body, having dried strangely after being soaked by the rain. I find my phone and check it, hoping there's a text from Ophelia, but there's nothing.

Pinching the bridge of my nose, I war with myself on sending her a text message or not. In the end, I decide not to do it yet and give her time.

Daire gives a stir on the floor, and I walk over,

bending to give his shoulder a rough shake. He grunts something out that I'm not sure is even a word. I give him a rougher shake, and his eyes blink open.

"Fuuuck, dude," he slurs. "Let me sleep."

I laugh, a rough cutting sound. "Nah, we need to talk. You can sleep later."

"Talk?" He yawns, opening his eyes fully. They're bloodshot and sickly looking. He drank way too much last night.

"Yeah, after your meltdown last night we need to talk. Get up and sober up." I give his foot a kick. "I'll make breakfast."

"Ugh." He gags, rolling to his knees and slowly getting up. "Don't talk about food right now."

"Fine, food for me. Water and Advil for you."

He gives me a thumbs up. "I'm about to sound like such an asshole, but you're going to have to give me a refresher on last night because I don't remember anything."

I narrow my eyes on him, looking for any hint of a lie and not finding any, which makes me wonder, was Ophelia completely wasted the night we met? I didn't think so, I would swear on my life she wasn't, and it makes me physically ill to think she might've been, and I took advantage of her.

"You okay?" Daire asks me, and I realize I must look as sick as I feel.

"Fine. I'm fine."

"I gotta go piss. I'll meet you in the kitchen." He stifles another yawn, shuffling to the downstairs bathroom.

I set out some water and pills for him on the island and get breakfast started for myself. He lumbers into the kitchen a few minutes later, dropping onto the barstool.

"Fuck, what happened last night?"

"Well, for starters, you got shit-faced."

"Really?" He shoves the pills in his mouth, gulping down water. "I didn't notice that part."

"You threw a massive party," I continue like he didn't say anything at all, "then you confessed that apparently you have a son and you married Rosie?"

"Oh, fuck." He covers his face with his hands, pulling them away to glare at the ring on his finger before taking it off and sitting it on the counter.

"Care to elaborate?" I pour eggs into a hot skillet for scrambled eggs.

"Not really."

"Are you really married?"

"Yup." He glares at the ring like it personally offended him.

"Do you have a kid?"

He hesitates a second before a shaky, "Yes," leaves him.

"What the fuck, man?" I try to focus on cooking my eggs but it's damn near impossible with this information confirmed.

"It's insane. I know."

"You knocked up a professor?"

He cringes. "I see I didn't forget that tidbit of information either."

"Nope. And you had no problem telling Ophelia that I was never supposed to be her tutor."

"Fuck. I'm sorry."

I raise a brow, sliding the eggs onto a plate. "Are you? You've been a dick this year."

"Yeah, well how would you feel if you saw a woman holding a child you know in your gut is yours? It's been hell, and I didn't want to say anything to anyone until I knew for sure. It's a whole fucked up mess. I'm sorry I took my anger out on you, but it felt like my life was imploding while yours was ... I don't know, heading in a different direction that took you away from me, I guess. I'm a selfish friend. There, I said it." He drinks the rest of the water while I slather butter on my toast. "Did I ... uh ... spill any other beans last night?"

"No." I pause, staring at my plate. "You alluded to

337

something with Jude and my sister, though." He looks out the backdoor. "Care to elaborate on that?"

"Not at the moment." He slides off the barstool and refills his water. Turning around, he props himself against the refrigerator like he can't hold himself up without it. "I really am sorry about that—telling Ophelia."

"Are you?"

"Well, mostly sorry. Is she pissed at you?"

"I … I don't know," I admit, sitting down with my breakfast. "She seemed hurt, confused. But not pissed." I shake my head, unsure if I really want my eggs now. "But dude, she doesn't remember the night we met. Like at all. And fuck, it's killing me to think maybe she was drunk and that's why. You know me, I would never take advantage of a drunk girl. That's fucking wrong."

Daire's lips turn down in a frown. "That's odd."

"Right?" I shake my head, my confusion growing. "I don't really know what to think about it."

"Are you going to talk to her?"

I give him a funny look. "Of course, I'm going to talk to her. She's my girlfriend."

"Right," he drawls slowly.

"I have a girlfriend," I repeat, getting his attention, "and you have a wife."

"A wife. Fuck." He rubs his jaw. "I have a wife. I'm

married to Rosie." He gags on the words. "Rosie." A shudder this time.

"Are you going to explain any of that to me? Were you drunk for the wedding too?"

"It was at the courthouse and no, I wasn't drunk."

"Dude," I shove my half-eaten plate of food away from me, "you've got to give me more information than that."

He gulps down the water he just filled the glass with and deposits it in the sink. "Rosie and I … we go way back. Like practically to the time, we were in diapers. Our families are close. Her dad is best friends with mine, and we lived in the same neighborhood."

He stops, and I expect him to pick back up with his story, but he doesn't. "And that's it?"

He shakes his head. "I guess you could say we've had a love-hate relationship over the years. And look," he shoves his fingers through his hair, "I'm not ready to be a dad, but I *am* a dad. I'm not about to watch my kid grow up thinking some other dude is his father. I'm going to be there, but look it's not as easy as saying it. I have to prove it, and unfortunately it's not smooth sailing for single fathers." He pulls out a chair and sits down at the kitchen table, his shoulders sag with wariness. "The lawyer I hired told me I don't stand much of a chance of getting any kind of custody without proof that I have my life together. He said a wife would make things a lot easier. Having my own home too. A proper car." He frowns at that, and I realize that means he's going to have to get rid of his motorcycle, or at least get something else. "So, I'll also be moving out. Rosie and I are getting a townhouse."

"And she knows about your son?" He nods in answer to my question. "What is she getting out of this?"

He shrugs. "Her family has wanted us together for a while, so I guess that."

"And your son," I pause, stumbling over the word, "do you ... what's his name?"

He smiles at my question, his eyes crinkling at the corner as he ducks his head down. "Sammy—Samuel. It's not what I would've chosen, but..."

"It's perfect," I finish for him, and he nods.

"I really am sorry about last night. It was a hard day."

"I take it yesterday is when you went to the court-house?" He gives a single nod. "I would say congratulations, but I don't think you want to hear it." He shakes his head, his shoulders sagging with weariness. "When do you move out?"

"Not sure yet. We have to find a place and get furniture and all that shit set up." He taps his fingers on the table. "Do you ... uh ... mind if Rosie moves in for a bit? It'll look better to the court system the sooner we're living together and sharing expenses."

"It's fine." I don't know how fine it'll truly be, but if my best friend is doing all of this to have rights to his child, then I won't stop him from doing what he can to get there.

"Thanks." He runs his fingers through his hair, getting up to make some fresh coffee. "I know I don't deserve you being nice to me right now. I haven't been a good friend. I should've told you what was up."

"Why didn't you?"

He sighs, adding a filter and grounds. "You were all wrapped up in Ophelia, and I guess I convinced myself that you wouldn't care about my shit, and that made me angrier."

I shake my head, shoving his shoulder before I grab a coffee mug from the cabinet and pass it to him. "Sounds like you were jealous."

"Of monogamy? Never." He gags.

I arch a brow. "You're married now, dude. Get used to it."

He sighs, watching the coffee pot fill up. "No sex for me. Not with my wife, and not with anyone else. Living the fucking dream, man."

But when he looks over at me, pouring his coffee

into the mug, and smiles, I know he'd do it all over again for that kid.

"I'm going to go shower and then try to talk to Ophelia."

"Good luck."

"Thanks."

I hope I don't need it.

TWENTY-EIGHT

Ophelia

I WAKE up to tears dried on my cheeks and pillow. The events of last night caught up to me once I got back to the dorm. Somehow, I bumbled around and yanked on my pajamas before crashing into bed and crying myself to sleep.

I'm hurt, confused, and a little bit mad.

Getting out of bed, I grab my shower stuff since I've heard both girls already take theirs.

I'm deterred when I open the door, and Kenna gasps when she sees me.

"Oh, no! What's wrong?"

"Huh?"

She bites her lip, setting her cereal bowl down on the coffee table. Uncurling her legs, she stands from the couch and comes over to me. "You look like you've been crying. You have, haven't you? Who made you cry? Was it Cree? Did he break up with you? I swear I'll rip his dick off if you want me to."

Her questions bombard me, but her final statement manages to get me to laugh. "That won't be necessary."

"So, it wasn't Cree? Who was it, then? Something had to have happened." She grabs my hand, forcing me to put my things down as she tugs me over to the couch. "Spill."

"Why?" The word rolls off my tongue, perhaps too quickly based on her frown and furrowed brow.

"Because we're friends, and friends tell each other things."

"We are?"

She looks surprised by my question which makes me feel like shit. "Yeah, of course we are. Why wouldn't we be?"

"It's just..." I flounder, looking down at my worn pajama bottoms with a hole in the knee. "I'm not good at making friends. Or keeping them. I'm sorry, it's nothing personal against you, or Li, or anyone else. It's entirely a me thing."

"Why would you think you're not good at making friends? You're fun to be around."

"I am?" I give her a funny look. I always feel like I'm raining on people's parade. I've lost count of how many times she's asked me to go to Harvey's, and I always say no because a loud bar is the last place I want to be.

"Yeah. I mean, you're quiet but that doesn't make you an awful person. There's nothing wrong with being a little bit timid. Trust me, my mom wishes I was bashful." She reaches for the blanket and wraps it around her shoulders. "Do you really think we're not friends?"

I bite my lip, deciding that honesty is the best policy. If last night proved anything, it's that.

Playing with the hole in the knee of my bottoms, I let it all out. "It's not that I don't think we're friends; it's that in the past, I would think I was friends with people only to realize that they were friends with each other and I was an outsider. I have autism and sometimes it makes it hard for me to fit in, or to understand social structures, and I think after being hurt repeatedly I just stopped assuming and sheltered myself." I wrap my arms around my body. "I have one friend from my childhood and that's it. And I've been okay with that, for the most part," I add, forcing myself to meet her eyes. I notice that Li has stepped outside her room and is listening. "It's been easier to keep a close circle and not get hurt than to put myself out there. But this year, meeting Cree, I think … it made me realize I was missing out on things, and it was my own fault."

Kenna gives me a sympathetic smile. "Sometimes we can be our own worst enemy and stand in our way."

"I think once I got diagnosed, I felt like all I was, all I'd ever be is my autism, but I see now that it's just one part of what makes me, *me*. Just like I love brownies and reading books. It doesn't change who I am."

"No, it's doesn't." Li comes over and joins us, sitting on the floor between the couch and coffee table. "I hate that you were scared to be friends with us."

"Don't feel bad," I beg. "Seriously, don't. It was my own insecurities plaguing me. You guys are awesome."

"We love you," Kenna adds. "You're a part of our group now, and you can't get rid of us that easy. Can we all hug now and make everything normal?"

I laugh, opening my arms. "I think hugs would be good."

Somehow the three of us manage to execute a hug. Calmness settles over me, a peace I haven't felt in a long time. Friends, I have real true friends, and I have ... or had Cree. I duck my head, my previous calm being tainted by sadness.

"Something's bothering you." Kenna squeezes my hand, her eyes pleading with me to open up and be honest. "What made you cry?"

Li's head bounces from Kenna to me, her eyes narrowing when she notices my red-rimmed eyes. Crinkling my nose, not happy with the idea of reliving last night I decide to just go for it. We've established we're friends after all.

I tell them all the details after we got to Cree's house after studying, what Daire said, though I leave out the part about his child and that he's married. He might not have a problem confessing everyone else's sins, but his aren't mine to tell.

"Hold up," Kenna crosses her legs, waving her hand through the air, "you're telling me that you hooked up with Cree, but have no memory of it, and this boy spent a whole year waiting for you, so he lied to be your tutor?" She laughs loudly, smacking her knee. "If I could be so lucky. That's so freaking cute."

I wrinkle my nose. "You think it's cute?"

Li shrugs. "Listen, it's more of a fib than a lie in my opinion. Cree is an English major, so it's not like he was jeopardizing your chance of getting help, and he's super smart. If anything, helping you would've harmed him with his busy schedule."

"But he did it anyway," Kenna pipes in, "because he wanted to be close to you. That's so romantic." She swoons dramatically.

"But you think he did all of this for Daisy?" I nod in answer to Li's question. "And you're not Daisy?"

"He says I am, but I don't recall that night at all. Even being at the bonfire."

"You were there." Kenna gives me a funny look. "You came with us. Hold on, I have a picture on my phone." She gets up and unplugs it from where it was charging. Her finger flies across the screen as she scrolls through her photos. "Aha, here it is." She taps on something and passes her phone to me. Sure enough, there's a photo of the three of us, bonfire in the background. "You were definitely there, but that doesn't explain why you don't remember."

Li frowns. "I hope no one slipped something into your drink."

I pale. "Do you think Cree—"

Neither of them lets me finish the question before they protest vehemently. "Not Cree. There's no way." Kenna shakes her head back and forth. "Honestly the fact that he lied to you about being your tutor shocks me. He's not that kind of person."

Sighing, I unfold my legs and stand from the couch. "I'm going to change and head out for a while. I have a feeling he'll show up here and I need ... I need time to think before I talk to him."

"We understand."

"Do you want us to tell him anything if he does come by?" Li asks.

I press my lips together, contemplating. "Just tell him, I'll talk to him later."

"That's it?"

I nod. "I don't know what else to say right now. We have a lot to talk about and frankly, I need a little bit of time before we do."

"Understandable." Kenna squeezes my hand. "Go get ready and get out of here for a while. Get some coffee. Eat a brownie." She winks. "Chocolate always helps me when I'm feeling down."

I feel tears prick my eyes again, but for an entirely different reason this time.

They really are my friends.

GRAVEL SCATTERS beneath my feet as I trek over to the barn. When I got in my car and started driving, this is where I ended up. I should've known this is where I'd come. Whenever I'm sad, or stressed, or angry, it's the barn and horses I find myself drawn to.

Inside, I spot Mary. She gives me a funny look. "It's the weekend, honey. What are you doing here?"

I shrug, looking around. "Just needed to be here."

She gives me a sad smile like she knows the confusion and pain in my heart. "They always make it better, don't they?"

I nod, walking over to Calliope. I swear she smiles when she sees me. "Hey, pretty girl." I pet her nose, leaning into her with my eyes closed. Instant calm spreads through my limbs.

Mary's boots scuff over the dirt, and I feel her come to a stop in front of me. Opening my eyes, I find her watching me with a curious expression.

"Do you want to talk about it?"

I exhale a heavy breath, my shoulders sagging. I give a tiny nod. If there's someone I can talk to about this with no judgment it's Mary, and I know any advice she offers will be genuine. She's a straight shooter. She doesn't sugarcoat things and I like that about her.

I hate it when people tiptoe around me. My parents are bad for that, even if I know it comes from a place of love, I just want them to see me as an equal to my brother, not someone they constantly have to worry about.

"Come on." Mary twines her arm through mine. "I made some fresh sweet tea. We can drink some of that and chat. Tom's not home so we don't have to worry about his nosey ass turning up his hearing aid to eavesdrop on us."

The visual of Tom sneaking around to listen in makes me laugh. Mary tugs me around to the side of the house, and we enter through the backdoor into the kitchen.

As promised, she pours two glasses full of sweet tea. I'm not a huge fan of the drink, but for Mary, I'll tolerate it.

She doesn't force me to talk, she waits until I'm ready and then the words pour from me.

With Mary, I start at the beginning. About my struggles growing up, how being around horses helped me to feel better. I tell her of my autism diagnosis and how my parents were relieved to finally have a label for me, but also worried because of what it could mean for my future, especially when their friends made it seem so much worse than what it actually is. I tell her about how I had to fight tooth and nail to actually attend college on campus instead of online, how my brother has had it so easy, but I've had to beg for normal things. I tell her about Cree, meeting him this year and falling so hard and fast for him that it's been a whirlwind. I even explain how sure he is that we met a year ago—leaving out the part about us apparently hooking up that night since Mary doesn't need *that* much information—but that I don't remember. When I finally stop talking, Mary just sits there. Her glass is empty. The ice melting.

I worry I've broken her, but finally she says, "Wow. That's a lot to take in. Give me a moment to gather my thoughts."

Wiping condensation off my glass, I do my best to be patient. It's difficult, but I manage to keep my mouth shut. Mary gets up and reaches for a tin on the kitchen counter. She pulls out two cookies and holds one out to me.

"Here," she says, and I take it, "I think we both deserve a cookie after all of that."

A small laugh bubbles out of me. Taking a bite of the cookie, I ask, "Do you think I'm completely crazy after dumping all of that on you?"

"Crazy? No." She breaks her cookie in half. "But honey, that's a lot to take in." I nod in understanding. I dumped a lot on her, even more than I did with Kenna and Li this morning. "Let's address one thing at a time, okay?"

She waits for me to reply. "Okay."

"I'm terribly sorry you grew up feeling like nothing you did was good enough for your parents. I can't speak for them, but I can say as a parent myself sometimes I prioritized things in the wrong way, and while I thought I was doing or saying the right thing for my children, I really wasn't. Being a parent is a difficult thing. There is no instruction manual. You should sit down and have a long conversation with your parents about how you feel. I think it would be really helpful for you."

She's completely right. It's something I've needed to do for a long time but avoided because I hate confrontation. "I will," I promise her.

She gives a reassuring smile, squeezing my hand.

"I'm too old to be giving you boy advice, but the memory thing, honey did you forget about falling off Calliope last year?" She's nothing but sympathetic, and the fact of the matter is I *had* completely forgotten about the fall. It wasn't a bad one and we all take a tumble from a horse now and then, it's just happens, so I dismissed it from my mind. "Remember, Tom and I took you to the hospital. They said you had a mild concussion and that it could cause minor memory loss. That's my best guess as to why you wouldn't remember that night. It sounds like maybe that was a day or so prior to when you would've fallen."

"Oh." A tiny gasp leaves me. "Oh," I repeat, a little louder this time. Her explanation makes complete and total sense. Now that she's brought it up, I remember the fall. I also recall the killer headache that came along with it.

"What's wrong?" Mary prompts when she notices my frown.

"What you said makes total sense, and I think you're right, but it makes me sad because that means I might never remember the night I actually met Cree for the first time. It's been over a year, and I still have no memories of that night, so it seems unlikely that at this point I'll ever remember."

"Oh, honey." She clasps my hand, giving it a squeeze. "You love this boy, right?" I nod in response. "Then losing the memory of one night, doesn't cancel out all the others you've made together. Those count just as much, if not more. Memories are a stepping stone through the mind. One missing piece means you stumble, you don't disappear."

"Wow. I never thought about it like that."

She smiles, her eyes crinkling even more at the corners than usual. "I'm glad I could help, sweetheart. Tom and I care about you so much."

"Thank you. You guys have been wonderful to me."

She pulls me into a hug, and I squeeze her back. I think I needed that hug more than I realized.

She places her hands on my cheeks, looking into my eyes. "You're going to live a beautiful life, Ophelia Hastings. I can't wait to watch you soar."

TWENTY-NINE

CREE

IT'S BEEN a week since I last saw or spoke to Ophelia in person.

I went by her dorm the day after everything happened, and she wasn't there. Kenna answered the door and said Ophelia wanted her to tell me she'd talk to me later. I wanted a more definitive answer than that. That's when I sent her a text message, asking when we could talk. She responded an hour or so later.

Ophelia: There are some things I need to take care of first. I need to talk with my parents about my

feelings on some things, and I'd like to talk to my brother too, if I can. I want you to know I'm not mad at you.

That was it and I haven't heard from her since.

It's been fucking torture not to text her back with each passing day, to beg her to talk to me. But I'm trying to respect her space and give her time to think.

"Dude, even after a fucking win you can't get her off your mind?" Daire shakes his head at me, walking out of the bathroom in our shared hotel room since we had an away game.

"Maybe I'm reading a text from my mom," I argue, putting my phone on the nightstand and plugging it in to charge.

"Are you?" He raises an eyebrow, pulling the covers back on his bed. Normally he would be out with the guys, picking up a chick for the night, but now that he's hitched, he's stuck here with me.

"No."

He chuckles, yanking the blankets up to his chin. "I knew it."

Our friendship has returned to normal, for the most part. There's a bit of awkwardness lingering since we've spent months with things being tense, but I'm the kind of person who believes when you forgive someone, you forget and move on. I'm not going to throw away an entire friendship with Daire just because he was going through some shit and didn't handle it in the best way.

"She hasn't said anything to me since last weekend."

Daire doesn't reply for a few minutes. "I'm sorry."

"Not your fault," I grumble out automatically.

He laughs, his whole body shaking. "It totally is, dude. Again, I'm sorry."

That gets me to laugh too. "Fuck, you're right, you bastard. This is all your fault."

"She told you she wasn't mad, though, so what's the hold up with talking to you?"

"I don't know." I pick up the book I brought with me, flipping to where it's bookmarked. I'm not sure I'm in the mood to read, but it would be a great distraction right about now.

My thoughts drift back to the night of the bonfire when we met, and how she said using the names Jay and Daisy might be a bad omen. I've never believed in that sort of thing before, but now I can't help but worry she might've been right.

Were we doomed from the very beginning?

"Cree, you're not even saying anything, and I can hear you worrying from over here." Daire sends a text and then plugs his phone in beside mine.

I set my book back down, crooking my arm behind my head. "I can't stop thinking about the fact that I might've lost her before I ever really had her, you know?"

"You haven't lost her."

He says it so boldly, without question, that I find myself rolling over and giving him a funny look. "How are you so sure?"

He runs his fingers through his hair. "Because anyone who looks at you the way she does, isn't going to let something this insignificant ruin you guys."

"She looks at me a certain way?"

He rolls his eyes. "Like you haven't noticed. Don't fish for compliments, this isn't a pond."

I snort. "Seriously, though, how does she look at me?"

"Like she's disgustingly in love," he gags. "It's disgusting and you're even worse."

I laugh, because he's probably not wrong. "I hate not talking to her."

"Jeez, I wish I could switch places."

"Why? Trouble with the wifey already?"

He groans, pressing the heels of his hands to his eyes. "She won't stop texting me non-stop with pictures of plates, and couches, and fucking utensils and shit. It's exhausting. We don't even have a place to live yet, and she's furniture shopping and wants my opinion on every little thing. I've told her I don't give a shit and to get whatever she wants, but she wants the place to be home for both of us."

I pause, thinking over what he's said. "Is that such a bad thing?"

He wiggles around, trying to get comfortable on the too-hard bed. "Yeah, it is."

"Why?"

"Because, I don't want it to feel like home. If the place feels solely like Rosie, there's no chance of me getting attached."

I let about thirty seconds pass in silence before I respond. "What exactly is it you're worried about feeling like home? The home you move into, or her?"

A pillow launched like a missile at my face is the only response I get.

THIRTY

Ophelia

THERE'S a light knock on my childhood bedroom's door, and my mom pokes her head inside. I sit on my bed, my legs tucked beneath me while I work on homework.

I came home last Sunday, feeling like an in-person visit was necessary after my chat with Mary. The conversation I needed to have with my parents wasn't the kind you had over the phone.

Now it's Saturday and I've been here a week — I did

my classes virtually while I've been here—and I need to head back to campus tomorrow.

But it's been a good week, filled with much needed and long overdue talks, some tears, and a peace I haven't felt in a long time. It's amazing how just opening your mouth and being honest can get rid of such an immense weight you've been carrying.

"Hey," she says softly. "I'm making omelets for breakfast. Do you want one?"

I close the lid to my laptop. "Yes, absolutely!" I'll never say no to one of her omelets. It's rare for my mom to cook, we've always had our housekeeper for that, but when she does it's either omelets or her mom's fried chicken recipe. "Can I help?"

She lights up at my offer. "Of course."

In the kitchen, she turns on some music, keeping the volume soft if we want to chat.

We work together easily, I chop onions, green peppers, and mushrooms, and she cracks all the eggs she needs into a bowl.

There's no weight on my shoulders like there used to be. No pressure to act a certain way. I'm free to be me.

"Where's Dad?" I ask, realizing I haven't heard him moving around the house.

"Oh," she hesitates, glancing out the large window

in the kitchen that overlooks the driveway. "He ran out for a bit. He'll be back shortly."

"Did he have to go to the store?"

"He had to grab something."

I finish chopping everything up and slide onto one of the barstools, resting my elbows on the counter. She starts assembling the omelets, the smell of the peppers cooking makes my stomach rumble.

I'll be sad to leave in the morning, but I'm also looking forward to returning to campus. This time has been needed, though, to grow and repair, and get things off my chest.

When I told them I always felt like such a failure in their eyes, especially compared to Augustus, they were horrified. Both have apologized over and over for ever doing or saying anything to make me feel that way, and their sincerity is genuine. I feel bad that I never spoke up in the moment, but that's something I've always had trouble with. Defending myself doesn't come easy, and that has nothing to do with being autistic. A lot of people are that way. I don't like to rock the boat.

"Do you mind setting the table?" she asks, nodding toward the cabinet where placemats are.

"Not at all. Is Dad going to be back soon?"

"Should be any minute. Go ahead and set the table for four."

"Four?" I question, wondering who else is eating with us.

"Mhmm," she hums, avoiding eye contact, which worries me. What if they've only pretended to be agreeable and are forcing a therapist on me? Oh, God, is this an intervention of some sort? "We have a guest coming."

I gulp nervously, but set out the placemat's utensils, glasses, and a pitcher of ice water and another of orange juice.

She plates the omelets, and I take two to the table while she grabs the others.

I turn toward the window at the sound of the garage door going up. My dad's SUV pulls into the driveway and straight into the garage. Sitting in front of my plate, I'm suddenly not all that hungry. Busying myself, I pour a glass of orange juice and wait, ears perked for the door into the house to open.

The moment it does, I look over my shoulder—catching my mom's smile out of the corner of my eye—then spot Gus walking into the house with an overnight bag slung over his shoulder.

"Gus!" I cry, diving out of the chair and running toward brother.

"Oomph," he grunts when my body collides with

his. He hugs me back, and in that hug all my worries melt away.

There's no therapist showing up.

No, intervention.

They got my brother to come up for the weekend because they knew I missed him.

His chuckle rumbles through the touch of his hug. He sits me down so my feet touch the ground, ruffling my hair. "I missed you too, sis."

Sticking my tongue out at him, I stand on my tiptoes so I can return the favor and ruffle his red hair. Fixing the mess I made of it, he nods toward the table. "Let's eat, I'm starving."

Dad comes in, kisses mom on the cheek and smiles at the two of us. "Are you surprised?" His question is for me.

"Shocked."

It's the truth. Gus showing up was the last thing I ever expected.

We sit down at the table to eat, and for the first time since I got my diagnosis, I feel like a full family of four and not an outsider looking in.

People can put us in boxes, give us labels, but we can also do the same to ourselves. It's crippling, but when you finally set yourself free it's liberating.

On THE HEATED BACK DECK, enclosed from the elements, Gus sits on the couch, and I lie on the twin-size swing. I've started and finished many books in this exact spot. It's been quiet for a while, neither of us feeling the need to fill the silence which is nice. I hate that I'm leaving tomorrow to go back to campus, and we won't have much time together, but on the other hand I'm grateful to have gotten to see him at all.

Setting my book down, I roll over so I can see him. He must feel my gaze because he turns and looks almost immediately.

"Whatcha thinking about over there?"

I smile at his question. It's one he's asked me a lot growing up.

"About how thankful I am that you came home."

He shrugs, taking a sip of his drink. "I'm always here for you, sis. I know I've done a shit job of showing that lately, school's kicking my ass, but I'm your big brother and that's what I do—I take care of you."

"I really am lucky to have you. Mom and Dad too."

Gus smiles, shaking his head. "Nah, Ophelia. It's us that are lucky to have you."

I've had a lot of time to think this week, about how much they've done for me that I didn't notice or thought they were doing because I was some sort of burden. The mind can lie to you, trick you, into believing so many things that aren't true.

I feel at peace now, stronger. I've grown a lot already the past few months, but now I feel like I can even more.

When I get back to campus though, the first order of business is talking with Cree.

I hope he's not too mad at me for not speaking to him this week and asking him to wait, but I wanted to have time to clear my thoughts and figure out what I want to say to him, where we go from here.

I didn't lie to him in my last text where I said I wasn't mad at him.

I'm not. It would be hypocritical if I was.

Even though now it all makes sense and I know I really am his Daisy, it doesn't matter, I still technically lied because I don't remember it at all. I lied to him the same way he did to me—to get what I wanted, which was a tutor, and in his case, he wanted … well, he wanted *me*, which blows my mind. Cree's a catch—he's insanely attractive in this wholesome boy next door way, he's kind, caring, smart, and a talented hockey player.

I really won the lottery when it comes to boyfriends.

If he's still my boyfriend after my radio silence.

But I needed this time. I needed to see my family, to get things off my chest, and to be on my own to see what I truly want.

"You want to talk about it?" Gus's lips turn up into a tiny smile.

I shake my head. There's nothing I want to say to Gus, because Cree is the one who deserves my words now. "No," I reply, "but I know I can."

"Good, I'm always here for you, sis. I love you."

"I mean, you did get on a plane to fly to see me for less than twenty-four hours, so I'd hope you do."

He throws a pillow at me. "Always a smart ass."

THIRTY-ONE

CREE

WE GOT BACK from our game early this morning, and I've spent most of the day trying to distract myself from the fact that I still haven't heard from Ophelia. Defeat is settling into my bones, along with acceptance that I might never hear from her again.

Do I understand it?

Yes.

Does it fucking hurt?

Unbelievably so.

I wish she'd at least give me the chance to talk, to

explain, but she's MIA. I'm back to never seeing her on campus.

Poof, she's gone.

I walk into the coffee shop, holding the door open for the girl leaving. She flashes a smile in thanks before I head inside to get in line. This place should just be a coffee shop, but now all it does is remind me of Ophelia. When I order, I get two brownies, not sure if I'll even eat one, but it feels like a goodbye of sorts.

Sitting down with my coffee and brownies, I pull out the book I've been trying to read for the last week. I've made hardly any progress. Last night I read maybe three paragraphs before I gave up and turned the lights out.

A throat is cleared, and I look up, shocked to find Ophelia standing in front of the table just like she did a few months ago. Only now, she's smiling from ear to ear, her red hair seems brighter, and her eyes glow with happiness.

Despite my desolate feelings, I find myself repeating the same thing I said to her in this very coffee shop, when she reappeared in my life after a year. It's only been a week, but the feeling of surprise at seeing her again is the same.

I grin slowly, making sure she doesn't disappear

from in front of me like some sort of mirage. "I've been looking for you"

Her whole being lights up as she smiles. "Is that so? Jay, right?" She pulls out the chair across from me and sits down, lacing her fingers together.

"That's right." I nod along, sliding a brownie toward her.

"For me?" She arches a brow.

"For you." She doesn't touch the brownie and we sit there, silence between us, but surprisingly it isn't awkward at all. That doesn't mean my tension has eased. "So," I clear my throat, "how have you been?"

Her eyes glimmer with barely contained laughter. "I've been good. I went home to see my parents. That's where I've been the last week."

"You went home?" For some reason that takes me by surprise, but I also feel relief that she was gone and not avoiding me.

"Mhmm," she hums, resting her elbow on the table and her head in her hand. "I needed to see my parents and talk to them. It was nice, and I think we're in a much better place."

"That's ... that's good." I'm reminded of the way Ophelia stuttered over her words when we first met, but now it's me doing it. "And how are you feeling about other things?"

"By other things, I'm assuming you're referring to yourself?"

I try not to smile but fail epically. "Yes."

She shakes her head. "You don't beat around the bush, do you?"

"Never." She doesn't say anything in response, her eyes flicking over me, and I can't help but wonder what she's looking for. Whatever it is, I hope she finds it. "You said you weren't mad at me. Is that true?"

"That's true." When she smiles at me, it gives me hope that everything is going to be okay. "At first I was hurt that you'd lie about something like that. I needed a tutor and you could've screwed me over with my class —" I start to argue with her, but she holds up a hand pleading with me to wait. "But the more I thought about it, I realized you wouldn't have done that if you hadn't known you could really help me."

"I would *never* compromise your education."

"I know." She lowers her hands to the table. "I think, if we're going to move forward, we need to be honest with each other."

"I agree." Leaning forward, the space between us becomes limited. I never knew a coffee shop could feel as intimate as it does between us right now. "Where should we start?"

"For starters, I don't remember the first official

night we met, and I might never remember it. I talked to Mary, and she reminded me of a small accident I had last year—"

"An accident?"

She nods. "I fell off a horse last year, it happens, but I did get a concussion and..." She trails off, shrugging. "I know I was there, Kenna showed me photos, but I don't remember it at all. I probably never will. Does that bother you?"

It stings a little, knowing that a night that changed my life isn't even a memory to her, but she can't control having an accident.

"It's not your fault you don't remember. There's nothing to be bothered about."

"Good." She exhales a sigh of relief. Glancing down at the brownie I slid her way, she smiles, tearing off a corner and sticking it in her mouth. "Are there any more confessions we should get out of the way?"

"I mean..." I give it some thought. "My middle name is Richard. Not much of a confession, but it *is* embarrassing."

"Cree Richard Madison?" When I nod, she laughs. "That's kind of cute, though."

"Are we good, Ophelia? Really, good? I want us to move forward, and everything to be okay."

"We're good. It would be hypocritical for me to be

mad at you when I technically lied too. But from now on, moving forward, we need to be honest with each other. Communication is key if we want this relationship to work."

"Communication, I can do that. I'll be the most communicative person you've ever met."

She laughs. "Is that so?"

"Absolutely. I don't want to end up dead like Gatsby over a misunderstanding. I want the ending he should have had."

"Some would say that's the ending he deserved."

"Nah," I argue, grinning at the girl I love, "anyone that loves someone like he did Daisy deserves better."

"And I'm the better you're looking for?" She arches a brow, chewing another bite of her brownie.

"You are."

Her smile lights up her face, her gold-green eyes shining with happiness.

She's everything. Has been since that night at the bonfire. Some people might think it's crazy to know that fast, but I think some of us are lucky in that way and recognize our person without second-guessing it. This is only the beginning of our love story, one that will span many chapters, but I'm looking forward to going on the adventure with her. After all, you never know what's on the next page until you turn it.

THIRTY-TWO

Ophelia

IT'S BEEN two weeks since Cree and I had our talk at the coffee shop. For the first few days after, I could tell he was unsure, waiting for the other shoe to drop so-to-speak. Like maybe I hadn't really forgiven him. But I reminded him we're mature adults, and the situation is over, in the past, and I want to move on and continue to grow what was already becoming a beautiful relationship.

"Are you sure you want me to come home with you to meet your folks?" He pulls his Bronco into the garage of his house. It's not the first time he's asked me this question, and I'm sure it won't be the last either when we fly back to where I grew up in just a few days.

"I'm sure. Are you?" I counter, raising a brow as I undo my seatbelt.

He purses his lips. "What if they hate me? And don't sass me, I might have to spank you."

I laugh, trying not to roll my eyes. "Oh, how the tables have turned. I felt the same way meeting your parents. You're going to be fine." I lean over, pecking him on the lips. He frowns and I can tell he's going to start arguing with me again, but we don't have time for this. I put a finger to his lips. "Daire and Rosie are moving out today, and we promised we'd help. Stop stalling."

He sighs, rubbing his hands on his jeans. I think a part of him is glad Daire is leaving after the rough start to the year he's had with his best friend, but also sad because it's the end of an era.

Daire ended up apologizing to me personally for his behavior that night and in general. I accepted, there's no need to drag out unnecessary drama, but we'll never be close and that's okay. We don't need to be. He's Cree's friend, not mine.

I already like Rosie. She gives him hell and puts him in his place. I don't think Daire has ever had a woman talk back to him the way she does. It's a sight to see when they really get going. And despite what either of them says, the chemistry between them is palpable. It's only a matter of time before they develop real feelings.

"You're right," he finally says, reaching for the handle. "Let's get this over with."

Inside the house there are a slew of boxes and plastic bins waiting to be loaded into the small moving truck outside. According to Cree, they found a town-house a few miles away, and Rosie's dad offered the full asking price in cash on the contingency that the previous owners had to be moved out by today.

"Knock, knock," Cree calls out. "Where is everyone?"

There's really no need at his question, because almost immediately we hear Rosie yelling at Daire. "I don't understand why any one person needs *twenty-three* pairs of the same sneaker just in different colors!"

Daire doesn't miss a beat, while Cree and I exchange amused expressions. "If you're going to nit-pick my sneaker collection, then let's talk about you having the same fucking lipstick in all different colors. Why the fuck do you need those?"

"Don't call my glosses and liquid lips *lipstick* that's blasphemy. Besides, I need different shades to coordi-nate with my outfits, and those don't take up nearly as much space as shoes." She sounds triumphant when she finishes her speech.

"I'm not getting rid of any of them. They go in the bin."

"Whatever you say."

Cree shakes his head. "They're either going to kill each other or—"

"Have really hot hate sex," I finish for him.

We venture upstairs into the lion's den and both appear relieved to have a buffer.

"Where's Millie and Jude?"

"Your sister said she was getting out of here to study," Daire grumbles, bent over in his closet pulling out what is obviously the twenty-three sneakers. "And Jude is supposed to be at the new place unloading some shit from his truck."

Rosie pokes his bent over butt. "Stop cussing so much. You have a kid. You're not going to get to spend time with him if they hear your potty mouth."

A low growl is his only response.

"What do you need us to help you guys with?" Cree interrupts before they can go at it again.

Daire leans back, squatting. "If you guys don't mind loading everything that's already packed onto the truck that would be great."

"You got it." Cree takes my hand, pulling me from the room just before they start going at it again.

It doesn't take too long to get everything on the truck, and then Cree and Daire are taking the bed apart and putting it and the mattress on as well, which is the final thing to be loaded.

Daire closes the back of the truck, and it clicks shut with a finality.

Daire clears his throat, getting a bit choked up. "Well, this is it, I guess."

"Dude." Cree blinks at him. "You're moving a few miles away, it's not the end of the world."

"Things are changing, that's all." Daire glances over to where Rosie speaks on the phone to her dad, I think. He shoves his hands in the pockets of his jeans. "Everyone's ... settling down. You have Ophelia." He dips his head at me. "I've got Rosie now." He rolls his eyes. "Not in a real sense, but it's still a ball and chain. And Jude's got..."

Cree narrows his eyes. "Jude has?"

Daire hesitates, wetting his lips. "A lot to sort through and a desperate need for a therapist."

Cree cracks a smile. "No lie detected. Don't be a stranger just because you're moving out."

"Never."

Rosie hangs up the phone and nods at the truck. "We need to go."

"Right." He clears his throat. "We have a house to move into. Well, townhouse. See you guys later."

Rosie waves at me with a beaming smile. "See you guys, later."

Daire goes around to the driver's side of the truck while Rosie takes her car.

Cree and I stand on the driveway, his arm slung around my shoulders and my arms wrapped around his warm hard torso as we watch the vehicles drive away.

"I feel like we're watching our kids drive off and leave us," I joke.

He glances down at me. "You want me to put some babies in you, Daisy?"

I jab his side with my finger. "Not *now*, but maybe one day."

"Hmm," he hums, "I can live with that. Besides," he grins that completely cocky grin of his, the one with the dimples and everything, "why have them anytime soon when we have so much fun practicing?"

I squeal when he grabs me up and tosses me over his shoulder, running into the house, and right up the stairs. He drops me on his bed and shows me exactly why we don't need to rush the future, the present is pretty fantastic as it is.

EPILOGUE

Ophelia
Two Years Later

SITTING in the box at the first home game of the season in D.C., I watch the love of my life skate onto the ice. He pumps his fist in the air, riled up by the cheering fans.

"Look at him," Cree's mom says from beside me, "that's where he belongs."

She's not wrong. Nothing compares to seeing Cree on the ice during a game. Getting to sit in the box and avoid the chaos is a godsend for me. I get to enjoy the game without the chaos of chanting fans.

"Eh, he's all right," Millie says from somewhere behind me, probably nibbling on something from the food table.

Cree's dad sits in a seat, eyes glued to the ice and completely ignoring us despite the fact that the game hasn't started yet.

After I graduated, I moved to Arlington, Virginia, taking up a teaching position at a local school. The location put me close enough to Cree that we moved in together. There's no telling if he'll stay in D.C. or where he could end up, but we'll figure that out together.

There aren't any more lies between us.

No half-truths.

No hiding.

When the game begins, I find myself on my feet the entire time. Never ever, did I think I'd turn into a hockey fanatic, but here I am. There's something addicting about watching a game, especially in person. Now, I attend every home game and some of the away ones when my schedule allows.

"Oh!" Cree's mom grabs onto my arm when he sustains a hit. "I never get used to that." She releases my arm, letting the blood flow return.

"Me neither." I bite my lip worriedly, but he skates on like nothing at all happened.

The game is an intense one, and by the end of it my hands are sweaty, but we manage to win by one point.

As the game comes to an end, we hang around in the box waiting until Cree can join us.

"Wow, I'm exhausted after that." His mom lets out a sigh, reclining back in her seat.

"And you didn't even play," his dad points out to her.

Millie shakes her head, smiling in amusement at her parents. "They're crazy," she mouths to me.

When Cree finally walks into the room, he looks happy but tired. His hair curls against the collar of his shirt, the sleeves tight on his muscular arms. He comes over to me first, pulling me into a hug, burying his face into the side of my neck.

"You played great tonight," I whisper in his ear. I feel his smile against my neck and when he pulls away his dimple flashes.

"Thanks, baby."

He hugs his parents and sister, thanking them for coming—as if they'd miss the first game.

Taking my hand, Cree leads us outside to the team's parking lot and his SUV parked there. He still has his

Bronco but wanted something bigger since we have friends and family visit a lot.

We all pile into the car, and as per tradition, get burgers for dinner before heading home.

The townhome in Arlington is old, rich with history, and it reflects both of us well.

Everyone heads their separate ways, and in our bedroom, Cree tugs me against his body.

"I was thinking about something today."

"What's that?" I place my hands on his chest, keeping him at a small distance because I know if I don't, he'll end up kissing me and forget all about whatever it is he wants to tell me.

"How lucky I am. To have this," he nods around us at the room, "to have you. To live this life, one some people only dream of."

"You don't have to flatter me," I joke, smiling up at him. "You'll get laid regardless."

He throws his head back and laughs. "God, I love you."

When he kisses me, I melt into his body.

He thinks he's the lucky one, but I think it's pretty equal between us. I never thought I'd find a love like the ones I read about between the pages of my favorite books, but here it is, and I'll never take it for granted.

Love is the greatest gift we have in this world, even though it's not always easy, it's always worth treasuring.

Want to know what Ophelia was thinking the night she met Cree? Get the free bonus story here when you sign up for my newsletter! https://dl. bookfunnel.com/5pw26zg09a

Broken Boys Can't Love
Jude & Millie's book coming in 2022.

ACKNOWLEDGMENTS

Wow, we've come to the end of another book. A book that wouldn't be possible without you, dear reader. There aren't enough words to express my thanks for going on this crazy journey with me and The Boys series.

Emily, Emily, Emily. Thank you, as always, for creating such a stunning cover. You always go above and beyond for me, not just with covers, but with everything. You're the best friend I could ever ask for, truly you're family. Thank you for always being there with me every step of the way.

A big thank you to my beta readers. You're both wonderful and I can't thank you ladies enough.

To my doggie Ollie, and my new doggie addition Remy, thank you for keeping me company and laying curled up beside me as every word is written. Your kisses are the best encouragement to keep going.